the Charmed List

the Charmed List

JULIE ABE

WEDNESDAY BOOKS
NEW YORK

First published in the United States by Wednesday Books, an imprint of St. Martin's Publishing Group

THE CHARMED LIST. Copyright © 2022 by Julie Abe. All rights reserved. Printed in the United States of America. For information, address St. Martin's Publishing Group, 120 Broadway, New York, NY 10271.

www.wednesdaybooks.com

Designed by Omar Chapa

The Library of Congress Cataloging-in-Publication Data is available upon request.

ISBN 978-1-250-83009-8 (hardcover)
ISBN 978-1-250-83010-4 (ebook)

Our books may be purchased in bulk for promotional, educational, or business use. Please contact your local bookseller or the Macmillan Corporate and Premium Sales Department at 1-800-221-7945, extension 5442, or by email at MacmillanSpecialMarkets@macmillan.com.

First Edition: 2022

10 9 8 7 6 5 4 3 2 1

To the readers discovering their own Charmed Lists.
May your tea always stay enchanted and your starry
nights shine bright.

To Jennie Conway, for charming this story from wisps
of thoughts into ink and paper (and cupcakes).

And to Emily, always. Every day is magical with you.

the Charmed List

Chapter 1

The warm summer air swirls in a cooling breeze as I bike down one of the side streets of downtown Palo Alto. There are some not-so-techy parts to my hometown, in the heart of Silicon Valley. Entrepreneurs swear that their best ideas were created sitting at the corner table of a certain café, and that startups are formed during walks through the Stanford University campus, as sunlight flows down through the leafy green oaks. Some visitors swear that there's a hint of vibrant energy in the air. People call Palo Alto a little quirky or even hipster . . .

But I know the truth. This city is *magical*. There are charms and enchantments hidden all over Palo Alto—if you know where to look.

I take a sharp left onto Ramona Street when I get near City Hall, and the street narrows, edged in by stucco buildings and cardinal-red awnings, marking our connection to Stanford University.

As I turn the corner into the plaza, there's a shout. "Hey, Ellie!"

I brake, rubber chirping against concrete, and grin. "What's up, Ana?"

Analise, the twentysomething owner of the trendy Simple Mornings Café, motions me over from where she's wiping down a table, her tanned skin shining golden under the sun. "Come by to celebrate the end of junior year?"

I point over my shoulder at my backpack stuffed with my laptop, a few sketch pads, and two textbooks for last-minute cramming. "Let me drop this off first. I swear, it's heavier than Totoro and the Catbus combined. Lia and I will be over here soon to plan our road trip."

"My new mango cupcakes are the perfect way to kick off your summer break—they're charmed with a spark of joy. Get back here before they're all gone!" Ana grins and waves me off.

My best friend, Lia Park, didn't have a third-period final, so she skipped out of the last day of school early. With my economics final, I wasn't so lucky, but I think I managed to scrape by with at least a B.

Either way, junior year is fading like the chalk-art sketches that Ana's drawn on the path outside her café to invite customers in. I'm not wasting any more time worrying about grades. It's officially the summer before senior year and I am *not* letting a second go to waste, starting with our epic road trip down to Southern California.

I slide to a stop in front of a seemingly plain oak door and lock up my bike at the rack. The door is covered in cascading ivy, and only the magic-aware can open it. Nothing about magic is plain or simple, but that's why we sorcerers hide it from the non-magic-aware. Or what Mom diplomatically calls "the general public"—those who don't know about magic.

The shops of Palo Alto's Sorcerer Square are in plain sight, but this ordinary-seeming plaza has a secret side. My favorite is my parents' shop, of course, where they sell the most energizing, freshly made tea in the city—with a hint of a joy charm. Plus there's Ana's bakery, where her just-baked cinnamon streusel cupcakes brighten up her customers' days and give them a shot of courage. We've also got what looks like a pharmacy (but is truly an apothecary for everything from bottled charms to elixirs that fix spells that go wrong); a clothing store (useful when you need jeans that have real pockets—and magical ones to hide charms and enchanted vials); an ensorcelled vegetarian South Indian restaurant with the most fragrant spice mixes ever; a cozy gem store filled with healing crystals and magic-gathering mood rings; and an enchanted fruit shop with dragon fruit that burns with a sugary fire.

And there's another store, opposite my parents' shop, but . . .

Let's ignore that one for now. Believe me, the whole city of Palo Alto would be better off if we didn't have *him*—I mean, *that* place—there.

Still, annoyances aside, I love this cozy plaza, where sorcery meets reality. It's home.

Sliding aside the curtain of ivy, I push in the wooden door leading to our living area behind my parents' shop. The bell above lets out a loud *ring!* An excited yap echoes, then curved nails skitter along the hallway. One second later, a fiery, furry ball launches at my face and into my open arms.

"Mochi!" My Shiba, bright orange-red and shedding more than a spell can contain, leaps out of my arms and prances around me on her long, graceful legs, wagging her curled tail so hard it looks like it might fall off. I try not to trip as she weaves about like I'm her human obstacle course. You'd think I'd been gone for a month, not just the school day. Little Mochi is ten years old now, but her eyes crinkle up the same way as when she was two and I'd found her shivering at Heritage Park, all alone and matted with dirt.

Remy, my fourteen-year-old younger sister, looks up when I pad into the kitchen, Mochi stuck to my legs like she's trying to become my fur. "Cam's here." Remy is just like Dad, with her thoughtful owl-eyes, rounded face, and thin, stick-straight hair, whereas I'm more like Mom, with her cat-eyes, sharp chin, and thick, slight waves that I'm constantly pushing out of my eyes.

Cam nods at me from the other side of the wood table, where he and Remy are working on yet another puzzle. It's jarring to see him at times, because his light brown hair and tanned coloring are exactly like his older brother's. But Cam's always peaceful, and would rather spend time with my little sister than anyone else, like celebrating the last day of their freshman year with this puzzle. With the two of them both being magic-aware, their puzzle isn't an ordinary one. Whoever puts in the last piece of this constellation-themed design gets a spark of luck that lasts a day. Remy is obsessed with working on these puzzles and collecting little tokens of luck. She won't tell anyone what she's saving them up for, but I'm guessing it has something to do with Cam.

"Jack says hi." Cam grins mischievously. I playfully steal

the piece from his hand. Narrowing my eyes, I slide the orange square straight into the section of the sun.

"There. If you win, give me part of your prize," I say. "With your brother around this summer, I'm going to need all the luck I can get." I don't say the truth: that I wish Jack Yasuda was off at an internship like last year.

Cam and Remy snort. They know that Jack and I do *not* get along.

"Good thing *you're* going away this summer," Remy says. "Jack's staying here to take care of the shop, so he won't be at the convention, either. You won't have to hate-stare at each other from across the booth."

I glare at them, and they laugh with so-cute-it's-disgusting synchrony. Jack and I were as close as Cam and Remy all throughout elementary school, but after Mrs. Yasuda passed away, Jack's dad started butting heads with my parents about the direction of Sorcerer Square (Mr. Yasuda is all for power and fame enchantments, while we Kobatas prefer joy and happiness charms, thank you very much). Jack followed his father's lead, and we stopped hanging out faster than you can say *our friendship is cursed*. He's ignored me ever since.

Somehow, placid Remy and Cam have stayed attached at the hip, even when our families brew up a storm, and they're usually the peacemakers. I'm usually peaceful too, but not when it comes to Jack Yasuda.

"Mom and Dad want you to check in," Remy says as I put my backpack on the open seat. "And Jack wants to see you after that."

My backpack drops out of my hand and off the chair, making a colossal *thump* on the worn wood floor.

"That was a joke," Remy informs me, unhelpfully.

"A bad one," I groan. "Any joke about Jack is *not* funny. Especially not if my laptop breaks." Mochi happily runs a circle around my backpack and then back to me, hyper as ever. Hopefully that sound was just textbooks and not my old computer, because then I'll have to look through the fix-it spell book to figure out how to repair it, and it's not going to be a pinch-of-magic type of project.

"Want me to check it?" Remy looks guilty; she knows we don't have the money to spend on a new laptop. She swoops down to help Cam set my backpack onto the chair. Cam's face turns pink when her hands brush against his. If I could see magic dust right now, I bet it would be like a blizzard in here between the two of them; their emotions are sparking like a storm.

"It'll be fine, I'll check later. I've got to go meet Lia." I ruffle her hair teasingly and she swats my hand away, smoothing down her bangs. She steals a glance at Cam, who's returned to studying the puzzle as if he's in desperate need of luck. I narrow my eyes between them, fully showing her *I saw that*, but she determinedly stares at the puzzle and refuses to meet my gaze, though her cheeks pink up. Hmm . . . they're fourteen. . . . Is it time for a summer romance?

Hah. Out of everyone I know, *I* need a summer romance before my younger sister does. As the plainest of the plain Janes of Palo Alto High School, I'm probably the last person who has yet to go on a real date.

Mochi prances down the hallway, leading me toward Elissa's Tea Shop. To the Mark Zuckerbergs and Elon Musks of the world (they or their families have all stopped by), Elissa's Tea

Shop is a Japanese café, but we magicals know that the matcha boba teas and steamed red bean cakes *actually* give joy. That hint of happiness in our drinks might be why we're the most popular tea shop in Palo Alto. Of course, the non-magicals don't know about the charms in the tea. Only that they feel lighter after drinking it.

There's a rumble of conversation as I approach the curtain separating our house from the shop. At first, I think it's customers, but Dad's deep voice is hushed. I pause.

"Eric Yasuda's still raising a stink about our exhibit at CMRC." Through the curtain, I can see him rubbing his hand over his bald spot. "He thinks only CharmWorks should sell their stuff. That our tea and Ana's cupcake mix and the rest of the stuff from the square are distractions."

This is the first year that my parents have let me drive to the California Magical Retailers' Convention in Huntington Beach, while they fly down. It's going to be the most epic road trip for me and Lia, even though she's not magic-aware. She thinks I'm just carting our booth to some boring old retail show. Lia is going down there to hang out with her cousins. But no matter the reasons for our trip, I'm ready for summer adventures with my best friend. I've been waiting for months to drive down to Orange County in my little Toyota Camry, the trunk stuffed with CMRC exhibit supplies, Lia and I with the windows down, hair streaming in the wind, our music blasting as we tour our way down the coast.

But that gripe about Mr. Yasuda. . . . Ugh. I didn't expect anything less. Mr. Yasuda's *just* like his frustrating son, stuck-up and uncaring about anyone else. This is a conversation I know far too well. Jack's father, Eric Yasuda, and their store, CharmWorks, are the biggest pains on the block. CharmWorks is basically the Walmart version of charm shops. They order in mass-produced charms and sell them in their storefront and on their shiny new website. To the unmagical, it looks like a stationery store—but their bullet journals are imbued with spells for power and fame.

Mom sighs. "And he keeps hinting that he wants to run for my Lead Sorcerer position. We know how well that'll go for the town. Palo Alto's full of ambition already, and he wants to add in more?"

Mr. Yasuda is trying to take away Mom's role? Being a Lead Sorcerer for a town is kind of like our version of a mayor, elected by the other magical residents, and sworn in by the county's magical supervisor. Mom is *amazing* at her work connecting charms with the magicless-in-need (without them knowing), and I can't see greedy, money-grubbing Eric Yasuda ever being altruistic enough for that.

It's something I don't even want to think about. I press my foot down hard on the squeaky board in the hallway, and their conversation fades out.

I pop my head through the curtain and Mochi sits patiently at the door. She's not allowed in because we sell food, and she's trained to know where to stop. Mom looks up from where she's packaging a box of matcha macarons, another of her creations. "Love! Welcome back from school. How was your econ final?"

"The worst, but I think I scraped by." I slide a macaron off the tray and Mom laughs, pretending to snatch it back. "How's the store? Need any help?"

Dad shakes his head from where he's cleaning the hot water boiler on the other end of the counter. "Nah, the lunch rush won't come in for an hour or so."

I lean against the counter, biting into the delicate macaron. It feels like I'm drinking a lightly sweetened, warm cup of green tea, sprinkled with a tiny contentment spell, one of Mom's specialties. The stress of econ and finals and junior year trickle away, like I've finally stopped and taken a deep breath. "So Mr. Yasuda's grouching about our CMRC booth again?"

Mom glances over at Dad, and I can tell they're still not ready to talk about Mr. Yasuda encroaching on Mom's role, or Sorcerer Square's plans for our combined stand.

Dad waves me toward the door. "No, don't worry about it, Ellie. You're all set to leave next week, as planned, with all our stuff. Go have fun with Lia today. Celebrate your last day of school."

As if my best friend has magical timing of her own, my phone buzzes.

LIA: At Ana's. Gonna eat all the cupcakes if you don't get here soon.

I chew on my lip, Mochi whining softly behind me.

The CMRC is an annual gathering of magical shops from around the state. This year's special—it's the hundredth anniversary of the convention—so our whole family is going. We and the other Palo Alto magical shops exhibit our wares for cross-promotion and in the hope of getting attention from distributors that want to pick up items for their online retailers, increasing our sales and the chance that our magical goods will go to a customer in need. Even though 95 percent of the world doesn't know about magic, our charmed goods usually find their way to the people who need them the most.

Mochi follows me down the walkway that she's allowed to go through along the wall of the store, far from the empty tables, and Mom uncorks a flask to pour out a cleaning charm into the air. It races after Mochi in a puffy little cloud of charmed powder, collecting any stray dog hairs it finds, before depositing itself in the tiny trash can next to the entrance.

At the door, I glance back at my parents. "Are you sure—"

Dad and Mom smile, their eyes crinkling, and wave me out. "Go enjoy the start of your summer, Ellie," Mom says. "Your last full vacation before you graduate! My, you grew up so fast."

"But don't cause any trouble!" Dad calls after me, in his usual warning, and I laugh. Me? Trouble? Realistically, *never*. Not like someone else I know. . . .

I grimace at the thought of my neighbor and push open the front door, striding out. I grip my phone tightly. The card slot in the back has my debit card and some cash, and I press against it, the sharp edge of the card imprinting onto my fingertips.

I turn the corner into the center of Sorcerer Square, where Lia's waiting, my head still buzzing with annoyance.

And it's when I'm not looking that it happens, that I stumble.

Smack into the worst resident in all of Palo Alto. In all of Silicon Valley, really.

No, let me correct that.

My least favorite person in the entire world.

Damn Jack Yasuda.

Chapter 2

The moment freezes in time as Jack slams into me. It's a slo-mo horror scene for teens everywhere: My phone arcs out of my hand, cash and card flying out, spinning through the air. And I think, *I'm never going to be able to get a new phone,* and, *Maybe there's a spell,* but no, I'm in public, I can't cast anything—

My phone smacks against the cobblestone path leading into the center of Sorcerer Square. Mochi and I race up to it, breezing by the person who ran into me.

It's facedown, and my heart is in my throat when I turn my phone around.

I groan. A jagged crack runs down the center of the glass screen like a lightning bolt.

A hand reaches out to pick up my phone from my tight grip, but I swat it away. It's a familiar hand. Calloused from electric guitar, but with long, graceful fingers that I itch to draw.

I turn to my right, facing Jack Yasuda head-on.

He's all dark and light. His perfectly mussed brown hair, lighter than mine because he's half-Japanese, half-Italian. His eyes that have specks of light brown, but shades of darkness, too. The tan of his skin from playing tennis on the school team. His slightly crooked nose from when we were kids and went ice skating at Winter Lodge, chasing each other around the rink, and he tripped over a bump in the ice. Somehow, it works on him.

He's gorgeous.

And I hate him.

I breathe in deep, trying to erase that instantaneous reaction of *oh, remember when we were best friends.*

He makes it easy. His eyes burn, as if angry thoughts are churning in his head like they are in mine. I would probably be able to write a book with the amount of insults I can come up with. *Your messy brown hair makes you look like a wannabe TikTok star.* Or how about, *You're so bad at directions, it's no wonder you walked straight into me.*

I mean, I can try to come up with insults. But with him, somehow, my insults sound more like pick-up lines.

Maybe I can insult how his perfectly fitted V-neck shirt is a little ragged at the edges. His hard-earned muscles from being captain of the school tennis team. The slim cut of his jeans. Hell, I don't know. The hair on his arms?

Why is he so impossible to insult?

Then I blink. His eyes are inches from mine, because he's kneeling next to my phone, and we're staring at each other, trading mental insults without saying a word. I think he's breathing in my air and I'm breathing in his and that's just plain *wrong.*

We are way, way too close for comfort.

His eyes narrow. And he opens his mouth, so I open mine because I'm not going to let him get an insult in first—

Mochi sticks her head in and slurps Jack's face in a greeting. He falls backward with a laugh, rubbing behind her ears. "Mochi likes me, don't you, pretty girl?"

My traitor dog. She wags her tail enthusiastically, and I grab her and sit back on the cobblestone path, turning away when she tries to kiss me, too. I don't want any licks until I brush her teeth, or it'll be like I got an indirect kiss from Jack.

I crook one protective arm around Mochi, who contentedly curls up. Possibly because I'm scratching behind her ear at her favorite spot, so she won't budge.

Jack crosses his arms to show off his muscles from tennis, which peek out from his short sleeves. Not that I willingly notice them.

"A great way to start the summer," I say dryly. "A broken phone."

"*You* slammed into me without looking and dropped it." His husky voice is deeper than the last time we talked, during a pained and awful team project during the middle of junior year. I wasn't joking about hating econ; he and his damn friends are why.

"Don't make this sound like my fault. You ran into me."

His eyes glitter as he shrugs innocently with a *What did I do?* gesture. Then he asks, "Well, does your phone still work?"

I swipe my finger on the sensor and it lights up, showing a sketch I did of me and Lia a few months ago, when we'd gone together to the Spring Fling dance. She's gorgeous; if I'm the plainest of plain Janes, she's the prettiest of pretty Janes. And even with that crack in the middle, my phone still works. I breathe out in relief. "Yeah, it looks like it's okay."

"I can try to repair the glass," he says, handing over the debit card and cash that I've dropped. My jaw nearly unhinges with surprise.

This is Jack? Is he actually offering to help? Did he somehow get brain-swapped with Cam?

"Dad got in a new set of upgraded Repair-All charms for us to sell to the magic-aware. They look like omamori. Take this with you, toss it onto your phone when you're back in your room, and it'll be as good as new." He pulls one out of his pocket. It's a bright red cloth rectangle, with a tiny white bow at the top, and looks like those Japanese amulets that temples sell. "Let me know how it goes. It'll be a good testimonial that it fixed your phone."

Oh, I'm a sales pitch. No surprise there.

"No, thanks," I reply shortly. I dig through the pocket of my denim shorts and pull out a small vial of Mom's handy fix-it concoction, no bigger than half my thumb. It's like the duct tape of all magical charms, a sort of fix-everything deal. The enchanted dust even has the aluminum-silver sheen of duct tape, too. "I can patch this up now."

"We're in public," he hisses.

I pointedly look around. "Do you see anyone?" The pathway that leads to Ana's tables in the center of Sorcerer Square is narrow and empty, and usually people take the plaza entrance at University Drive, the main street. One wall is my parents' shop and house; the other is the concrete back wall of CharmWorks.

"Still, we're out in the open." He's as insistent and stubborn as his father.

"Weren't you the one who offered me your omamori charm?"

"For you to use at home; magic is way too flashy to use here—"

"I'm going to see Lia in a few minutes. It'd be too weird if the crack is gone when I see her tomorrow." I stare back at him. "Stand watch and cover me up."

He glances around, grimacing, and inches closer, scanning the entrances to the path. I regret my words immediately. I can smell his mint-and-clean-cotton scent.

Too. Close.

But if I'm going to restore my phone screen, I need to focus. Instead of pushing him away, I uncap the silvery concoction. It feels like I'm taking a huge breath of air inside my parents' shop, filled with green tea and frothy, just-steamed milk, like one of Dad's matcha lattes.

Carefully, I tip the vial over the top of the glass, and the charmed powder slides out. It sparks, like tiny, infinitely small liquid fireworks as it finds the break, and I breathe in with delight, watching the magic work. Even Mochi, still in my lap, is transfixed by the sparkling light.

"Magic is always so pretty," I whisper to myself. Raw magic dust—which the magic-aware can see and collect with a pair of charmed, rose-tinted spectacles—can be refined by our spells into little enchantments: a raincoat that dries instantly after a downpour; a flower lushly evoking a warm memory of a loved one; a fix-it charm to smooth out cracks like these.

The spells that we can cast are small-scale—just a nudge—but like with my phone, these tiny little changes are beautiful.

"It's magic," Jack says, matter-of-fact, as if my statement is stupid. Then he spins around. "Ellie, quick, Ellie—"

I stuff the vial into my pocket and wipe furiously at the sparking magic, feeling it tickle my skin. Raw magic floats in the air around us, but only the magic-aware—those who are either born into magic or marry into it—can ensorcell the bits of dust into something like this fix-it elixir. However, once it's been turned into its refined form, it's visible, just like how its effects can be felt—but I *can't* let anyone who isn't magic-aware see it.

"Well, this wasn't what I expected to start off my summer," a smooth, velvety voice drawls from the pathway leading to the center of the plaza.

I peek around Jack's long legs. "Oh, Lia!"

My best friend since middle school brightens as she sees me, and Mochi scrambles off my lap to race around her, whining with happiness.

"See, Mochi likes everyone," I mutter, but Jack simply ignores me.

"Did you fall?" Lia asks, pushing past my neighbor as if he doesn't exist and offering me her hand. She pulls me up and protectively wraps an arm around my shoulder, glaring at him. Her immaculate flicks of eyeliner could be daggers.

He looks slightly nervous, but who wouldn't? Lia's one of the fiercest girls I know, but even one pointed look from her melts half of the high school into a state of pure euphoria.

Back in seventh grade, Jack said to me in front of our whole class, "Why are you trying to follow me around?" He straight-up pretended I didn't exist after that, and my grand delusion that he and I were friends disappeared pretty fast. A few weeks later, some girls teased me during lunchtime, calling me "Ellie-Invisible." I hated the way the rest of the class looked over with pitying glances. But Lia, who'd moved from Southern California the week before, sat down next to me, shrugged, and said, "Well, I'm invisible, too, I guess."

And we've been inseparable ever since.

"I dropped my phone," I say. "And Jack was helping me check that it still works."

Lia looks down from her four-inch advantage. I can almost hear her quizzing me on this later. *Jack helped you? Since when did hell-in-human-form freeze over?*

"I bumped into her," Jack says, and I nearly fall over again. He's . . . admitting he's at fault? Then, typical Jack, he adds, "Ellie had her head in the clouds. She didn't notice me."

Ah, it's like a hidden thorn on a rose. This is the Jack I know. When not obsessively bragging about CharmWorks' success like his father, he finds it fun to take digs at me. Lia snorts under her breath. We both know him all too well.

She knows about my past with Jack and she's supported me when I've gotten snubbed by my ex–best friend, and I've stuck by her side in the days that she's lonely and hurting from the sting of missing her parents.

Back when she was eleven, she had a countywide violin competition; she'd been called a musical prodigy by the local paper and she was the crowd favorite to win. Before it started, she kept looking out of the wings for her mom and dad. Her grandma had brought her there, since her parents were carpooling from their offices the next city over.

Lia waited and waited, strange worries twisting her stomach as she played her first piece. Her parents usually messaged their group chat if they'd be even a minute late. During intermission, she snuck out to the audience to ask. Grandma smiled strangely, waving Lia away from the two empty seats, like she was trying to conceal a gaping hole. "It's okay, they'll be here soon. Don't worry. Focus on your final piece."

As she played, her fingers felt like ice around the bow. She got second place, and when the curtain fell and the rest of the violinists were cheering backstage with their families, Lia's grandmother came to find her. Her eyes darted nervously around, and Lia knew something was really wrong.

"Where's Mom and Dad?"

"It wasn't appropriate to explain to you earlier. You needed to focus on your performance. You were supposed to get *first* place, the prestige—"

"*Where are they?*"

It was too late.

If Lia had gotten to the hospital ten minutes, thirty minutes, an hour earlier—when her grandmother had lied and said it was all right, that everything would be okay—she would've been able to hug her parents one last time. She would have heard the words they'd begged the ER nurses and physician assistants and doctors to tell her, despite the blood loss from the car crash, despite their barely there coherence.

That they loved her, that she was the center of their world, that they wanted her to be happy no matter what—

She never got to say goodbye.

That was the last time she played violin.

Ever since I've met her, she's made it clear: she's really fun and easygoing—until someone lies. Last year, for her sixteenth birthday, I'd tried to arrange a surprise birthday hangout—a day at the pool, stuffing ourselves with Ana's cupcakes for lunch, a sleepover at her Aunt Miki's apartment to cap it all off—but she could tell straightaway that I was keeping something from her . . . and she'd drawn into herself so fast that I blurted out the plans right away.

There are no—well, *almost* no—secrets between me and Lia . . . other than magic.

I swallow the lump in my throat, trying not to think of the lies I have to tell to hide a part of me that I'll never be able to share, not without getting kicked out of magical society. She's the one who sticks by my side, no matter what.

And I can't even tell her the truth about my life.

"It doesn't matter, anyway, my phone's mostly okay." I wave the screen at Lia. There's only a tiny chip on it, right on top of the clock. Mom's fix-it elixir didn't have enough time to mend it completely, but at least the hand that I used to wipe off the charmed dust is baby-soft and smooth.

"Ready to plan our road trip?" Lia asks, grinning at me. "Let's go."

I slide my phone into my pocket and wrap my arm around Lia's waist. "See you later, Jack."

Jack opens his mouth as if he wants to say something. Probably something like, *I don't know why you were so clumsy and wasted my time*, similar to what he said to me at the start of our econ project, in front of all of his friends: *I don't know why we have to be in a group together.* His friends laughed so hard, thinking his cruel words were a joke.

He wasn't kidding around. The tears I cried that night

joined the ocean I've cried since he stopped being the person who knew me better than I knew myself. But that's the old me. I'm over Jack, starting today.

Or maybe he wants to say, *Can I come with you all?*

Hah. The exhilaration of using magic in the open streets is addling my head. He'll never say that to me. Not anymore.

Back in the day, he and I used to have eating contests with Ana's cupcakes, and we'd run around Palo Alto causing trouble with our extra stroke of courage.

Or we'd help Jack's dad sort out the stock at his store—they sold homemade charmed stationery, back when Mrs. Yasuda was still alive. Once upon a time, there was an actual soul in CharmWorks' products.

We'd "help" my mom and dad taste-test recipes. And by "taste-test," I mean we snuck Mom and Dad's latest creations out from under their noses. Sometimes that was a smart move (like the red bean cake with a hint of euphoria), but sometimes it didn't end up so well (the caramel pops that stuck to the roof of our mouths instead of helping things stick in our memories).

Some days we'd even work on collecting raw magic dust, the heart of every charm. It's a lot like collecting rain, but it comes out of strong emotions, so we'd wear our parents' old chipped, rose-tinted spectacles and search around kids' birthday parties for fallen sparks to scoop into our vials, or try to make each other laugh so much that a spark would slide off our shoulders. When we collected the raw dust in our jars, the magic prickled at my fingers like static.

That's how my childhood felt with Jack: a series of magical sparks.

Until it ended all too fast.

I suppress the sugary-sweet nostalgia, like it's a candy that's turned sour. That's long gone. And this is now. *Now* is me and Lia instead of me and Jack.

We've drifted apart, and there's no way I'll understand Jack Yasuda ever again.

He glowers at me as Lia and I walk past, Mochi close at our heels.

Chapter 3

The wicker swing seat in the tucked-away crevice outside Ana's café feels like a warm hug as Lia and I slide in. The swing rocks softly under us as we kick off our shoes and pick up our cupcakes.

This corner is covered by a maple tree and a cardinal-red awning, overgrown with ivy. Mochi curls up near our feet to nap in the sunlight flickering through the green leaves. It's hidden from the tables with the red umbrellas in the center of the square—and this is our favorite place to hang out. Around the patio, Ana and her staff are rushing between tables, all of them outfitted in pale-red aprons with Simple Mornings' cheery sunrise-theme logo embroidered on the chest.

"Cheers," Lia says, tapping her creamy red velvet, gluten-free cupcake against my mango one.

I grin back. "Cheers to summer road trips . . . and wish lists."

"Oh?" Lia says, raising an eyebrow. "Did you have plans for us today? Another list of supplies for our trip?"

I laugh. "No, I already got enough packs of Jagabee to get us across the US, not just through California." These are my and Lia's snacking weakness. Japanese potato chips but in the shape of fries and a *million* times tastier. I have to wipe my chin to make sure I'm not drooling at the thought of them.

"I don't know, though, you've seen me demolish those," she replies. "So what's this list?"

I scroll through my phone to pull up a list and then stare at her, holding my screen to my chest. "Don't laugh. I know you're going to laugh."

"Because you're always so cute as a planner?" Lia pops in a mouthful of cupcake, the crumbs as red as her scarlet lip stain. After all, she's the fiery one; I'm the one who draws up schedules and lists. "Ellie, you know I love that about you."

"Okay. . . ." I take a deep breath. I'm ready, but I also want to crawl under the swing and hide forever. I'm a 24/7, would-hide-in-the-walls-if-I-could nobody.

Though when I see Lia, the center of attention in class, or the other students laughing with their friends, and I'm sitting by myself, sketching on my phone . . . I wonder what I'm missing.

I've spent all junior year perfecting this list. I think of all the times when people say hi to Lia, but they don't even look at me. And each time Jack sneers when he's bringing in a shipment for CharmWorks and I'm bringing in the sign for my parents' shop, and I get tongue-tied like I don't know what to say. Because even if I don't act like it, being invisible . . . it *does* sting.

I have to break through my walls starting this summer. It's my last chance before senior year starts, and I want to spend *some* part of high school as a person I'm actually proud of. It's hard to feel like myself when there's a huge part of me others can't know about—magic. Remy and Cam have always had each other to talk about charms, but I lost my closest friend that I grew up sharing all those moments with. Now, though, I don't want my past to hold me back from being myself anymore. I hand over my phone and my best friend bends her head over it. Her dark hair, dyed pink at the ends, falls over her face, and I desperately want to see her expression.

I know this list by heart, because even if I'm a wallflower, I . . . I want to change.

THE ANTI-WALLFLOWER LIST

1) Conquer (aka survive) the Giant Dipper at the Santa Cruz Beach Boardwalk
2) Pierce my upper ear cartilage and (hopefully) don't faint
3) Crash a wedding with a +1
4) Revenge on Jack Yasuda
5) Go on a picnic date
6) Win a contest, any contest
7) Dance under the stars with someone
8) Make my art Instagram account public. Maybe.
9) Have a fake model shoot to use as a senior yearbook photo
10) Sneak onto the beach for midnight s'mores
11) The perfect first kiss
12) A summer boyfriend (or maybe for more than just the summer?)
13) Fall in love

Lia's still got her head tucked down when she stops scrolling through my list.

"Thirteen total?" she asks, her forehead creasing. "I thought you always said thirteen is unlucky."

"I'm hoping some of these bucket-list items that feel cursed will turn out to be more charmed. To change things for me, you know." My cheeks are probably red; it feels like summer cranked up the heat. I should've grabbed some of Ana's homemade ice cream. Instead, I start tearing at the paper cupcake liner.

She flashes a smile at me. "Let me read this one more time."

As she scans over the list again, my paper liner looks like it's going through an industrial shredder.

Finally, finally, Lia passes my phone back, her laser-strong gaze focused on me. "Why? Why this, now?"

"I . . . I've always wanted to do this. It's a mix of things I've been looking forward to all year . . . and stretch goals that'll break me out of . . . being so shy."

My best friend bites down on her dark-red lip. "Like your art Instagram. You're *actually* going to make it public?"

She's been harping on me forever to let her see it. But outside of AP Art, it feels so *weird* to show off my work to anyone.

I nod slowly, and my stomach feels like a quivering bowl of jelly, instead of stuffed with cupcakes. "I refuse . . . I refuse to be invisible forever." I glare across the square at the backside of CharmWorks. "I refuse to let other people get the upper hand."

Lia bursts into a grin, throwing her arms around my shoulders and squeezing me in a big hug.

"I love this. I'm going to make my own list." She pulls

away to look at me, her eyes dead-serious. "Wowza, Ellie. Actually riding *the* roller coaster? *Finally* making your art public? Who *are* you and what have you done with my best friend? Let's make this happen."

My heart swells with joy, and it isn't from Ana's charm on the cupcakes. This summer's going to be perfect. This is going to be the summer when my Anti-Wallflower List becomes a reality.

Then Lia's eyes brighten, and my stomach drops. I know that look. She's ready to start some trouble.

"We're leaving for the road trip in three days. We don't have much time. Let's ride that roller coaster today."

Chapter 4

Moments later, we're packing up Lia's car for the hour drive down to Santa Cruz.

Remy is up in her room, casting quick-dry charms on the beach towels so we'll dry off in an instant. Cam's back at his house, above CharmWorks, where he's packing bags of snacks and an ice chest full of drinks; he's also casting a charm to make sure the cold packs don't melt in the heat. They're both staying out of sight of Lia, or else they would've been in our kitchen casting the charms together.

But Lia and I are busy anyway, cleaning her old Toyota RAV4. We're giving it a quick wipe-down, inside and out, before the four of us cram inside.

I wish I could use Dad's Car Clean magical dust for this. Every Sunday, he pulls our old, cranky Toyota Camry into the garage, closes the door, and pours a vial of the green powder onto the roof. With a quick spray of water, it foams all over the white paint, wiping the dust off from top to bottom.

I think Lia would get kind of suspicious if I borrowed her

car for five minutes and took it into the garage with me. So, we clean the non-magical way.

Remy trots out with a tote bag of towels, each neatly arranged like a sushi roll, and sets it in the back. "Are you ready?"

I grab the handheld vacuum from Lia, shove it onto the shelf, and toss the rags into the laundry basket. "Ready. Where's Cam?"

My younger sister looks up at CharmWorks' second story. "I thought he'd be done already. He's usually faster at"—her cheeks turn pink, and I know she was about to slip up and mention magic—"getting ready."

Lia frowns slightly. Sometimes, I do wonder if she notices. She's almost caught me a bunch of times. Each and every time, it feels like I'm burying myself deeper and deeper in lies, and I can't dig my way out of this.

The closest call still burns fresh in my memory—it was just a few months ago, right before spring break.

During a lunch hour when Lia was eating with some friends from drama class (she'd invited me, but I didn't know any of them), I'd holed up in the art studio. I was getting lost in the lo-fi music humming out of the tinny speakers and echoing against the high ceiling as I'd opened up a brand-new set of acrylics.

There's something magical about painting. It's the closest thing I've felt to the enchantment of casting a spell. The thick tubes of creamy paint, especially when they're fresh. The sleek tips of the brushes I like, the dark fibers contrasting with the bright colors.

It's in front of the canvas that I feel like *me*. It's a feeling I can't capture elsewhere, really. It's like all that blank space is a mirror, and for once, it sees me—the true me.

And I'm not invisible.

Here, the paint, the art, it makes me real. Into somebody who leaves a trace.

But what was the perfect color for this new canvas?

I picked up all the tubes, musing over how much red and yellow to mix for a perfect sunset orange. When I unscrewed the tops, the shiny, gleaming paint greeted me like a familiar friend.

The door opened, slamming against the wall, and a couple tumbled in, their hands all over, mouths attached like they're respirators for each other. My hand squeezed the tube involuntarily, sending paint splattering out, seeing the girl's hands weave through his messy dark brown hair—

Jack.

I blinked. It was Ally and Ian, the goth couple who fought and made up every other day in my art class.

"Here?" Ally giggled, twirling a lock of his hair around her finger. "I mean, I know Mrs. Mitra doesn't come back until class starts, but . . . that only gives us ten minutes."

Ian leaned in. "We've done it in five before."

She smacked him playfully on the chest but left her hand lingering. Then she traced her fingers down, down—

Hell no, I don't need them getting it on. In front of me and my once-sacred art haven.

I cleared my throat, my face burning red.

Their heads snapped up.

"I thought the studio was empty." Ian grimaced.

Is that an apology? Shouldn't this be more embarrassing for you than me? Why am I the only one who cares here?

"Who is she?" Ally whispered. "Did we summon a ghost?"

Wow. Okay, I'm not even real now?

"*Hello*—I'm standing in front of you two." But I'd spoken too quietly, my mouth hidden by the slant of my canvas, and they didn't hear me.

Ian laughed, his voice low as he wrapped his arm around her waist. "She's been in our class all semester. Don't you know her name?"

"You tell me first. I bet you don't know." Ally snickered.

"Ooh, you caught me," her boyfriend replied, but he didn't sound remotely embarrassed. Maybe because of the noisy, *wet* kissing that quickly ensued.

I glanced over at the door leading to the courtyard, the escape *away* from them. I took a step and my shoe squelched as loud as their make-out session.

My eyes dropped down to the ground, and I stared at the red paint splattered over the concrete. *Dammit.* I'd squirted some of the paint out of the tube and onto the ground.

It'd take forever to clean up, unless . . .

I checked the pocket of my denim shorts and, sure enough, under the secret flap, I had a paper packet of CleanCharm, a heavy-duty cleaner that looks like a packet of sugar. With one sprinkle, it zaps away minor messes. Usually, I kept it on hand for accidental period stains, but . . .

Maybe it could get me away from listening to this couple make out. That would be worth every penny. I could run out to the courtyard, away from them.

I glanced around. The coast was clear other than the couple, and they *obviously* weren't paying me any attention.

I tugged the CleanCharm out of my pocket and tore it open, tipping it over the paint. The white powder tumbled to the ground, taking on an iridescent gleam.

Just as the door to the courtyard opened, and a familiar voice said, "What was *that?*"

My heart thudded as I spun around.

Lia.

She hollered across the art studio, her voice echoing against the high ceilings, "Get a room, Ally and Ian. A *private* room."

Ally detached from Ian, blushing. "Oh, hey, Lia." She'd had a crush on my best friend last year, and apparently some feelings still lingered.

Ian grimaced, glaring jealously at Lia. "Let's go." The door slammed shut behind them.

But then my best friend turned back, squinting at the concrete ground. "Did I see . . . did you use *sugar* to get rid of paint?"

"I, um, dropped a piece of red paper." I stuffed the wrapping of the CleanCharm into my pocket, just before the paper vanished (it was a full-service charm—it even recycled itself). *I'd have a hard time explaining disappearing paper.*

Lia looked at me strangely. Sweat prickled my neck as my cheeks burned, a telltale giveaway. She knew me well enough to figure out something was up, but I *couldn't* tell her about magic.

"That make-out session was a little too much for my eyes," I blurted out.

Lia let out a loud laugh. "Yeah, that was a front-row seat I never wanted." Seemingly satisfied that I was on edge because of Ian and Ally, she added, "So, can I see what you're painting?"

I bit my lip. "It's not any good—"

Bzz! The bell rang, signaling the five-minute countdown before the next period.

Saved by the bell. I breathed out with relief. Lia sees a lot of my artwork, but I still get that naked-and-itchy uncomfortable feeling when I share my pieces with anyone.

"Shoot," she groaned. "I'm not ready for my test. Meet you at Ana's later?" Lia gave one last lingering look at where the red paint had splattered over the concrete, shaking her head. But she disappeared as my classmates milled in; she'd been working so hard to maintain her top-of-the-class rank in AP Physics, and she couldn't afford to be late for a test.

But that afternoon, she sat me down for a talk outside Ana's café and said, "Hey, you know you can tell me anything, right?"

"Of course. And I tell you everything." My stomach had burned with my lie.

The thing is, I *can't*. I can't tell her about magic. With concerns of enchantments getting in the wrong hands, plus the amount of raw magical dust decreasing these past few decades, the World Government of Sorcery decreed the general public can't be brought into magical society. You can be born into it, of course, like Remy and I were. Or, like when Dad was introduced by Mom into magical society, someone who's not magic-aware can marry into magic and find out about it (once they know about it, they can't unknow it).

Short of Lia and I getting hitched, if she were to find out, I'd risk being forbidden from touching a single speck of charmed dust ever again. I'd be cut out of our monthly family hangout where we go to Fisherman's Wharf late on a Saturday, once the tourist crowds are back in their hotels after having filled the pier with joy and wonder (which manifests as raw magic). Those are the best evenings, when we fill up on bread bowls stuffed to the brim with clam chowder and then spend the full-moon-drenched night on the empty pier, gathering the thick, swirling clouds of raw magic. I wouldn't be able to spend late nights with Remy, cozied up in my room with magic-infused globes floating around us as we watch the latest episode of *Demon Slayer* projected on my ceiling, while sipping charmed mugs of yuzu honey tea.

I'd miss that . . . but that's not the worst part.

If Lia finds out about magic, about the magnitude of this secret that I'm keeping from my best friend . . . after our promises *specifically* about telling each other everything . . .

She'll know I lied to her face, day in and day out. That I'm no better than her grandma, who she doesn't talk to anymore.

"Dad's not letting me go," a voice groans, pulling me out of my thoughts. Cam slumps on the curb, looking surprisingly dejected for his usual levelheaded self.

"Seriously?" Lia grumbles. Remy just sighs; Mr. Yasuda has always been such a grouch.

"Supervision, cost, *blah blah blah*," he says, mimicking Mr. Yasuda's deep and intimidating voice. I shudder.

"Look, I'll be there," I say, reasonably. "There's no way we're going to get in trouble. Want to try one more time? I'll say I won't let you out of my sight or something. Plus, the boardwalk is free admission. It doesn't get any cheaper than that."

Then, when Lia's phone buzzes, drawing her attention away, I mouth at Cam, *I'll cast some magic.*

He looks at me hopefully, nodding eagerly. I fight my grin. Even though Cam's already fourteen and taller than I am, he's been around so much that he almost feels like my younger brother. "I'll try asking my dad again. It might work like a charm," he says with a wink. A few weeks ago, I cast a *Say Yes to Opportunities* charm I found in one of Dad's old spell books—it only took a few pinches of dust—and we think it stopped Mr. Yasuda from raising a stink about Cam staying over for dinner for the fifth night in a row. Mr. Yasuda always tries to cook, but even his curry and rice tastes bitter and off compared to what Mrs. Yasuda used to make.

I nod. "Right, right." As he heads back to CharmWorks, I clear my throat. "I forgot my phone. I'll go grab it."

"Your phone's in your hand." Lia looks at me strangely.

"Oh!" I laugh. "I meant I forgot my ch—chicken burrito. That, uh, Dad made for me. I'm hungry."

Our stomachs are stuffed with the cupcakes we ate before rushing out of Simple Mornings with the plan of roping Remy and Cam into our Santa Cruz trip. I think I even have frosting still on my face.

Her forehead wrinkles, sensing something's up, and panic swells up in me. *I don't know what to say, I don't know what to say . . .*

Then Remy blurts out, "Lia, I need your advice about what

to wear at the start-of-summer party at Minami Vu's house.
Everyone's going, but I don't like wearing swimsuits . . ."

My best friend is momentarily distracted by my sister—
who sends a *Hurry up!* look over her shoulder—and I slip into
my house, Mochi's nails tip-tapping alongside me as fast as my
racing heart.

Chapter 5

My room is quiet and calm, a welcome haven from this hectic last day of school. It's a little cramped, but it feels truly like *home*. Everything from my packed bookshelves along one wall, stacks of sketch pads in the corner, my closet crammed with more art supplies than clothes, strings of fairy lights strung across the ceiling, and the big window pouring in warm light fills me with simple joy.

I glance over my shoulder to double-check that Lia didn't follow me in. But I'm alone—even Mochi disappeared, probably to search for a bone—and I stop in front of my bookshelves.

Just being near all these beautiful books reminds me of the feeling I get when I'm in front of a blank canvas holding a palette filled with smears of colorful paint. I run my fingers across the smooth paper jackets of the spines, sinking into daydreams of the worlds and characters hidden between the covers, until I stop at *Spin the Dawn*, one of my absolute favorites, with one of the most gorgeous covers I've ever seen.

As I walk over to the window seat and settle in the sun's glowing midmorning rays, I thumb my way to the title page. Though I want to immerse myself in Maia's adventure and forget all about the roller coaster and my Anti-Wallflower List (it's way too tempting), I close the book and tap on the spine. *Tap, tap, tap.*

When I open it again, instead of the luxurious scent of paper and ink, there's a pair of slightly scratched-up, rose-tinted glasses with a thin wire frame and a tiny glass vial nestled in a crushed red velvet backing.

But when I pick up the vial—the glass charmed so that I can see the raw magical dust that would otherwise be invisible to the naked eye—I groan.

"Shoot." The bottle is empty; I forgot to refill it after last night's concentration spell to study for my econ final. I pick up the vial, giving it one hopeful shake. A few tiny sparks of magic shimmer, but there's not even enough to cure a case of hiccups. Dad used up the rest of the dust we gathered on our last trip to Fisherman's Wharf for a set of new teas he and Mom are testing out. I'm going to have to collect some on my own, quickly.

I wipe down the pair of glasses—a hand-me-down after Mom got a set through her work as the Lead Sorcerer of Palo Alto—and put them on, with my eyes closed.

A big breath and then my eyes flutter open—

Oh.

Raw magical dust swirls through the air, soft and gentle like crystal snow. Suddenly seeing magic flowing around me is like diving underwater—overwhelming my senses with wonder. Most of the time, I can't see it because we magic-aware only use rose-tinted spectacles to gather raw dust; magic's sharp glow causes headaches with too much exposure.

Usually, I'd restock my vial at Fisherman's Wharf or, if I had more time, I'd set the glass out on a sunny day—along with a few rose quartz crystals for manifesting abundance—and let it fill with magic. But I need the dust *now* if I'm going to cast that spell for Cam.

I eye the dust shimmering around me. I can gather just enough—

I jump up, trying to catch a few sparkles with the vial, but they swirl right out of my reach. I groan. "Don't move!"

Thankfully, Lia isn't around to see me, because I look like Mochi dancing around for a treat. It's like trying to grab a snowflake with my hands; magic dust always seems to have a mind of its own. During our Fisherman's Wharf trips, Mom uses a few spells to make the dust slow and easy to collect, plus with the amount of joy in a tourist spot like the pier, there's a ton around.

Ever so ungracefully, I leap around after the swirls of magic, trying to capture enough. I only need a few pinches, which shouldn't be too tough, especially in a house like ours that's teeming with emotion. I lunge after another speck. "Ooh, gotcha!"

There's a snort from outside my window and I spin around.

My room looks out onto the alleyway and the house on the other side. Being two stories up, there's no way anyone can see inside except—

Jack leans on the frame of his window, arms crossed. "So, you're not just casting spells in broad daylight anymore. You're collecting magic where anyone can see?"

I want to crawl into my bed and never be seen again.

His damn window faces mine. It was something we loved when we were younger. I used to sneak out of bed and to the moonlight-drenched seat. The two of us would lean on our window frames, an alleyway apart, as we read each other stories until our eyelids drooped and our heads pillowed on the books.

But that was the never-to-happen-again past.

And he's the last person I want to see when I'm hopping around like the Easter Bunny.

My face blazes with embarrassment. "Anyone walking below in the alleyway can't see into either of our rooms. So your attempt to get me in trouble is sorely out of luck."

His forehead furrows in a deep frown, like I've said something that bothers him. But I can't read his eyes that flash with light and darkness at the same time. Jack is a stranger now. Yet, even from across the alleyway, I can see his fingers grip his window frame. He opens his mouth, likely to insult my fantastic, Olympic-worthy bunny hops, but I beat him to it—

"Leave me alone, Jack," I say sharply. *You're the one who frowns every time you see me. Stop talking to me. Stop noticing me. Stop making me notice you.*

He drags his hand through his hair and starts to say something—

Then, from his side, I can hear the faint sounds of Mr. Yasuda yelling, "Jack? *Jack!*"

He spins around, yanking the curtains closed. Through the open sliver, I can see Mr. Yasuda stomping into Jack's room.

"What's up, Dad?"

"I hope you weren't talking to that Kobata girl. They're the competition." Mr. Yasuda is as sweet and charming as ever. I once heard Mom and Dad comment—when they'd thought I was out of earshot—that the only nice thing about Mr. Yasuda was his wife.

"It's not a competition when we're outselling the rest of the square."

Mr. Yasuda snorts, sounding like the toad that he truly is. "That's my son. That's right. With our dedication and hard work, sales are shooting through the roof. We just have to keep at it."

And Jack simpers, "Of course, Dad. CharmWorks is my top priority. I promise."

His father laughs and continues talking; he always likes to hog the attention.

I couldn't even start my summer vacation without having to see Jack *twice*. During my econ final, I was so focused on getting a passing grade that I was able to ignore him and his popular group of friends. Unfortunately, today's luck ended the moment he bumped into me.

I try to catch another few floating specks, but my head aches from wearing the rose-tinted spectacles too long. Glittering dust swirls at the bottom as I shake the vial; I have enough anyway.

The curtains snap open, and Jack glares, crossing his arms. His father has disappeared, probably to return to CharmWorks and continue his goal of outselling the rest of Sorcerer Square, just for bragging rights.

I stare straight back, not even pretending that I haven't

heard every single word he and his father have said about me. I open my mouth to say something, but he's too fast—

"Don't collect magic in public," he hisses under his breath. He shoots me one last warning look and slams his window shut, the lock clicking as he gets in the final word.

I growl under my breath, turning my back to his house. But he's reminded me that I don't have much time, and Cam needs my help fast.

Quickly, I pour out some of the raw dust I've collected into my palm. I don't have any time to make it into something fancy, but I open up Dad's dog-eared *Hope for Hard Times* and thumb my way through the pages. I have to find the right incantation, because I'm not licensed like Mom to cast charms without the proper spell book. The last time I skipped a single word of a charm, my polish-and-clean charm broke everything it touched, including Mom's ikebana vase. My parents are pretty relaxed; they've never grounded me, thankfully. But Mom wasn't particularly happy about that one—I had to work at the shop to pay it back.

Say Yes to Opportunities.

Not for the first time, I wonder if I should cast this on myself. But I don't want magic to change me, not for my wish list. And with how stubborn Mr. Yasuda is, I need to use it on him so he'll agree that Cam can go on our trip.

Requirement: two pinches of raw magic.

Spells range from a pinch (like curing hiccups) to a gallon (a house-wide cleanup). I'm sure there're recipes that call for more magic, but there's not enough magic in the world these days to do things like saving lives or instantly electing a better president, so even a pinch or two is a pretty big amount.

INSTRUCTIONS:

1) Visualize what you would like to have happen.
2) While holding the vial with two pinches of raw dust, incant:

Say yes to opportunities that you least expect;
Now is not the time for one to reject.

3) Guide the spell-infused dust toward those in need of opportunities.

Well, that's simple enough. Okay, first, *visualize.*
A world where Jack and I don't throw barbs—
Dammit. Not that. I couldn't care less about Jack. I glare one more time at the now-empty window across the way.

I try to clear my mind, and I think of going to the boardwalk with Remy, Cam, and Lia. *Rumbling noises of the arcade, the scent of cotton candy in the air. Heavy crinkly bags of saltwater taffy, gleeful shouts of riders soaring overhead.*

Yes, I think as hard as I can. *Let Cam go. Say yes.* Carefully, glancing down at the spell book to make sure I don't mess up the words, I chant, "*Say yes to opportunities that you least expect; now is not the time for one to reject.*"

The vial of dust warms in my hands with a faint summer-blue glow. I pour it out in my palm and blow it at the Yasudas' house, watching it shimmer as it glides through the walls and hopefully toward changing Mr. Yasuda's mind.

With that, I breathe out deeply, sighing. I've cast my spell—as well as I could, given the circumstances.

Damn Jack Yasuda. Seeing him twice in a day is two times too much. I sure as hell hope I don't see him the rest of the summer.

I go back down to the garage—after a quick detour to the kitchen—with a chicken burrito in hand. Lia gives the burrito a skeptical look, but doesn't say anything other than continuing to give Remy advice on what to wear for that start-of-summer pool party.

Five minutes later, the back door of CharmWorks bangs open. Cam stands in the doorway, his lean body slouching even more than before.

"He said yes. I can go," Cam says, but it sounds like his dad told him he's got to work in the shop all summer.

"Then what's wrong?" Remy asks. "Don't tell me your dad had some catch—"

"As long as I go, too," a voice growls from behind Cam. "You owe me for wasting a day of my summer, bro."

Jack freaking Yasuda glares at all of us, his lips pressed in a frosty line.

"You didn't have to say yes," Cam grumbles under his breath.

Dammit. My spell backfired in the worst way possible. Seeing Jack Yasuda three times in a day is a curse. I narrow my eyes at him, and he meets my gaze straight back. Stiff, awful silence fills the air, and even Cam winces as he glances between his brother and me.

"Well," Lia says, finally. "This is going to be fun."

෴   ෴

The Santa Cruz Beach Boardwalk *oozes* summer. The bright sun shines without a cloud in sight and the faint scent of cotton candy drifts through the air. From the far end of the beach, I can hear the faint screams of riders on the Giant Dipper, the boardwalk's famous wooden roller coaster.

"This," Remy breathes out, eyes bright, "is the best way to kick off our vacation."

Cam nods, his face lighting up as my sister smiles. They're so oblivious to how much they like each other.

Not that they need help with their love lives. If anyone needs help, it's me.

We stroll onto the boardwalk and down the line of rides and shops along the beach, the sand soft and warm, and the water glinting playfully next to us. It's perfect.

"So, what are the chances we'll find a cute date here?" I ask Lia, who grins back. Maybe I can get started on number 11: The perfect first kiss.

Jack coughs from behind us, like he's choked on his breath.

"You okay there, chaperone?" Lia glances over her shoulder.

He waves her off. "I'm fine."

My best friend turns back to me. "Anyway, *I* count as a cute date." She pouts, and I can't disagree with that. I loop my arm around hers as something catches my eye.

"Saltwater taffy!" I squeal, pulling her into Marini's at the

Beach. The candy shop's sweet, chewy taffy is a boardwalk staple and our favorite way to kick off our visits. Only the magic-aware know that the local surfer—and sorcerer—applies summer vibes charms to some of the taffies, chilling you out for the day.

We speed past the taffy-pulling machine, which is already churning out a new batch of strawberry-pink taffy, and past the stacks of chocolate-dipped everything (pretzels, strawberries, even bacon), beelining straight to the crinkly bags of taffy.

Five minutes later, we're back outside, clutching our goods.

"You ditched us," Remy calls from where she and Cam are sitting on one of the benches, across from Marini's.

I hand over a wax bag filled with sour watermelon gummies. "Yeah, but I got this for the both of you." My younger sister grins like a cat that's surrounded by an ocean of cream. Cam snags one from her and starts chewing.

"That much candy, all for yourself?" Jack says from where he's leaning against the railing separating this part of the boardwalk from the beach. His voice is quiet. *Judgmental.* The prickle of annoyance that spears me doesn't let me walk away.

"Sorry, *Dad.* Are you going to say it's not healthy or something?" I glare.

He shakes his head. "Does it matter what I was going to say?" Pushing off, he saunters past. "C'mon, let's keep moving."

"Downer," Lia grumbles under her breath, and I wholeheartedly agree. Even Remy looks a little annoyed.

"Sorry," Cam says, glancing between the three of us.

I nudge him. "I'll *try* to tolerate Mr. Sunshine's company if it means we can hang out with you, too."

A throat clears, and we all jump.

Jack's waiting at the entrance of the arcade, looking bored as ever.

Did he hear me? I wonder, my insides curling up. Then I remember my list. *Does it matter?*

I brush past him, dragging Lia in with me. It doesn't matter if he heard or not. We all know he's coldhearted anyway, and deserves every word of what I said, if not more.

～～

Lia and I are playing Skee-Ball in the somewhat dark arcade when I drop one of the smooth Masonite balls. "Ew, there's gum on this one." It rolls onto the floor, the digital display flickering at the corner of my eye. "Dammit."

This machine's old, one of the models that only goes up to 50 points, so I'm not surprised these balls have been through a lot. Still, someone's old chewing gum is nasty.

"I'm gonna beat you," Lia calls after me, taking her time to aim for the 50-point hole as I search through the crowd for the ball. We're usually so close to each other that it's a tie, but with this setback—

The ball rolls to a stop at a pair of tan flip-flops. A tall guy picks it up, peeling off the gum by its barely-hanging-on wrapper and tossing it into a nearby trash can. He holds it out to me, clean. "This yours?"

He's around my age, with green-brown eyes, golden-brown curly hair, and tanned skin. In board shorts and a loose V-neck, he looks like the epitome of a Santa Cruz surfer boy. But his crooked smile draws me in, making me stop instead of just grabbing the ball with a quick thank-you.

A handful of guys and a couple of girls stop behind him.

"What's up?" one of the girls asks, then she sees me. "Ooh, Ezra, she's cute."

I blush madly, thankful for the semidarkness of the flickering lights, as I grab the ball from his outstretched hand. "Um, thanks for the help."

"Mind if me and my friends play on the open lanes?" this Ezra guy asks, with a cool nod toward the five free lanes to our left.

"All yours." I wave my hand like I own the place. Could I be any more dorky?

They scan their prepaid cards, and then Ezra, who's ended up in the lane closest to me, says, "Do you two want to join our game? Say, first to get the highest score?"

Lia winks. I know she's memorized my list, and we're thinking, *number 11: The perfect first kiss.*

I will *not* let myself just blend into the walls here. "Sure," I say. Lia and I finish up our game—I barely notice that she wins by a landslide—and swipe again. My card slot flashes red; I'm low.

"Use this." Ezra leans over. He's got the scent of salty beach air and a simple sweetness, like puffs of cotton candy. Maybe I did get one of the lucky taffies from Marini's. "Play a game on me."

I protest, but it's too late. My machine rolls out the balls, ready and waiting. Ezra glances side to side between all of us. "On your mark, get set, go, go, go!"

We shout, laughing as we start, and one of the guys yells with fake indignation when his ball rolls over the ball-hop and into the gutter. Ezra's at my side, carefully aiming each shot, and I'm trying to stay focused on mine, but I'm completely distracted, scoring 20s and 30s instead of my usual mostly 50s streak.

Cam and Remy come up from behind. "Hey, what're you all doing?" Remy calls over the clamor of dinging machines and rolling balls. "Want to head outside to the beach?"

I grit my teeth, gesturing toward Ezra and his friends. "We're—going—to—beat—them—"

"No way!" one of the guys calls back in a joking taunt.

"Oh, you won't beat *my* score," Ezra adds, and I can almost feel Remy's gaze of surprise burning into my shoulders. Me? Talking to strangers?

And then I feel a darker, deeper burn on my shoulders. This time, I glance around and see Jack. His eyes are narrowed as he takes in me and Ezra, who's nudging me playfully to try to keep me from getting the perfect shot. *Ugh.* He's here to watch Cam, not monitor me. I turn back to the Skee-Ball machine and my abysmal score, trying to ignore his annoying presence.

I laugh ruefully when the buzzer rings, signaling the end of the game. I've played horribly. One of the girls from Ezra's group of friends cheers. "A perfect set of 50s!" She catches Lia eyeing her in surprise, then flexes her arms with a wink. "Good aim from archery."

"Hey, do you play tennis at Gunn?" Jack asks Ezra. Gunn's our rival high school.

My potential summer fling runs a hand through his hair and nods. "Yeah, varsity. I'm Ezra, one of the co-captains." Then it's his turn to squint at Jack. "You're the captain at Paly. Damn, didn't recognize you out of uniform, Jack. What's up, dude."

The guys do that bro-hug thing, with back slaps.

Ezra nods at me. "What's your name, by the way?"

"Ellie. Thanks for paying for my game."

"No problem." He shoots me another one of those crooked grins that makes me think of *number 11: The perfect first kiss.* "Want to go for another round, Ellie?"

"Sure, but let me do a refill first." I wave my arcade card at him.

"I can pay for another game for you," he says, but I shake my head, my heart leaping as I hurry off. I call over my shoulder, "But you can pay after I beat you next time!"

I like the way he laughs, cool and smooth, like the waves hitting the beach outside.

This is it: the start of my perfect summer romance.

ᐁ   ᐃ

Three games later, I'm still losing—but I totally blame Ezra. He keeps nudging me when I'm trying to roll the ball up. I *think* that's supposed to be cute. My flirt radar is rusty from never being used.

Lia keeps winking when he does that, and that makes me flustered. I'm getting closer to fulfilling my bucket list. I might actually get kissed.

This strange way my stomach flips when I think about that . . . it feels *right*.

After the fourth game, we take a break, loitering around the machines as a group of elementary school kids take over, screaming at the top of their lungs. Jack starts talking to Ezra—of *course* my neighbor is taking all of his attention—in a low voice, to the side.

No. Way.

I'm not letting damn Jack Yasuda ruin my summer romance. I stalk forward, bumping into Jack with my shoulder, none too gently.

"Ouch—oh, Ellie." He doesn't seem to be surprised. He should be jumping with guilt, worry, *something*. But instead he raises an eyebrow, as if trying to tease me. "Leaping around everywhere still?"

I ignore him, smiling invitingly at Ezra. "Wanna go play a different game? We can try something else."

"Well—" Ezra glances between me and Jack. Jack shifts toward me like he's trying to stand in front of me. And his face loses that teasing look really fast, turning into a glare at the surfer for some reason.

It's almost like he's trying to protect me.

He hasn't done this since fifth grade, when the most popular, richest, and prettiest girl (seriously, where is the justice in the world?) in the year below us, Minami Vu, made fun of my overalls.

"Those are so last year," she'd sneered, with her perfect button nose pointing up in the air. Her mother is a venture capitalist, and Minami always wears the latest styles before they even start trending on Instagram. I'd been proud of my green corduroy overalls. Hell, I didn't even know overalls *had* a year. But Jack loudly commented, "*I* like overalls. They look good on you, Ellie." Then he'd shifted in front of me, facing the girl, and she flushed all red.

The following week, she wore the *exact* same green corduroy overalls to school. For some reason, he never complimented her on them.

But we're not in elementary school anymore. I'm definitely seeing things. I glance over at the Skee-Ball lanes, where the archery girl's chatting up Lia and the rest of Ezra's friends are still hanging out.

"Or, even better," I say boldly, ignoring Jack's pointed glare. "We can go out into the boardwalk and ride the Giant Dipper."

"You—you're going to ride the Giant Dipper?" Jack cuts in.

I ignore him, stepping closer to Ezra. "So?"

"Sounds like a plan, El." Ezra breaks into a grin, waggling one eyebrow. My stomach drops like I'm already on the roller coaster.

Jack speaks up. "Ellie—I thought—"

I pull Ezra by the arm, looping my hand around his elbow, tugging him away from my neighbor. "Let's get out of here."

Chapter 6

I can't miss the huge wink Lia throws my way as she distracts the rest of the group with promises of greasy, summer-perfect food. The rest of them go off—Lia manages to pull Jack after her even though his forehead is furrowed like he still wants to get in the last word to ruin my potential date—to load up on buckets of garlic fries and cones dripping with decadent ice cream.

Usually, I'd be right on the plastic bench with them, devouring the fries and making my hands stink with loads of delicious garlic.

But I look up at the red-and-white roller coaster in front of me. The Giant Dipper in its full glory.

It feels like my head is already spinning.

It's a wooden roller coaster, made around a hundred years ago. So it doesn't have extreme loops like modern-day, wild, flipping-upside-down coasters. It shouldn't be too bad, right?

But it's on my list for a reason.

I've always been nervous around heights. Anything above

one or two stories makes my stomach feel like it's going to simultaneously shrivel up and explode.

It got bad when I was six. We were taking a weekend trip to see Uncle Jeremy, who lives down by the Santa Cruz coast, and he thought it would be funny to take me on the most famous ride on the boardwalk.

I should probably mention that he *loves* daredevil things. He's gone skydiving with each of his five ex lovers, and bungee jumping is an ideal way for him to spend a vacation. So roller coasters are *nothing* to him.

But the ride—even though I was tall enough to ride it and all that—was *way* too much for six-year-old me.

Even sitting in the stopped car, everything looked so far away. It made me realize that if I fell, I'd fall a long, long way. My parents and Remy were standing beyond the barrier, tiny as ants as they gaped at me—they'd gone off to pick up a bag of saltwater taffy. Dad's mouth opened and closed worriedly as he tried to call something over to me, but his voice was lost in the sea breeze. They probably thought Uncle Jeremy was going to take me on the kiddie teacups knockoff ride, but no, this being my wild and adventurous uncle.

The car began to chug slowly toward a dark tunnel, and I breathed out, my hands dripping with sweat. "Is this what a roller coaster is like? It's the perfect speed."

"Hah!" my uncle boomed with a laugh. "This is just the beginning!"

Roller coasters looked so fast from the outside, but maybe this ride was different. No matter what, after I got off, I'd get to run to Mom and Dad and get a big hug and—

A whoosh of wind swirled through the dark tunnel. As

we chugged upward, slow and steady, Uncle Jeremy was still chattering away about how fun coasters are, how much I'd been missing out. I let out a tentative laugh. This roller coaster wasn't too bad, I could—

Below the car, gears clicked ominously and—and—

In front of us, a light glowed, and I caught a glimpse of how high up we were. It felt like thirty stories high, and I couldn't see Mom and Dad anymore. I'd thought people looked like ants before; now they didn't even seem to *exist*.

"Wait," I said, sweat coating my face. "Uncle Jeremy, how do we get down from here?"

My uncle let out another booming laugh, and—

The world fell out from under us as we dropped down, down, down, my brain feeling like it had evacuated the planet.

I broke into an ear-piercing shriek.

We plummeted as the coaster swerved in a hairpin turn, and I—I—

I peed in my pants.

There were more rickety turns and drops, but I don't really remember much. Just the wetness of my pants, the scream that I couldn't stop. We were planning on driving back home the next day, but Mom and Dad took us back immediately.

For nights after, I'd wake up crying, feeling that sudden drop of the roller coaster, that absolute fear, the sweat coating my skin, sour bile in my mouth. Remy and I slept together in my parents' bed, snuggled between them, and my nightmares faded.

But that knee-jerk, vomit-inducing feeling when I look at a roller coaster—*the* roller coaster—hasn't changed. I always feel like I'm six years old again, small and lost in the world.

On the platform, I stare at the Giant Dipper's bright blue car. This might be the very same seat I peed a puddle in all those years ago. I half expect Uncle Jeremy to pop out of the line of waiting riders and bellow, "Are you wearing a diaper this time?"

"Get in," the tired attendant says, waving me forward. Ezra clambers into the car, his flip-flops loud and clacking. He slides into the seat like it's nothing.

Still on the platform, I roll on the balls of my feet, like I'm at the edge of an Olympic-height ten-meter diving board.

Ezra and the list . . .

Safety . . . comfort . . .

Ezra . . . and the list . . .

Safety . . .

"Has anyone gotten off the Giant Dipper midway?" I turn to the girl. "Uh, asking for a friend. To make sure you have protocols and all that."

She shrugs, picking at a thread coming off her uniform. "I don't know, I just do the safety checks. You don't want to ride? Go that way."

The exit gate, on the far end of the platform, looks like the golden gates of heaven. Or if there's no heaven, then the doorway of a bookstore. I eye it longingly.

"C'mon, Ellie," Ezra calls.

I bite my lip.

He reaches over, tugging me in by the hand, and my heart swoops. He sees that I'm scared, and he's trying to comfort me.

I stumble onto the bench seat next to him, smiling widely in thanks. I know this list is all my own thing, but some romantic encouragement can't hurt, right? After all, two of my summer goals *are* falling in love and getting a boyfriend. This is just one step toward that.

"We're holding up the ride," he mutters, glancing around. "I thought we'd have time to take a selfie here, but everyone's staring."

"Oh." I look around, and he's right. People are mumbling under their breath, craning their necks to see what's happening.

"Good, you're in," the attendant sighs, cranking down the safety bar over our laps.

I blink. It's a glorified iron bar that clicks down, locking into place over our thighs.

"Wait, this is it?" I squeak. "Where's the harness? You know, so we don't fall out? Where's the—"

"This is our standard safety belt, inspector-approved, etcetera, etcetera," the girl says. "But I think your seat's that way."

Again, she gestures at that heavenly exit gate. At my side, Ezra shifts, his eyes furtively glancing back at everyone staring at us.

"No," I say, trying to sound calm even though I'm shrieking inside like the six-year-old me who just got off the roller coaster with Uncle Jeremy. "I'm good, thanks."

"You're welcome?" the girl says tiredly and saunters over to the control panel. She says some announcements about not moving, not standing up—why the hell would anyone try to *stand* on a roller coaster, isn't sitting *enough?*—but my head is spinning too much to absorb anything.

The car starts slow as the gears click into motion. *I can do this, I can. I—*

"Eep!" I cry out as the car starts accelerating.

And we plunge into darkness.

"Hell, no!" I throw away all my dignity and clutch onto the side of the car. "I shouldn't have done this, I shouldn't have—"

"It's okay, it's okay," Ezra says, surprisingly comforting. "Look at me, El."

El? Who's El? I wonder in a delirious haze, and then he reaches out, the faint light from the end of the tunnel illuminating his outline. He turns my face toward his.

I really would prefer to be scanning around for dangers, for potential hazards so I can leap out of this car if it looks like we're going to crash and go up in a plume of smoke, and—

He leans in, and I can smell the ocean-wash of his hair.

I freeze.

Is he trying to *kiss* me? In my moment of near-death fear?

Maybe . . . my heart melts a little . . . *is he trying to make me forget about how scared I am?*

He slides closer. "El, the moment we met, I was drawn in by your exotic beauty. You're like someone I've always longed to meet, I—"

I can't miss the way his hand is a little *too* sweaty. Like just-dipped-in-the-ocean sweaty.

And *exotic*? What the hell? Exotic is for high maintenance cars, not people.

The roller coaster shifts as we go up an incline, and I let out a yelp, sliding farther away from him on the bench seat.

"Don't be scared." His voice grates like sandpaper. "El, c'mon. This is nothing."

Who the hell is El, *anyway? And just because it's "nothing"*

to you doesn't mean it's "nothing" to me. I grit my teeth. "Me?
Scared? Never."

*This is your summer romance, this is your summer
romance—*

*Is this really going to be the spot of my first kiss? I'll finally
make out with a guy, but also pee in my pants five seconds
later?*

Ezra leans closer, just as the car pulls out of the tunnel and
into the brilliant summer light—

There's too much blue sky, holy spells and curses, there's
way too much blue sky.

We're about a thousand feet above the ground—or at least
that's what it feels like—and the crowds below are little ants
scurrying around.

Ezra's still trying to pull me back to kiss him. "El—"

Beyond the other cars in front of us, there's no more track
that I can see. We're not going up anymore (which is a relief).

. . . but it means we're going down.

I bite down on my scream. Shoving his hands away in favor
of holding on to the safety bar, I pull it low across my lap as
hard as I can. Because if I do, I mean, I'll stay in this damn
flying car and not hurtle off into the blue, blue sky and up into
heaven, right?

Or maybe hell because—

"*Ahhh!*" I scream as the car plummets down.

Approximately ten long hours later, after I faint about five
times, the roller coaster clatters to a stop and the tired attendant drones, "Please wait until your safety bar lifts up before
exiting."

It's probably more like two minutes. I didn't actually faint, and my pants are *dry*. Still, the moment that the iron bar eases (and I manage to pry my pincer-grip hands off), I dart for that beautiful, beautiful exit.

Outside, on solid ground, I put my hands on my knees, breathing in and out.

"Are you like, scared of roller coasters or something?" Ezra slides his arm around my waist. "Hey, talking about scary—the other day, I ate an In-N-Out burger with chopped yellow peppers from their secret menu. That heat is out-of-this-world ridiculous and—"

I guess it's nice he's trying to comfort me. Still, I tune him out as I savor the strange euphoria warming my chest—and try to stop the uncomfortable sloshing in my stomach.

Ezra pauses his monologue to finally look at me. "Wait, are you going to puke?" I keep ignoring him as I try to return to some feeling of normalcy.

I did it. I rode the Giant damn Dipper.

I press my hands to my stomach. I'm still in one piece. I think.

My body feels like it's flipped inside out.

Is this what brave people feel like all the time? Like they're at the edge of dying?

"*Ellie?*" Jack stands in the middle of the crowd. A family pushing a stroller has to weave to the left to avoid him, and the dad shoots him an annoyed look.

But he's ignoring all of them. His eyes are wide as he steps closer to me. "Are you okay?"

Ezra laughs him off. "Dude. Calm down. It wasn't brain surgery."

"Ellie's deathly afraid of roller coasters," Jack snaps, his eyes dragging down to where Ezra's arm rings my waist. "Especially *this* one."

"Really?" Ezra raises an eyebrow. "C'mon, this coaster is for little kids."

I breathe in a gasp of the salty boardwalk air. I'm still getting used to the damn beautiful feeling of solid ground underneath me.

"Here." Suddenly, Lia's extracting me from Ezra's sweaty grip and guiding me away. "Let's sit down." My best friend leads me to a bench facing a pair of couples playing beach volleyball, and pushes an ice-cold water bottle into my hand. "Drink."

The movement of the volleyball arcing back and forth over the net makes me queasy, like I'm back on the roller coaster watching the world swing around me. I close my eyes as I drink the water, the near-freezing chill centering me.

"I don't know how I survived," I moan, splashing some water on my face.

"If I didn't know about your list, I'd ask what the hell you were doing." Lia laughs. "You knocked the roller coaster off your list *and* flirted with a cute boy."

I brighten slightly at that. It feels like I rode into hell and back, but she's right.

There's a buzz of voices behind us. Lia and I look back toward the exit of the Giant Dipper. Jack and Ezra are talking, but something about the way Jack's gesturing up at the roller coaster and then over at me doesn't look so friendly.

"What's gotten into Jack?"

"They know each other from tennis, right?" Lia says. "Maybe it's some friendly team rivalry?"

Hah. Jack? *Friendly*?

I head back to them. Jack's standing at his full height, almost six feet, to tower over Ezra.

"Hey, want to go grab some food?" I ask Ezra, nudging him in the side. "I don't know about you, but I'm kind of obsessed with the garlic fries here, and—"

But Ezra takes a step back, like I'm suddenly infectious. "Uh, nah . . . I remembered we're meeting a few friends . . . on the other side of the boardwalk . . ." He coughs awkwardly. "I, uh, gotta go."

"What? Why?"

Ezra's eyes shift between me and Jack, and I don't understand that look. Just a minute or two ago, his arm was wrapped around my waist and it seemed like he was willing to spend all day hanging out and be a potential candidate for number 11.

"Yeah, um," Ezra stammers. "I . . . I got plans already. Sorry."

Was it because I was a wimp during the roller coaster? Embarrassment burns through me, making my stomach feel like it's full of acid. So much for my list. My daydreams of a sweet cotton-candy summer kiss under the blazing sun burn out faster than I can say *Jack Yasuda shut down my date before it really started.* I don't even bother asking Ezra for his number. He's already walking backward in his urge to get away from me.

Moments later, Ezra disappears down the boardwalk, his golden curls like a trophy disappearing from under my fingertips.

"What the *hell*, Jack," I hiss. "Thanks for chasing my date away."

"You really call that a date?" Jack says. "With a guy like him?"

Okay, I don't know if Ezra and I really had chemistry. And I'm not too sure about that whole "exotic" thing. But there was a chance he and I could've been something.

Until Jack blew it all up.

I snap, "Better him than a guy like you. Why the hell did you have to go and chase him away?"

My damn frustrating neighbor growls, "Ellie . . . it's not like what you think, he—"

I shake my head with disgust. "Why am I not surprised? Oh, wait. Because you're *always* like this."

"What do you mean by that?" He takes a step toward me, but I glare, warning him not to come an inch closer.

"Whoa there, guys." Lia waves her hands between us placatingly.

But I'm seeing red. How can Jack act like he doesn't know how he's been all these years? Leaving me behind. Always ignoring me unless it's convenient for him. Laughing about me with his father. I realized I was a nobody because of *him*.

"What did you say about me to him to chase him off like that? That I'm a loser at school? Wow, thanks, Jack."

"Ellie, I—"

I don't want to hear a single excuse. "Go watch Cam. Do what you're *meant* to do, not screw up my summer." I spin on my heel, Lia calling my name behind me as I push through the crowd, careful to stay well away from the direction Ezra was headed. I'll just embarrass myself if we see each other again.

I stride down to the sand, and Lia finally catches up, looping her arm into mine. "Ellie . . ."

"I can't believe him," I hiss. "I'm pretty sure he said something about me to chase off Ezra."

"Damn Jack Yasuda." Lia shakes her head. Seagulls screech loudly overhead, jarring and sharp, like the thoughts tumbling through my mind as I angrily walk down the sand. Even the cold water running over my feet doesn't chill me out.

"Yeah, I'm not letting him get away with that." I stop, turning to her. "It's time for number four. It has to happen before we leave for our road trip. I'm getting revenge on on Jack, and he's going to think twice before he ever screws around with my life again."

"I'm in." Lia's eyes sparkle. "He's obsessed with his electric guitar. How about something to do with that?"

"Maybe, but it'd be tough to get to his guitar." I wouldn't be able to find a way into the Yasudas' house without Cam's help (and I don't want to rope him into this; if something goes wrong, his dad would get mad at him) or magic (which I can't do because of Lia).

"Fair . . ." Lia and I continue walking down the gritty sand. "Darn it. What's his weakness?"

"His obsessive need to please Mr. Yasuda. It's always about CharmWorks' sales numbers, CharmWorks outselling the rest of the square, CharmWorks being the most successful business in Palo Alto, just so he can show off to anyone around him and act perfect all the time— Oh, I've got an idea . . ."

Earlier in the week, I'd been wiping down the glass window front of Elissa's Tea Shop, and Jack had come out the side door of his dad's shop, dragging boxes to the recycling with the part-time girl at CharmWorks. She's a magic-aware sophomore, only a year younger than us, and she looks at Jack with stars in her eyes. And Jack kind of puffed up the moment he saw me, not-so-casually making a point of saying hi, so I'd see her with him.

Was he trying to show her off to me?

I don't know, and I don't care.

But I do know now—based on the way he had self-consciously run his fingers through his brown hair—that he cares about what she thinks of him.

After I tell Lia about this encounter, she grins like the Cheshire cat. "What're we going to do? Clearly, we have to embarrass him a little, right?"

I nod. The sun burns down on my neck, hot and angry like the revenge I'm going to serve up to my neighbor. "Jack got in the way of my summer romance, so I'll just have to do the same for him."

Chapter 7

Revenge of this level requires subterfuge. We can't plan at my house, not with Mom and Dad popping in my room all the time to offer their latest tea creations—even though Dad's roasted green tea macarons with a hint of strength make me feel like I can conquer the world.

Instead, on the day after my eventful first (and likely only) successful roller-coaster ride, we curl up on our swing at Simple Mornings, Mochi faithfully lying out in the sun in front of us. Her ears flicker when Ana pops over with a tray to offer us her favorite agua de coco, still in the freshly cut coconut shell, as well as a plate piled with mini cupcakes. "Come on, have some, won't you two? You've got to try this, so refreshing for the summer."

After Ana feels reassured that we've got enough food to last us five lifetimes, she bustles away to check on another patron.

We sip the clear coconut water through the compostable straws (of course, Palo Alto), and for a second I feel like I'm lying out on the beach, the salty air fluttering my hair. A tall boy is strolling toward me through the sand and—

Oh, right. Jack *stopped* that daydream from becoming reality when he chased Ezra off.

"Okay, plans." I set the coconut onto the small table in front of the swing with a thump, jumping straight into business. Lia nods, picking up a gluten-free guava cupcake and biting into the pink-orange fluffy frosting. "We want to embarrass him. Not cause too much trouble—"

"Unfortunately," Lia says, licking buttercream off her finger. "I'm still not forgetting the way he snubs you all the time at school. Ugh, I hate that way he looks down on you!"

Me too. He never used to be like that. . . . Before, he and I were almost stuck together at the hip, and during class the teachers would have to separate us for group projects so we'd socialize with the other kids.

"So let's get under his skin." Lia devilishly chomps down on the rest of the mini cupcake. She takes another long draw of coconut water. "We're hitting the road on Friday morning, though."

That's only two days . . . less than forty-eight hours to get revenge before we head off on our road trip.

"He doesn't like mice," I say. "We know that much." Back when we were seven or eight, Jack and I had heard stories from his great-grandparents about being in the World War II internment camps. His great-grandma had explained that when she was a little girl, the mice would come crawling out at night, and Jack has been scared of them ever since. It's up there with spiders, which he avoids like his life depends on it—and it kind ot does, after his leg swelled up a ton from a bite, back when we were nine years old.

"We could do something about that," Lia says, waggling her eyebrows. "Freak him out with a twitch of a mouse..."

"It might be mean, though..." I trail off, tearing at the paper liner of my mini cinnamon cupcake.

"Mean? What're you two up to?" Ana kneels next to Mochi, running a hand through her fluffy fur.

"Nothing," Lia says sweetly.

"Summer plans," I add.

She shakes her head and plunks two boxes full of mini cupcakes on the glass table. "Bring these on home, one for each of your families. Gluten-free acai cupcakes, with a new buttercream frosting I'm testing out."

"Ooh, my favorite! A fresh batch?" I can almost taste the sweet tingle of the fruity acai, tangling with a hint of coconut and that dollop of extra honey that Ana uses in the frosting. Mmm. She knows acai is one of my favorite flavors at her shop. What Ana doesn't know is that acai is my go-to because she weaves in a hint of bravery when she purees the fruit. And, being a shy nobody, I need all the bravery I can get.

"And..." Ana pauses, studying both of us.

"Something up?" Lia smooths down her hair innocently.

A patron signals Ana, gesturing her over to their table.

"Whatever you two are up to, think twice. Sounds like trouble to me," she says, before hurrying off.

Lia and I look at each other, sharing a grin.

"Trouble is *exactly* what Jack deserves," I say.

∽   ∽

That afternoon, Lia and I begin setting up the prank of the century.

First, we stop by Books Inc., one of our favorite local indie bookstores, across the street from our high school. Not only do they have an awesome selection of books (Remy could stay here all day; she's been thinking about applying for a part-time job), they also have a small selection of nifty toys.

When Lia and I stopped in earlier in the year, during our school lunch break, something in the toy section had caught my eye: a box full of realistic-looking rubber mice, solar-powered by little hard-to-see panels on their twitching tails. One raced inside a plastic box, showing how it runs around for ten minutes after you press the button on the bottom. They even squirmed like real mice.

And they're still here.

Perfect.

"No books today, Ellie?" the bookseller says, ringing up my basket full of mice. My family's been going here for as long as I can remember, and most of the staff know us by name.

I'd special-ordered an enchanted tour book of California for the drive down, but I can't bring that home in front of my magical-unaware best friend. "Well—"

The bookseller winks and lowers her voice. "Our team will deliver *that* to your house later; your parents bought a few new charmed cookbooks, too."

"But we can't leave without a book," I protest, looking around. There are non-magical books I've had on my to-read list forever. And leaving a bookstore without a book is *unthinkable.*

"Ellie's right." Lia strides over, placing the paperback edition of *Dear Martin*, one of my favorites, onto the counter. She grins. "We'd *never* leave without a book."

∾ ∾

On Thursday morning, the day before we head out on our road trip, we're setting up the final touches on our prank.

Lia and I have snuck up the outside stucco stairs to the rooftop above CharmWorks and the Yasudas' house. We've got our bucket of mice, a bottle of sealing foam to shut the door . . . We're ready for business.

Now it's time to wait.

Exactly at 10:30 A.M., Jack and Zareen, the part-timer, pop out the side door for their early lunch break. Lia and I grin at each other from where we're situated on the rooftop, directly above the exit. They stroll down the alleyway, not noticing the two of us posed like gargoyles, happily watching as they disappear around the corner.

"Enjoy your lunch break while you can." Lia snickers.

We don't have any time to waste. Lia and I hurry back down the stairs, leaving our blue bucket of mice on the rooftop. Mr. Yasuda is still inside, so we have to move quietly.

Quickly, we look up and down the alleyway. It's before the lunchtime rush, before people use this path as a shortcut between the shops. But we stay on our toes, with Lia keeping watch.

I get to work, pulling the cap off the spray bottle of expanding foam. Carefully, I pull open the back door of Charm-Works and peek inside.

It's been years since I've been here. There's a set of stairs immediately to the left that go up to the Yasudas' living space, and a long hallway leading down to the shop. Back when I hung out with Jack, the walls were maple wood, caramel-colored and homey. Now they're painted over in pure white, blindingly bright, soullessly corporate, and *cold*.

Just. Like. Jack.

"Is someone in there?" Lia asks.

"*Shh!*" If there *was* someone, she would've caught their attention.

I don't know how to explain how much CharmWorks has changed. Instead, I say, "No, the coast is clear. Let's get this show on the road . . ."

I shake the spray bottle and attach the clear nozzle for the foam.

Then I take a deep breath. We're not going to cause too much trouble . . . only a spray or two to make it tough to open the door for a minute. Enough for us to shower Jack and Zareen with (fake) mice.

Psst. With one puff, the foam starts expanding on the sill. I ease the door shut. The off-yellow foam bubbles and begins to harden immediately.

"That's it?" Lia asks, peering over my shoulder.

"It'll keep the door shut." Lia doesn't know that I've altered this foam to melt off in about thirty minutes, nothing permanent. I don't *actually* want to get in trouble.

"Oh, shoot!" Lia says, suddenly. "Someone's turning into the alley—"

Without another word, we scramble toward the stairway and dive for cover.

My heart pounds as we hear footsteps approach. Are Jack and Zareen back already?

Lia tugs at my sleeve, motioning for me to crawl back up the stairs. We have to get back to our bucket. Sweat pricks at my neck as we sneak to the roof.

Just as we make it to the top, a cheery whistle echoes through the pathway. We slump against the wall with relief. It's only a customer, swinging a bag from my parents' shop, stuffed full of tins of freshly roasted green tea and boxes of their pastries.

"Thank goodness, I thought we were caught *for sure*," Lia says. She quickly reapplies her soft-pink lip stain; she'd told me earlier she was going for the look of innocence if we get caught. Lia passes the lip stain to me, but I shake my head— because there's another set of footsteps.

We tense up and I chance peeking over the ledge. Zareen is clutching white cups from the trendy frozen yogurt shop around the corner. Jack's lugging a few bags from the local grocery store that look heavy.

But that's not what catches my eye.

Zareen and Jack are laughing about something. Jack's head tips back, and his eyes close, as if he's breathing in a moment of temporary bliss. I freeze, staring at him. I don't think I've seen him laugh in years.

I haven't made him laugh in years.

But that weird tickling feeling in my stomach . . . it's not jealousy. It's . . . it's just . . . annoyance, pure and simple. I hate how different he acts around everyone other than me, and this is more proof of how he's changed, how much we've drifted apart.

"Who is it?" Lia gets up to look. I shake my head, motioning for her to keep her head down.

"It's them. They're back. Another fifteen steps . . . ten . . . five . . ."

Zareen darts forward to try the door and frowns. "That's strange. Did we lock it on our way out?"

Lia peeks up next to me, her smile as sharp as her eyeliner as she hands me the bucket. "Ready?"

"Wait—only Zareen's in reach. . . . He's got to try the door first. Let's see him try to use those tennis muscles of his," I growl.

Lia pauses. Then: "I never realized you noticed his muscles, too. But if we're on the topic—"

"Shut it."

Lia snorts. She and I peer down, trying to track their movements. But they've both stepped backward, out of reach.

Jack doesn't even try to open the door. He trusts Zareen, without having to test the lock for himself. Dammit. I bet if that was me, he'd push me out of the way to yank it open with his stupid, ugly arm muscles to prove a point.

I groan under my breath. "Okay, now—wait—they're both moving away, they're too far—"

Zareen waves at Jack to stop, and my heart leaps as she says, "Don't worry, I'll go around and open it up. Stay here, those bags weigh a ton."

"Dammit," Lia moans. "She's supposed to stay *here* . . ."

"We'll just have to witness his complete humiliation on his own."

"I don't mind that either." Lia pops her head up and grins. "And he's right underneath us now, waiting for his dear co-worker. *Perfect.*"

"Ready, then?"

We look at each other. My grip's sweaty on the plastic bucket rim. This is the moment I could back out. Say this is too cruel.

But Jack has hurt me more than he'll ever realize. I think back to lunchtime in middle school, expecting he'd come by like he always did. Sitting at the sticky table all alone, the other kids whispering as Jack strode by, head turned away as if that would make it so I couldn't see him . . . as if he hadn't suddenly decided to ditch me for his "cool" friends.

But he'll laugh with Zareen, chat with his tennis buddies and the popular kids at school . . . he'll pretend like I never mattered, any day.

No, I've never forgotten. And without Lia, who's next to me for this prank, I would've been completely friendless for the rest of my school years.

I won't back off. This is the least of what Jack deserves. "*Go*."

We peer down, excitement thrumming through my veins, and tip the bucket over.

The mice fall, brilliantly alive-looking, their rubber legs waving helplessly as they tumble, tumble . . .

Straight onto his head.

And he lets out an ear-piercing, completely satisfying *screeeeeech*.

We couldn't have aimed any better.

"What the hell?" Jack's shout echoes through the otherwise empty alley. Then his voice raises an octave. Another definite screech. "Mice?!"

"This. Is. *Beautiful*," Lia singsongs in my ear and then dashes toward the stairway for a better vantage point. I have to press my hand to my mouth to muffle my laugh as I follow her. She's got her phone out, taking a video of this.

I get an ominous prickle . . . a recording . . .

Jack backs away from the door, the thirty or so rubber mice lying on the ground. Like the manufacturer described, the mice twitch upright. *Oh, how I adore you, dear little solar-powered mice. A magic of your own.*

Lia and I crouch in the stairway, shaking with laughter.

He lets out a faint gasp.

Enjoy the show, dear, sweet neighbor boy.

"Stop! No. Get away!" Jack yelps as a mouse crawls over his shoe, spinning in a circle. He doesn't seem to notice their movements are stiff and jerky, not smooth like real mice. Instead, he keeps backing up, digging in his pocket for something, and a sickening feeling fills my stomach.

"No, wait—" I half stand, raising a hand out to wave him off, to stop him somehow, but Lia grabs at my arms, dragging me down.

"Don't blow our cover!" she hisses, craning back over the stairwell to see if he's noticed us. "Shh!"

I should cover her eyes. Something. But she's got my arms pulled tightly down, and I can't wrench them out, and everything is happening too quickly—

"Leave me *alone!*" Jack throws a paper packet onto the ground.

I can't let this happen. I shout, "Jack—"

"Ellie!" Lia drops her phone as she tries to muffle me, but fear courses through my body, like the mice themselves are crawling up my spine. She shakes her head, letting out a laugh. "Why's he throwing a sugar packet at them?"

No, no, no.

Because it's not a sugar packet.

It's a bright red omamori, like that charm Jack had been talking about when I'd broken my phone screen. . . . There's the sound of a rip of fabric and—

A giant *whoosh* of air propels down the alley, out of nowhere. My hair flies in my face, but I don't need to see to know what's going to happen next. Next to me, Lia gasps with surprise. "What the *hell*?"

The gust continues down the alley, churning the dust in its path, and sweeps around Jack in a full circle, sending all the mice flying. It immobilizes them, killing their circuits.

The toy mice lay scattered around the alley, legs up, still as can be.

"But, they were supposed to last for ten minutes . . ." Lia breathes out. "Impossible . . ."

Impossible, if not for magic.

A golden light swirls around Jack, a solid barrier against any of the mice.

But the spell has already taken care of them, and he spins around in confusion as he stares down at the ground. "They're not real? What the—"

"What. Was. That." Lia takes a step into the alleyway, squinting at the light and at Jack, who slowly turns to face her, understanding dawning on his face, and just as quickly turning into pure horror.

"No, no." Dread makes my stomach burn like it's sloshing full of pure acid. I follow her down the last steps, my heart pounding. How can I explain this away? How can I scientifically reason away a charm that bizarre looking?

Feet away, Jack stares at her, silent in shock, as the gold barrier surrounding him fades.

"Did—did you see that, Ellie?" Lia shakes her head. "That looked like, no, it couldn't be—But, that was impossible . . ."

Then she glances between me and Jack, her intense curiosity melting into confusion as she sees the horror on both of our faces. I try to turn away. But there's a flash of recognition in her eyes. She can tell that there's something the two of us know about, something to do with his so-called sugar packet.

"Wait . . ." Lia says, slowly. I want to scream. I want to stop time. I want to do anything to change the past. She swallows. "Did—did you do *magic*?"

Just then the back door swings open, our foam shriveled and melted on the doorsill.

Mr. Yasuda walks out and stands in front of us, arms crossed. He's overheard her.

Chapter 8

"Magic?" Lia bursts out in hysterical laughter. "You're . . . you're joking. You're trying to pull a prank on me now, aren't you?"

I shake my head, internally begging for her to understand. But it's not just me who needs her to understand.

It feels like we're in an interrogation cell. It's actually the Yasudas' living room, but it's all stark without the coziness of our home. Instead, it looks like the spread of an interior design magazine, white-painted bricks, exposed piping overhead, cold, bare windows. Last time I was here, Mrs. Yasuda was still fighting the lung cancer that'd suddenly and rapidly taken over her life. Last time I was here, it looked like a home.

Lia's sitting at the glass table, my parents on each side of her as if they're scared she's going to run off, and Mr. Yasuda's at the head of the table, staring her down. I'm across from her, with Jack next to me.

I try to speak. "It was a harmless prank—"

"I do not have *time* for these excuses," Mom snaps. "Now that you've gotten us all in trouble."

"Wait . . ." Lia's eyes widen. "Are you *serious*? Like, magic actually exists?"

She looks around the table, looking for someone to crack their stormy frown and burst into laughter. Maybe for Cam or Remy to jump out with a camera, snorting about how she looks like she's starting to believe us.

But nothing saves her from the truth.

"I'm sorry, Lia," I whisper. "I've always wanted to tell you . . ."

"All those times I was crying over my parents!" she gasps, as if hit by a flood of icy-cold water. "You knew . . . you knew I was in pain! You could've turned back time, stopped the truck that hit them, sent them a warning, helped knock some sense into my damn grandma, *something!* Just *anything* to show you care about me!"

Sitting next to her, listening, was the only magic I could give her. After her weekly therapy sessions, when she'd been drained and withdrawn, I'd offered her soothing chocolates, and Dad's matcha snowflake cookies . . . but when the memories had hurt the most, she'd been too sad to eat, too tired to care.

"You could've done something for my parents," Lia cries, her voice rising and rising. It's like a screeching violin, so out of tune, so out of place, and this anger, this *rage* is nothing like the Lia I know. The Lia that I never wanted to look at me this way. "Why didn't you save them?"

I would have done anything I could. Even if there was any chance that giving up my magic would help Lia, would stop her pain forever, I would have done it immediately.

Mom shakes her head. "We can't do magic like that; we wouldn't have been able to stop that car crash. It's impossible."

Lia slams her fists on the glass. "Or you could've helped me so I"—her voice breaks—"so I could've said goodbye."

Her skin welts red, and I want desperately to reach out, to hug her. "I—"

Lia shoves her chair back angrily. "Don't you *dare* even talk to me."

"Whoa, whoa," Dad says, trying to add a sense of reason into his words. "Lia, Ellie was banned from telling you. That's why she's getting in trouble now. There's going to be consequences. Ellie might never get to use magic again. And . . . and if there was anything, anything at all we could've done for your parents, we would've already done something, dear. You're like a daughter to us, too."

At that, Lia's eyes widen, the lines in her forehead brittle as breaking glass, and she bursts into tears, clutching at my mom. "But . . . but you're *not* them! I'll *never* see them again!"

"There, now," Mom says, shooting a glare at me over Lia's head. "Let's go get some rest, why don't we—"

Jack hurriedly gets up. "The guest room . . . here . . ." He strides down to the first door in the all-white hallway. It's the room his mom used back when she was sick.

Mr. Yasuda begins to protest. "But no one uses that—"

"It'll relax her," Jack says pointedly, cutting off his father. There are probably still strong calming charms on it, even years after she passed. Maybe—maybe they all expected Mrs. Yasuda would be around for longer.

My heart wrenches as my parents shuffle Lia into the room.

I take a step forward, but Dad looks over his shoulder and shakes his head sharply. His eyes admonish me. *Not now.*

"Lia—"

"I don't want to talk to you!" she cries out.

And that's that.

My dad shuts the door behind them, and the click is a sound of finality.

I slump back to the chair, wishing I had a calming charm of my own. My chest aches. What can I do? What should I have done? Was there something I could've said differently?

But I deserve this.

My best friend doesn't want me by her side, because I hid the truth from the one person I swore to tell all my secrets. Even worse, I'm the one who opened up her scarred memories and made her believe, for a painful, excruciatingly hopeful moment, that things could be different.

I might be losing all my magic, too, because of this mess-up. I won't even have charms and spells to help her feel better in the future.

And it's all my damn fault.

❧   ❧

Mr. Yasuda, Jack, and I sit numbly at the glass table, and I stare at the scratches on the surface. Lia's sharp cries reverberate through the walls, louder than my parents trying to calm her down. My best friend's voice stabs me, laced with a bitter pain I can't help.

Maybe thirty, forty minutes later, my parents step into the hallway. It's quiet now.

"Lia's doing a little better," Mom says, with Dad carefully

shutting the door behind them. "We gave her chamomile tea with a drop of a relaxation elixir. . . . She's taking a nap. Mind if she rests up here?"

"Fine," Mr. Yasuda says gruffly. Even a cold guy like him wouldn't dare push her out now.

"Let me make a quick charm for peace," Mom says. As the strongest—and cleverest—magic-user in our family, she's the only one licensed to cast spells without having to refer to one of the magical tomes that Dad, Remy, and I have to resort to, and she can easily convert raw magic into a charm.

She pulls out a vial of raw magic dust from her pocket and closes her eyes, wrapping her hands firmly around the full glass. To anyone else, it might look like a prayer, but as the magic-aware know, it's something wholly different.

Mom mutters a long-winded spell under her breath. A few minutes later, the raw dust turns a soft green, filled with her intent of peace. As it glows bright as a beacon, she tosses the contents of the vial onto the door. It coats the white paint, making the door shimmer with a pale celadon green, before fading away.

Now Lia's securely enclosed in the peace charm, and I can breathe a little easier. Hopefully she won't be as mad when she wakes up.

"Thankfully, she agreed to sign the temporary contract," Mom says, pulling a folded piece of paper out of her pocket, and Mr. Yasuda's shoulders ease with relief. When Jack and I frown in confusion, she explains, an edge to her voice, "It's a short-term version of the contract that someone who falls in love with someone with magic has to agree to. Since I'm only a Lead Sorcerer and not an actual Judge, I can't make it lifelong."

She groans, rubbing her forehead. "I'll have to appeal immediately. Or else . . ."

Mom glances over at me and then Jack, her eyes sharp.

Oh. That's why Mr. Yasuda's all wound up. He's only worried about his son getting in trouble, not how Lia's been hurt.

"What's the contract do?" Jack asks.

"They're not allowed to tell anyone about magic," Dad says. "Or they'll lose their memories. No hints, written clues, anything." He stares sternly at us. "Very similar to how you two would be instantly banned from magical society if Lia hadn't signed that temporary contract."

I gulp. I can't imagine life without charms and spells. It'd be like imagining life without Lia.

Mom clears her throat. "The Judges coach them through a set of lessons, similar to the Saturday classes you took as a kid, explaining the reasoning, but it often takes a while for new magic-awares to understand that our magic is small charms, nothing that—that really saves lives. They have to fully agree."

Mr. Yasuda stares down at the glass table and so does Jack. And my stomach drops. They, like Lia, have had a loss that no amount of enchantments could help. Nothing was enough . . . enough to make a difference. Our magic is special because it can brighten someone's day, but it can't *save* a person's life.

This is why magic isn't publicly known—there are too many limits to what magic can do, but if enough power gets into the wrong hands, a charm can turn into a curse. Some recent worldwide troubles—a global stock market crash from a man greedily trying to pad his own pocket, missing election ballots and the wrong candidate elected after a local mayor fudged the numbers—have been from non-magicals with bad intentions getting a hold of the wrong magic. And seeing how greedy some folks can be, it's better that magic stays a secret.

"I'll work on the full license paperwork as soon as I get home," Mom says briskly. "I'll have to move fast to make sure you two can keep your magic." Then she glares at us again. "Though I'm not really sure that you deserve it."

I wince, the guilt weighing heavily on my shoulders. Seeing Lia like this has shaken me up; *this* is why we can't share magic with the general public.

Mr. Yasuda looks up, the darkness in his eyes clearing enough for him to speak. "I'll help you, Eleanor. It's my son's fault."

Mom shakes her head. "I believe he is not alone in the blame. He may have cast the magic, but it wasn't unprovoked."

"I'm so sorry, Mom." I hate this pit of guilt in my stomach; I hate how I can't wipe out the memory of the way Lia looked at me in absolute fury. The prank was supposed to be a harmless joke. And now . . . "Isn't there anything I can do to make up for this, at least a little bit? I can help with the paperwork or—"

"You *knew* the dangers of others finding out about magic," Dad says, his voice cold.

I knew. I knew it was wrong, but I never knew how horribly wrong it was until I saw Lia's wild, intense hope shattered by the belief that I didn't help her in her time of need.

If I could've helped her, I would have. I glance at the shut white door. Not that she'll listen to what I'll say, not for a long time.

"Yes." Mom's voice is like a dagger, flying swiftly through

the night, cold and ominous. "Lia won't be going with you on the road trip after all, not with how much training she'll have over the next week to learn about being magic-aware. Not with how much I'll have to work to make sure you don't lose *your* magic."

I splutter. "But—but—she and I have been planning the road trip forever!" My bucket list is *meant* for our adventures together.

"Well, she's not going. And now I don't trust *you* to go alone," Mom hisses.

"But—" I sit back in my seat, in shock. Mom and Dad have to take care of the shop, Remy is too young . . .

Mom looks over at Mr. Yasuda, as if confirming something. He nods.

"It would be appropriate for the two of you to spend time reflecting upon your actions," Mom says.

"What do you mean, the two of us?" I blurt out. I have to go with Mr. Yasuda?

Mom switches her glare to Jack, who's sitting frozen next to me as if he can't believe what he's hearing, either.

"*Us?*" Jack looks sick at the thought.

This is the one time that he and I willingly agree on something. I add, "*He's* the one who cast magic. Can't I . . . can't I go on my own? Can't we get separate punishments?"

I don't want anything to do with Jack Yasuda. I'd rather do *anything* else than be stuck with him.

"No," Mr. Yasuda says, with crystal-clear conviction, as if he and Mom have exchanged thoughts silently. "The two of you will drive the Sorcerer Square's exhibit crates down south to the CMRC, together."

Mom nods sharply. "When your father and I fly down for the convention, there had better be a perfect, smoothly running stand with all items from the crates on display. Or you're not allowed to see Lia this summer."

My jaw drops. *No.* This was my summer *with* Lia, not the summer my parents stop me from hanging out with her.

Dad adds, "Instead of visiting around California, you can pick up the distribution route that your mother and I were going to do next week. It'll be much easier this way."

The distribution— Wait—*no.* My parents take little road trips on Mondays, the day the tea shop is closed, to drive out their matcha powder to magic-aware shops around the Bay Area.

"But—"

"We have client visits that Jack and I were going to do," Mr. Yasuda pipes up. "It would save me time—and money—to have Ellie drive Jack to them, and I can contribute that to Lia's magical education instead."

Dad claps his hands. "Perfect. The classes and licensing aren't free, after all."

My parents are nailing me into a coffin of summer hell, one hammer stroke at a time. Me? And *Jack?* Having to work for our parents' shops . . . *together?*

"But—"

"As your parents, we have to sign the paperwork to allow you to keep your magic-aware status after this huge mess-up," Mom snaps. "If you cause another issue, it's *our* powers on the line, too."

"We'll let you know, once the convention is complete, if we'll sign the papers," Dad says.

Jack presses his hand to his forehead. "I need my magic."

No, *no*. But I can't go *with* Jack. I try one more time. "I really am sorry. But I think we'll reflect on our actions best if I go alone—"

My parents firmly shake their heads, their shoulders set and their eyes narrowed. I gulp. They're not going to budge.

Mr. Yasuda stares down at us coldly. "Enjoy the road trip, kids."

Chapter 9

Early the next morning, I wake up as streaks of orange-yellow sunlight paint themselves on the ceiling. I grab my phone, using my stylus to sketch out the view above. The textured rubber tip slides across the screen just like pencil on paper, gentle and soothing. *When we're on the road trip together, I'll be able to sketch lots of illustrations like this, and Lia—*

And Lia won't be there.

The nauseating sourness in my stomach bubbles up again. I was barely able to sleep last night, thinking of Lia's tear-stained cheeks, and how I'm going to be separated from her for the next week without a chance to apologize.

The most we've ever fought is about who gets the last Jagabee, and we always end up splitting it in half. We just don't fight; we've always been such good friends, and I don't know how to fix this distance and strangeness between us.

I peek out the window at the alleyway between my parents' place and CharmWorks. On weekend mornings, Jack and I used to turn flashlights off and on, sending each other messages through Morse code until our parents would let us run off to the park to play. . . . I blink, rubbing at my eyes. The light's on in Jack's bedroom, which surprises me. Isn't it early? Maybe he's already getting ready.

Then I look at the clock on my phone and roll out of bed. It's 6:00 A.M. Unlike most high schoolers, Lia's always rattling around at the crack of dawn, either testing out some new makeup or eating breakfast with Aunt Miki, who commutes early in the morning to her software engineering job at Tesla in Fremont.

Mom and Dad are sleepily sipping at their tea when I walk down, their eyebrows rising when they see me.

"I'm going to take Mochi for a walk," I say, and my dog nearly tap-dances along the wood floor, her nails clacking with delight. My parents still have grooves of frowns etched on their foreheads; they haven't forgiven me.

"Good," Dad says, gruffly. Then he adds, gesturing at a plate on the table, "Take one."

It's a pile of onigiri, Japanese rice balls hand-pressed into the shape of a triangle, with something savory inside. Even if they're mad, my parents still take care of me. My chest clenches thinking about the trouble I'm causing them. But the nausea that's still heavy in my stomach makes me shake my head. "I'll grab some later for the drive. Thanks."

Mochi is surprisingly docile during the walk, as if she can tell I'm not my usual self. As we amble along Bryant Street, she doesn't yank me to greet people like she normally does, though her tail wags, hopeful for attention, whenever someone glances her way.

She follows me down the quiet street, and I turn this way

and that, in the familiar path I've taken thousands of times before. Before I know it, I've arrived.

I pause in front of Lia's four-story apartment building and draw a deep breath.

I'll apologize. We'll talk things out, and I'll explain again that I was forbidden from telling her about magic—I mean, if she doesn't go through with the training, I'll be banned from magical society.

After she forgives me, things will be like before; she'll ease this frustration that's burning in my chest with a few choice words about Jack. When I tell her about how I'm nervous about being stuck with my damn neighbor for the road trip, she'll say something funny, make me laugh. And, hopefully, I'll be able to comfort her.

I knock, and I hear the faint shuffle of bare feet on the tile floor. Mochi whines excitedly; she knows we're at Lia's place, and that Aunt Miki, who might still be home, will lavish her with compliments about how beautiful she is and maybe even offer a scrap of her scrambled eggs.

But no one answers.

"Hey, Lia, it's me," I call. She and I drop over at each other's places all the time, so this is the norm for us.

Then—silence.

Didn't I hear footsteps? I check my phone. It's almost seven o'clock, time for her second coffee of the day. She's got to be home, so why isn't she opening the door?

My stomach drops. Is . . . she ignoring me?

Lia and I usually shoot each other text messages, but I decide to call instead. Maybe she ran out to grab coffee, so if I can find her in time, we can eat together.

I press her name on my phone and wait for the call to connect.

It rings. *Brrring. Brrring.*

And then, louder, it rings from *inside*. Through the cracks of her door, the melody of "I Wish" by Hayley Kiyoko plays for a split second, before abruptly shutting off.

"Lia . . . ?" I call.

No answer.

With a long look at the door, I sigh. Then I pull up our text message chain.

> **ME:** Hey, friend. I really am sorry
> about not being able to tell
> you. Miss you, L.

No response, no read receipt, nothing. I wonder if she sees the pop-up notification and dismisses it. Or if she's muted our conversation.

Years ago, when Jack suddenly disappeared from my life, my heart hurt like hell. It felt like I'd been ghosted, like he'd broken up with me even though we were only friends.

And now, with Lia, that same empty, aching feeling spreads through my bones like wildfire.

I lost a once-good friendship years ago, and I don't want to lose another.

But another text message pops up.

> **REMY:** Are you on your way back? Mom and Dad think
> you're trying to flake out on the road trip. Jack's
> almost ready to head out, too.

I glance at Lia's door again. I have to go. I want to mend things between us before I leave, but if she won't talk to me, what choice do I have? Mochi whines when I tug her with me as I turn away, my heart heavy.

Chapter 10

My family's Toyota Camry is sitting in the driveway, ready for the trip, but I feel like there's something missing.

Gas? Three-quarters of a tank is enough to get us to Gilroy.

The itinerary? I check the Notes app on my phone. A bunch of stops for CharmWorks and my parents' shop, then an overnight stop in some town called Pixley, before heading down to Huntington Beach in Southern California. All stops, unfortunately, with Jack.

My duffel bag? Packed and secure.

Thirty cardboard boxes stuffed into the trunk of the Camry thanks to Mom's expansion spell, filled with all sorts of goods from Sorcerer Square—everything from my parents' tea, Ana's jarred cupcake mix, to CharmWorks' most popular bullet journals, pens, and notepads? Check.

Spare tire? Check. It's somewhere in the magical car repair kit.

Tires pumped? Check.

Ten boxes of CharmWorks' specialty line of newest stationery, crammed into the back seat, for Jack's sales visits? Sadly, check.

I stare at my little white car that should be collapsing under the weight of these things. But what I notice more is what's missing.

At some point yesterday, Lia pulled her stuff from the passenger seat. The scarlet headrest, the box of gluten-free snacks she'd assembled in case she didn't feel like another lettuce-wrapped burger. The USB-powered mini fan, because my AC is wimpy.

All of that has been cleared out.

Instead, the passenger side is as bare as the day Mom drove the car home from the dealership on Middlefield Road.

I check my Instagram. Lia hasn't posted anything recently. I wonder if she's blocked me from viewing her stuff. I glance up at the car again and sigh.

"So, are we driving or are we going to stare at the car and hope it teleports us?" a husky, early-morning voice says from behind me. The faint scent of just-washed laundry wafts over me, smooth and clean. "Morning, Ellie."

Jack is carrying a duffel bag over his shoulder. I motion for him to throw it in the trunk. Even though it's jam-packed, he manages to stuff it on top of some of the exhibit boxes.

I stiffen when the garage door leading into my house opens. Mom and Dad stroll out, deep in a conversation about next steps for Lia's magic-awareness education. When they see us, they stop short.

"All ready to go?" Dad asks, scanning over the car the same way I did. But he doesn't seem to notice what's missing.

I clear my throat. "Yep." I wonder if they'll let me hug them, but then I drop my hands. "Everything's packed."

"Dad and I put a tracker on the car," Mom says, her arms crossed. "So we'll be able to see where you are. Don't you dare cause any trouble, or you'll be grounded for the rest of your life *and* you'll be banned from magical society."

My jaw drops. A *tracker*? "That's not necessary—"

"What's necessary is that you *won't* cause trouble. Personally, I didn't even want you to go on this drive, but the repercussions of your actions have left me no choice." I clamp my mouth shut as Mom adds, "You're lucky you don't have to go through all this paperwork for Lia, but I do. If I didn't have to do all that, and if your dad didn't need to take care of the shop, then you wouldn't even be heading off on this road trip."

"It's not like it's going to be *fun* anymore," I protest, and Jack makes a noise from next to me. Maybe he feels insulted or something, but I don't even care.

Mom pinches her forehead and takes a long, deep breath. "Do this right, Ellie. For the sake of your family, please."

My stomach feels like it did at the crack of dawn, standing in front of Lia's front door, bubbling with nausea. It's not just me who might get in trouble. Mom—as Lead Sorcerer—has her job on the line.

I wish my prank hadn't ended up like this. I wish there was some kind of magic that could turn back time. To fix things. To go back to years and years ago, where I could've broken out of my wallflower shell then, and none of this mess would've ever happened.

But I'm sore out of luck.

"We'll see you in Huntington Beach," Dad says, his eyes going from me to Jack. "And the booth better be set up right, all items intact."

Jack nods stiffly. "I've got the layout; I'll make sure it's done."

I glare at him. *He* will make sure it's done? Oh, if Jack wants to take responsibility like that, he can do it all himself.

Footsteps slap against the concrete, and Mr. Yasuda says from behind me, "Don't forget any of the sales visits for CharmWorks' latest line of goods. Our clients will be blown away by our innovative, *popular* products."

My shoulders stiffen. I'm going to have rocks for shoulders if I don't figure out how to loosen up around the Yasudas, regardless of whether Mr. Yasuda sounds like a walking infomercial.

Before Jack can butt in about how he's so responsible, I smile as politely as I can. "Right, I've mapped out the five stops. I'll have Jack send you updates as we reach each stop and he meets with CharmWorks' clients."

Mr. Yasuda looks momentarily impressed. "Sounds like a good plan." *You think you can take all the credit?* I narrow my eyes at Jack, who meets my gaze. *Think again. I'm not going to give up that easily. I'm not going to be a nobody anymore, and especially not around* you.

Cam and Remy hurry out of our house, Jack's younger brother hefting a wicker picnic basket. Savory, delicious scents waft out of it.

"Wait, wait," Remy calls. "We packed lunch for the two of you."

Despite how grouchy I feel about having Jack come along, some of that annoyance fades when Cam sets the heavy basket into my arms.

"Drive safe," Remy says, giving me a hug. Then she leans in. "I hope you two will talk it out."

"Talk what out?"

She only says, "Give us a call if you need help, okay?" Then she turns to give Jack a hug and murmurs something in his ear, too.

What in the world does she mean?

"Good luck," Cam says, drawing my attention away. To my surprise, he presses something in my hand. It's a tiny glass vial, the prize from the solar system puzzle he and Remy had put together on the last day of school. He winks, his light brown eyes the same shade as his brother's.

"But you won this—"

His lips curve up in a knowing grin. "With my brother, sometimes you need all the luck you can get. But give him a chance, would you? Listen to his side of things, too."

Cam's too nice; maybe some good luck is what I need to survive this trip. I slide the vial into the pocket of my denim shorts, then squeeze him in a hug. "Thanks, Cam. I'll try not to leave your brother on the side of the road."

Cam snorts as Jack and I get into the car. Jack glances over at me with a grimace and immediately rolls down the window, as if he can't bear to share the same air as me.

See, this is why we can't get along like normal people, I want to tell him. I roll my eyes, waving at everyone gathered in the driveway: my parents, who still look grouchy; Mr. Yasuda (who always looks grouchy); our siblings waving like their arms are about to fall off; and then Mochi, who's whining because she can't see me anymore, and she wants to go along for the car ride, too.

As I drive down University Avenue toward the 101, I glance in the rearview mirror at the familiar sights. There's too much that I'm leaving behind.

I'm going to complete my damned bucket list. When I complete it, Lia will see that there's more to me than charms and spells. My magic was a part of me that I could never share, but it's not what made me and Lia get along so well. This time, I refuse to lose a best friend just because I don't know how to speak up for myself. And I'll fight to make myself into someone Lia will be proud to call her friend—her *best* friend—with or without magic. And if I can make that happen, maybe I can find some way to make her forgive me.

Chapter 11

I'm enjoying the soft, beautiful chorus of one of my favorite songs, "Euphoria," crooning through my car's Bluetooth speakers, when Jack cuts in, shattering my relaxing drive. "The first CharmWorks stop is in San Jose."

"What?" I blurt out, slightly more aggravated than I mean to be.

"For my sales visit—"

"I know." I motion at my phone propped up on the dashboard, navigating us—like magic—to the exact shop in San Jose we're supposed to go to.

We've already stopped by five shops to drop off my parents' tea, throughout Mountain View and Santa Clara on our way down the 101, and I'd programmed the next stop into my phone. It's taking us to the right place, whether Jack believes it or not.

He's silent for a moment. "I take a different route."

Well, guess who's driving. Not you, Mr. Passenger Seat. If

I were gutsy enough to give him a piece of my mind, I would. Lia would speak up, if she were here—

Dammit.

I get off the highway and turn onto Taylor Street, zipping through a commercial area until I get to the Japantown of San Jose. It's one of three remaining historical Japanese American areas left in California, after Japanese Americans were released from the internment camps of World War II, and it's nowhere near as vibrant as it used to be. But it's still cozy, with cherry blossom–patterned flags fluttering from forest-green lampposts along the street of mom-and-pop shops.

I parallel park in front of Shuei-Do Manju Shop, one of the best traditional Japanese sweet shops in the area. They're known for their manju and mochi, soft and chewy rice cakes stuffed with tasty fillings ranging from peanut butter to traditional red bean. It's so good that the emperor of Japan ate manju from their shop during a visit to the US.

I'm patting my chin to check for drool when the back door of my car slams shut. Jack has already jumped out of the car as if he can't stand my driving (which is very safe, thank you) and is balancing three of the CharmWorks stationery boxes. He jerks his head at a shop a few doors down. "I have to drop by there. I'll be back soon."

He's heading to KEIKO-M, the trendy store that draws shoppers from all over the area to Japantown for its "surprise boxes"—monthly subscription boxes filled with five top beauty, fashion, and lifestyle items, curated by the owner, a former actress and model. KEIKO-M directly imports the hottest items, so rather than having to go through Amazon or a third party, the boxes get delivered straight to the customer's doorstep. I've always wanted a KEIKO-M box, but I haven't had enough money for the monthly forty-dollar price plunge.

Even though the shop is known for its pale-green mail subscription boxes, their brick-and-mortar store is the perfect place to pick up well-loved favorites from previous boxes or to try hot new products that are available in such limited quantities that they won't get shipped out in a KEIKO-M box. It's only ten in the morning, and shoppers are already bustling around with their pale-green wire baskets piled high with items.

Jack yanks at the door, trying to pull it open while balancing his boxes. I stare at him and sigh. Why's he so stubborn about not getting any help?

I get out of my car and follow him. I catch a box before it slams onto the concrete. Tucking it under one arm, I pull open the door for Jack and motion him inside the shop.

"Thanks," he says, with a touch of surprise.

Why does he sound shocked? I'm carting his butt all the way down to Southern California. Helping him get through his stops faster means we'll arrive at Huntington Beach earlier. It's a win-win: I'll be able to spend less time with him.

Then a voice calls, "Is that *you*, Jack Yasuda?"

A slim, tall Japanese American woman steps out from behind the counter, motioning for a team member to take over the iPad register. She's in her midtwenties, but she looks like she stepped out of a 1950s fashion magazine with her tortoiseshell cat-eye glasses, pale-green circle skirt, and hair smoothed up in a way that looks slightly retro.

My jaw drops. This is Keiko Mayu, the namesake and

owner of KEIKO-M. And she knows Jack on a first-name basis.

"I've missed seeing you!" Ms. Mayu says, waving for Jack to unload the boxes on the counter. "I'd gotten your message that you'd come today; it really has felt too long."

"You know I can't stay away," Jack says, with one of his classic smiles. It's slightly crooked and irresistibly charming, and Ms. Mayu *melts* under his gaze.

Ugh, ugh, ugh.

I nudge the corner of the box into his side, *hard*. He pulls the box from my grasp, his calloused fingers brushing against my skin, and I nearly jump backward to avoid the strange sensation of his touch.

"Oh, your girlfriend?" Ms. Mayu says, beaming at me.

Jack is momentarily speechless.

And I desperately look for an exit. Or can I hide in one of the boxes? And never be seen again?

I'm wearing ratty denim shorts and a white V-neck under a loose, pale-blue, unbuttoned top. Which would be shabby cute, but my hair is in a mangled low ponytail and, overall, I look like a complete mess. I hadn't expected to meet someone during the drive down. Especially not *the* Keiko Mayu. And this is not definitely not the outfit I'd wear if I wanted to be mistaken for someone's girlfriend.

Then Jack breathes in, quickly regaining that one-thousand-watt smile and his composure. Which is good, because I'm positive I'm sinking into the tiled floor, inch by inch. *Walk all over me. Just don't notice me, please.*

"She's my driver." Jack runs his hand through his hair,

winking at Ms. Mayu. And *wow*, his eyes are even crinkling at the corners, like he's Mochi in front of her dinner bowl.

He's good at his job, for sure.

I roll my eyes as he starts into an elevator speech, opening the first of his boxes. "Our latest line, and it's been flying off the shelves, featured in over a thousand Instagram bullet journal posts within one week of sales. The theme for summer is sunflowers, and we're planning on maple leaves for fall. The early designs have been well received by our Instagram influencers that I've connected with."

The lady is nodding like she's lapping up his every word. "Count me *in!* I love this sunflower design, it's perfect for summer. Can your father send over a few boxes in a week?"

A smooth smile tips up his lips. And his whole face light up in a way that makes my chest tighten. He's disgustingly handsome, and I can't stand this.

How can he be so nice to her and so cold to me? It's as if that frosty, nagging guy in the car, offering up unnecessary directions, no longer exists.

I feel like a third wheel. I slip out, going to the manju shop a few doors down, checking my Instagram again. Lia's posted a picture of her hanging out with some girl I don't know, and my eyes blur. It didn't take her long to find a new friend.

When Jack gets out thirty minutes later, I'm brushing the telltale rice powder off my lips, the sweet flavor of the classic red bean manju still dancing on my tongue. Instead of staring at my text message chain with Lia (my previous message is still unread), I'm doodling aimlessly on my phone, drawing everything from Shuei-Do Manju Shop's irresistible sweets to

Mochi curled up at Simple Mornings to a pair of hands that I can't seem to get off my mind. "I was wondering where you went," Jack says, his brows raising as he saunters up to me. What—is he going to be condescending (as usual) about how well CharmWorks is doing?

Without a word, I slide into the car and buckle up. Quietly, he gets into his seat, and I can feel his curious gaze on me, the way he opens his mouth to say something, and then closes it, as if thinking twice. Then he clears his throat. "Dad's been pretty worried about the sales of this new line—it was a big investment to hire an artist and pay them a solid rate, plus the actual production and supplies. . . . It's a project I've been working on, and I need this to succeed for CharmWorks to take on more private-line projects like this. We've got a potential investor looking at us, so I really need CharmWorks to do well this year. Sorry I made you wait so long, Ellie."

He . . . he actually sounds *sincere*. But I don't trust this guy who wrecked my entire summer with his stupid need to use magic without checking if anyone was around. Lia's not here, and she's mad at me in part because of him. I don't want to hear his excuses.

"Okay. Tell me next time how long you'll take." I shove the plastic box with the remaining mochi at him. "Anyway, have something to eat. We have a few more deliveries before we can take a break. After the Gilroy one, we can have that lunch Remy and Cam made."

His eyes light up. "Wait, this is a sakura mochi. How did you remember—"

I glance down and curse internally at the faintly pink,

round dessert, pale as a cherry blossom petal. *How did I remember his favorite?*

His mom used to take us, Cam, and Remy down to San Jose to go around Japantown, picking up bentos from a homey restaurant to eat at the park, and then we'd stop at Shuei-Do Manju Shop. Every time, without fail, Jack would choose sakura mochi. The times that there was only one left in stock, the rest of us purposefully ordered other sweets, just so Jack could get his favorite. And his eyes would shine with delight as he munched on the pink rice cake, the way he's smiling now.

But I shove that memory away. "I bought whatever they had. Don't forget to message your dad about how the visit went. He wants regular updates."

The glow on his face cuts out. "Right," he says stiffly.

After he taps out a quick message on his phone, I hear the click of the plastic container from the manju shop. Finally, my shoulders ease a bit, even though my phone's navigation promises heavy traffic ahead.

I regret giving away my emperor-approved dessert to my enemy, but it's a small price to pay to make him shut up.

But why does this silence feel so strange now?

Chapter 12

Next up is the last drop-off for my parents' tea in the Evergreen area of East San Jose. Our deliveries are all in the local Bay Area, unlike Jack's sales visits that stretch down the coast. Mine are simple, routine stops. I'm not perfecting my sales pitch like Mr. But-Wait over there.

The strip mall is a plain white square surrounding an open area with walkways in the middle, twisting around thick redwood trees. Jack and I are walking around the outside when he pauses in front of the garden path. "The coffee shop, right? I think the café is through there."

"I *know* where I'm going." I shift the heavy boxes of tea in my arms.

"Wouldn't it be a shortcut if we walked through these trees? And c'mon, let me carry that box."

This drop-off is kind of bulky; Café Thăng Long goes through a lot of our tea. Jack offered to hold one of the boxes, but I'm weighed down with two. And trying to ignore how much my arms ache.

"I'm fine. Things are fine. Everything is fine," I tell him through gritted teeth. He might be right. *But . . .* I've never gone that way before. I've been here countless times to drop off our tea and check out the piercing shop's cute window display around the corner. The path along the outside is paved and smooth and—

"C'mon," he says, teasingly. "Take a chance. Live on the wild side."

That stabs me.

Somewhere deep down inside, I *think* he means it as a joke. But this is Jack. He doesn't do "nice." Not to me, not anymore.

"I take chances," I snap. I pivot on my heel and stalk through the redwood trees.

To be honest, this winding walk is probably just as long as going around the building. But it's beautiful here, with a slight breeze coursing along the packed dirt path. There's also an added benefit of seeing trees instead of Jack (who's hurrying behind me, trying to catch up), giving me a moment to breathe.

Until I trip over a thick root. "Oh—"

"Watch out!" Jack is at my side in a flash, his hand reaching out, but I tumble hard.

On the first day of middle school, I was so nervous about meeting my classmates and only having two classes with Jack, instead of being by his side all day.

But Jack and I were late; we'd taken the wrong turn, so by the time we'd locked up our bikes, the first bell had already rung. My hair was a sweaty mess as we ran to our classes, not even really sure if we were in the right building.

Just when I'd found the right classroom, I hurriedly yanked

open the door, but it flew open faster than I'd expected, and it
threw me off balance. My new classmates burst into laughter
at the sight of me pitching forward—

Jack caught me, steadying me with a smile that was only for
me, with a warning look at the rest of my class, which quieted.
The teacher shooed him off to head to his room, but he only left
after I promised I was okay.

"Are you all right?" He's kneeling next to me, from where
I've fallen on my backside next to that damn tree root.

There's a strange expression on his face. Almost like our
first day in middle school—*concern?* No, it can't be.

Then I spot the cardboard boxes behind Jack, toppled on
their side, and my stomach lurches. If I've damaged the tea,
Mom and Dad will ground me for the rest of my life.

I scramble past Jack, and collect the boxes, turning them
over and wiping away specks of dirt.

Miraculously, they're safe and undented. I breathe out
with relief as the tension rolls out of my shoulders surprisingly
fast. Mrs. Nguyen has probably cast a few relaxation enchantments over this garden area; that's what this is. It's probably
floating on the breeze, along with the familiar, gentle scent of
warm cotton.

Wait—when did the scent of Jack *ever feel relaxing?*

"Ellie?" Jack repeats. I think I've been lost in my memories. "Are you okay?"

"I'm fine. It's . . . it's time to go." I brush myself off and
gather the boxes. I hurry past him, not stopping until I get
to the front of Café Thăng Long, the popular East San Jose
coffee shop known for its to-die-for creamy Vietnamese coffee. What most people don't know is that its decadent drinks

and desserts are dusted with a magical powder for strength—in whatever form needed: physical or emotional. I think I need a coffee for *both* after dealing with these heavy boxes and Jack.

It's already jam-packed with the midday crowd. The doorbell rings as I make my way inside. The motherly owner, Mrs. Nguyen, looks up from behind the counter, smiling cheerily; she reminds me of a chirping bird with her high, light voice. "Ah, the beautiful Elissa!" She quickly calls for one of her staff members to take over the register, and waves me into the shop.

My cheeks burn as I follow her into the back room. "Hi, Mrs. Nguyen." Even though I've told her I go by Ellie, she still *always* calls me "the beautiful Elissa."

Jack is close at my heels, holding his box, and Mrs. Nguyen tilts her head. "Ah, a boyfriend? But you would be so perfect for my son, Jon—"

I shake my head quickly. *No, this is the boy whose friends say I'm invisible, even though I'm here in front of him.* "Just Jack—"

"CharmWorks! Eric Yasuda's son, aren't you?" Mrs. Nguyen nods knowingly, pulling open the metal door to their storage space. She's always up to date with the latest gossip in the magic world.

"Yes, ma'am." My neighbor shifts, holding the box of matcha powder, and Mrs. Nguyen flutters to a shelf, motioning us to drop it off on the empty wire rack.

"Thank you, thank you!" Mrs. Nguyen chirps. She winks in a not-at-all-subtle way. "Elissa deserves only the best in a boyfriend, though. My son, Jonny, would be such a good match. Though it's nice for Elissa to have help, yes?"

Jack raises an eyebrow and I cough, remembering our argument at the car about who should carry what. "Right, right."

Mrs. Nguyen nods eagerly as I go over this latest delivery, showing that we've brought the full order of thirty tins of matcha powder. Even though their namesake is their Vietnamese coffee, they also like to whip up an amazing matcha latte that rivals my parents' creations.

I can feel Jack's gaze on my back. The other deliveries were smaller—just a box or two—so he hadn't accompanied me inside. But now, in this small storage space with Mrs. Nguyen buzzing around and him so close, it feels like I need fresh air.

A boy around Remy and Cam's age pops his head in the storage room. "Mom, we need you up front, I think the espresso machine's stuck."

Mrs. Nguyen beams at her son with pride. "Jonny! Look at who it is!"

He glances over. "Hey, Ellie! How're you doing?"

I peek around Jack, who's standing between me and the doorway. "I'm doing great, just got stuck on this road trip down to the convention."

"That's awesome you're going there," Jonny says brightly. "I've always wanted to go. I was thinking of maybe asking Remy if she wanted to road-trip down there with a few friends next year."

"Remy!" Mrs. Nguyen's eyebrows are raised again. "The younger Kobata girl? She is quite smart, I've heard. Likes puzzles, was it? But Ellie is right here, Jonny! You two should go on a date!"

The boy blushes, and I think my face is flaming red, too.

"Um, well," I blurt out. "Mrs. Nguyen, if you have to go up front, I can stack up the rest of these boxes. We have to head to our next stop."

"Maybe a date after you get back?" Mrs. Nguyen looks eagerly between the two of us.

Her son groans, covering his face. "Mom, you're worse than a dating app. You think there's a match everywhere."

"Ah, but the best part of my life is love!" Mrs. Nguyen pushes her son out of the storage room. "Fine, fine, dear, hard-working, beautiful Elissa, I'll keep my lips zipped . . . for a little bit. But think about the date with my son, yes? And don't leave without saying bye to me!"

As she shuffles away, I can hear Jonny grumble, "I can't believe you said that! In front of Ellie!"

When the door swings shut, Jack, who's been quiet through all of this, says, "So, Jonny?"

I train my eyes on what I'm doing, stacking the tin boxes of matcha powder onto the shelf.

Jack steps closer to help me, his warmth so palpable in the cold storage room. "Ellie," he says teasingly, "what if, for the rest of this trip, you pretend you don't hate my guts?"

I nearly drop a tin straight onto the ground. He easily catches it with one hand, setting it back on the shelf.

Who is this flirty guy?

"This coffee shop has a great front display," he says, almost to himself. "But it's neat they also serve your parents' tea. I wonder if they'd be interested in selling stationery, too."

Memories of how he suddenly ditched me swim up in my mind, his reassurances to his father that he'd never willingly spend time with me. My heart pounds angrily in my chest as I turn, looking up at him.

He's just being nice to me to figure out how to push a sale on Mrs. Nguyen.

"Let's just get through this trip," I reply.

His eyes darken, so black and fathomless that there's a hint of emptiness. For a flash of a second, I see the Jack I used to know. The Jack who used to be vulnerable, who used to worry out loud about his mom, who cried more than I did when I had to get surgery to fix the scar on my lip again, back when I was four, because he was scared I was in pain.

That glimpse disappears like it never existed, and his face shutters. Back to the fake Jack, this stranger. I don't want to continue this conversation; there's nothing left to be said. I push past him, out of the storage room. "We should get going."

"Right." His voice is flat. "Let's go."

On our way out, Mrs. Nguyen loads us up with frosty cups of Vietnamese coffee, the ice clinking irresistibly. With that, we're done with the last of my parents' deliveries. Now it's just Jack and CharmWorks' drop-offs.

Outside Café Thăng Long, I glance at the garden path, and pointedly walk the other way.

"Damn, this coffee wakes me up." Jack trails behind me. "The shortcut is—"

"Faster, if we were going straight through." *I know.* I spin around to finally face him, even though my stomach's a quivering mess that has nothing to do with Jack. I dangle the keys from my fingers. "I'm going to drop by one of the stores around the corner. Want to wait for me in the car?"

He looks at me. "Are you okay, Ellie? You look kind of pale."

"I'm fine." The tremor in my voice doesn't convince either of us, judging by the puzzled look on his face.

"I'll stay with you," Jack says. *Don't say you're concerned about me; that's a lie.* "It's . . . it's boring waiting in the car."

Okay, now *that's* a lie.

But I don't have time to think about Jack.

Clutching my iced coffee, I stop in front of the store I've been looking for. The windows are slightly tinted, but they've got a few glass cases out for display, and there's a big black leather chair. Only a basic sign hangs above the door: PIERCINGS.

"Whoa, Ellie." Jack clears his throat. "When I said 'take a chance,' I didn't mean to pierce yourself on a whim. You *hate* needles—"

"This is my choice," I snap. "You have no veto powers over what I do to *my* body."

Jack splutters. "I didn't mean that— It's a needle— You—"

I don't have time to listen. Indecisiveness and worry tear at my thoughts. I down the Vietnamese iced coffee, hoping for *any* kind of strength from the bitter sweetness, and toss the cup into a nearby recycling bin.

Cold air washes over me as I pull open the door. I hope I'm making the right decision.

～～ ～～

A woman pops her head out of a back room when I walk in. Jack's stammering something behind me, an apology, maybe. But my head's buzzing too much to listen.

Am I really doing this? The piercing? Finally?

I've wanted an upper-ear piercing for as long as I can remember. Except for the fact that, when I got my earlobes pierced at thirteen, I fainted.

I had to have a few surgeries when I was younger. I was born with a cleft lip, where the lip doesn't fully connect in the womb. There's no magic big enough to fix something like that. The first surgery was when I was three weeks old, and even though there's no way I could possibly remember that surgery, Mom and Dad say I've never been comfortable around blood or needles ever since. As I got older, Jack was at my side for the lip revision surgery at four years old and the post-op visits. Mrs. Yasuda and my mom would schedule our annual doctor appointments for shots together, and he'd hold my hand, chatting about his guitar or making up awful, cheesy jokes so I'd forget about the nurse swabbing my arm with alcohol, the needle sharp and ready on her tray. But after Mrs. Yasuda passed away, Jack stopped going with me to those doctor visits, and I had to tough it out on my own.

I fainted a few times, not that I'd ever tell him that.

Quickly, I glance at the armchair. It looks sturdy enough to hold me if I lose consciousness.

The worker leans on the glass display of navel studs. "How can I help you?"

Her scarlet-as-blood name tag says *Ruby*. I shiver at the thought of blood . . . blood coming from my ear.

"I don't have an appointment, but I was hoping I could get my ear pierced."

"How old are you?" Ruby puts her chin on her hand, like I'm an interesting show. "We don't pierce underage kids without their parents. It's California law."

"I—I know. I'm sixteen." There's a wobble to my voice that I wish I could erase. "But . . . I made an appointment a while back . . . and my parents weren't going to be able to make it since they work on weekends, so you'd emailed me the permission form that I got notarized. So I have that."

"When kids cancel, I figure it'll never happen. No offense." Her hand opens and closes like a claw, flashing her bloodred nails. "Paperwork."

I pull my phone out of my pocket and flip open the wallet case.

From somewhere behind me, Jack makes a noise of surprise. "You're serious about this."

I ignore him as my fingers rest on the folded form, peeking out from the inner pocket. The paper has been folded over so many times. After way too many shifts at my parents' shop, I've sat at Ana's café and pulled it out, running my fingers over the official stamped seal. I've always adored how upper-ear piercings look; it's *extra*, something more than the ordinary earlobe piercing.

Maybe I'm giving way too much thought to this. But I've also spent way too long thinking about how I'm not really who I've wanted to be.

I take a deep breath.

Am I ready?

Short answer: *no and hell no.*

Jack's still standing in the doorway of the shop, looking confused. "But—*why?*"

That answers it for me: I'm never going to fulfill my Anti-Wallflower List if I give up here. Lia will never see me change. I'll just spend another year looking at the notarized form and folding it up again, stuffing it back in my wallet as if being out of sight means it would be out of mind.

But it's always going to be on my mind.

I pull the paper out, unfold it, and smooth out the creases. "Here it is."

"Well. It's real." Ruby nods her head toward the chair. "Pick your piercing and then jump in."

Moments later, the sharp scent of isopropyl alcohol makes me dizzy as I lean back in the cool leather chair. Ruby is prepping my ear, making sure it's clean.

For. The. Piercing.

The walls spin around me as I catch sight of the needle on her tray. It's the length of my finger and wicked sharp.

"Oh, we have a woozy one here." Ruby shakes her head. "It's never too late to stop. I never pierce anyone who doesn't want it. I'll give your money back if you walk away."

The fifty dollars I've paid are tempting to run off with. I can use some of it on another Vietnamese coffee and a snack, and then I can drive on south like I'd never given up.

Give up . . . give up . . .

"I'm fine," I rasp.

Ruby snorts, shaking her head. Then she points Jack toward a black stool next to my chair. "Distract."

That leaves me and Jack basically face to face, because there's no way I'm going to look at her handling that scary-long needle.

"So." Jack shifts uncomfortably. "Um, distract. Yeah, so our next stop is Gilroy, right?"

I grunt.

"The Garlic Hut," he says.

"You suck at distracting," Ruby interrupts. "Truthfully."

Jack's ears turn red. He clears his throat.

"Try a story. Something funny. Something *interesting*. Anything is better than 'the Garlic Hut in Gilroy,'" Ruby says. "The standards are low right now."

"She's right. You can just go outside," I croak. Ruby and I have gone over the placement, the piercing, everything. So all that's left is the actual stabbing of my ear. I mean, the piercing. And judging by the way Ruby's moving around, it's going to be any second now.

"Okay," he says, dramatically taking a deep breath as if *he's* the one getting his ear pierced. "So, why were you trying to flirt with that asshole at the boardwalk?"

My jaw drops. I've got to be hearing things. I—

"Wow, there," Ruby says. "That's a new form of distraction I haven't heard before. I like that. I thought you two were a couple by the way you look at each other but—"

I panic-stare at her and she snorts. "Never mind, you do you, keep talking."

I stammer. "It . . . it was . . ."

Jack says, maybe to Ruby or maybe to himself, "Ellie's not usually like this, for sure."

"How would *you* know what I'm like?" My cheeks flush, and I barely notice Ruby lining up the needle. People love to label me. What about what I want to label *myself*? Especially Jack—he's pretended not to know me for so long.

Jack grins. "Well, we'll have to debate later on that."

"No, we won't!" There's no way I'm going to let him ignore me. I'm going to throttle him as soon as—

"You're all done." Ruby places a mirror in front of me. "What do you think?"

Already? I turn my head to look; my skin's a little pink, but there it is—the star-shaped silver piercing is on my right ear, at the exact spot I'd chosen. I breathe out in surprise, giving it the label *I* want. "It's perfect."

Jack smiles smugly, standing up from the stool. "And I was the perfect distraction."

I'll ignore *that*.

Chapter 13

As I drive past the outskirts of San Jose, the bustling city surrounding the highway fades into the occasional neighborhood, and then eventually gives way to brittle, patchy brush and fields of dried, golden grass. The blue sky overhead is deceivingly beautiful, as if I'm not stuck within throttling distance of Jack.

"Mind if I make a call?" he asks.

I jerk my head in a nod. "Go for it."

He presses his phone to his ear. "Hey, Minami."

A voice, bright and cheery, buzzes back through the line, but I can't hear the words. Is it really Minami Vu from our high school? They sound so friendly. . . .

"Video chat? Now?" He glances over at me.

"Go for it." I wave, and he presses a few buttons on his phone.

"Who's that?" Minami's on speakerphone, and I glance over to catch a glimpse of her dreamy wide eyes and perfect, heart-shaped face, all framed by artfully messy bed-head hair spun up into a bun. She's semifamous on Instagram for her envy-inducing, globetrotting lifestyle (the most frequent comment is always "I want to be you!"), though she and Lia are probably tied as the most crushed-on girl at school.

"Remember?" Jack prompts her. "The road trip."

"Right, but who is *she*?"

"No one," Jack says quickly.

Ow. Dammit. It shouldn't hurt like this.

"Isn't that Ellie Kobata from Elissa's Tea Shop?" Minami cranes her graceful-as-a-swan neck as if she can see around the corner of her phone. Given that she's magic-aware and talented, maybe there *is* some sort of charm she's figured out. It would explain how she always seems to know the latest gossip. "I thought you said you don't like her."

Including. That. Gossip.

"Minami!" Jack lets out a strained laugh.

I clear my throat. "Hi, Minami."

"Ohh. You can hear me?" Minami grins. "Sorry, Ellie."

With a sharp pang, I realize Jack hasn't even bothered to correct her.

I don't like you two either, Jack and Minami. Go be a cute couple elsewhere.

It's like I'm back in AP Art again, watching Ian and Ally make out in front of me. Ah, the things I would say if I weren't a wallflower.

Minami sighs. "Jack, I really, really wanted to talk with you. Let's catch up later?" Then she adds, as if it isn't obvious, "Privately."

I don't have to look at his phone to know she's serving up one of her doe-eyed gazes. Jack clears his throat, injecting a niceness to his tone that he'd never use for me. "Of course."

"Bye!" Minami says cheerily. "See you later, Ellie!"

He stops the call and starts rapidly texting instead. "I hope Dad shipped out that new set of stationery for her mom's order," he says, seemingly talking to himself. "No, I'm sure he's got it handled." He pauses to look over at me. "I'm sorry about the phone call; I'm not trying to ignore you."

I almost make the car screech to a halt. "Keep entertaining yourself. Continue your phone date with Minami. We don't need any hanging out here. No fun and games on this ride."

The instant I say that, I bite my lip, wishing I could take back those words. Jack sits up straighter in his seat. Clearly, talking with Minami got him in a better mood. He shifts toward me, curiosity woven through his words. "Fun and games?"

When we were younger, we'd get carsick all the time, so we used to make up games to keep our minds off our churning stomachs. But—why would he want to talk about this now? Maybe he's desperately trying to make sure I don't leave him on the side of the road after what Minami's just revealed.

"I see . . ." Jack looks outside. "Something blue and new."

That was our favorite game. We had to search for something around us, and then make up a rhyme about it. The other person had to spot it or they'd get tickled. This game worked well until we got to the tickling part, because that always made us extra carsick. But we still played it as our faces turned green from the bumpy ride.

"Blue and new . . ." I repeat his clue before cursing at my-self. Dammit, why'd I fall into this?

"C'mon, don't make me tickle you."

"I promise to eject you from my car if you even *try*. Then the only blue and new thing you'll be facing is the sky as you walk your sorry ass back home."

"I bet you would've cursed me if your hands were free." Jack snorts. "But, actually, you got it. I was talking about the sky."

"That's like level one. *Way* too beginner."

I catch his grin from the corner of my eyes. "Sure, but it's your turn."

Dammit. I've roped myself into the game. "Pink and bet-ter than a soft drink."

"This is the answer." He lifts up the remaining half of his sakura mochi. "Want it?"

My mouth waters. He waves it in front of me, and my lips part automatically—

Just as he pops it into his mouth.

"I should have kept that for myself," I grumble, and my stomach echoes my thoughts.

"Oh. Shoot." He actually sounds sorry, which sounds so weird. He's trying to play Mr. Nice Guy after that awful phone call. "We can stop and eat lunch?"

I shake my head in a clear *no*. Game's over, I'm too hungry now.

"Are you sure?" he asks. "Wasn't that just your stomach I heard?"

I give him a generous helping of my side-eye, and he lightly taunts, "Okay, okay. I know how you get when you're hangry.

I'll leave you be." He reaches forward and turns up the volume to the Mirei Touyama song piping out of the speakers.

But the constant presence of my neighbor remains through the congested hour drive into Gilroy, the garlic capital of the world. When I stop for gas at the first station I spot, Jack steps out and walks over to my side of the car while I'm trying to fill up.

"Hey, Ellie," he says as he tosses the empty plastic container from Shuei-Do into the recycling. "I can drive."

I'd agree in an instant if Lia asked. But I don't trust Jack. He doesn't do anything to be nice. I stab the nozzle into the gas tank. "It's my car."

He frowns, and then motions at the dripping car wiper in his hand. "Mind if I wash down the front windows?"

I grit my teeth. A million flies and mosquitos have splattered onto my windshield in the short drive. "Fine."

Jack scrubs at the front, and even the side mirrors. Then he tries again. "Don't you want to switch off? You've driven for a few hours—"

My chest clenches as I pull the gas nozzle out of my car. "No. I hate when guys think they have to be all masculine and drive." Most of all, I hate when Jack thinks he knows what's best.

He freezes. "I didn't mean it like—"

"I'll drive." My voice is cool.

Jack opens his mouth as if he's got a death wish. But, thankfully, he shuts it and nods. His broad shoulders are stiff as he uses a paper towel to wipe the window-washing fluid off the wiper.

We get to the Garlic Hut—a small café a block or two away from the Gilroy Outlets—forty minutes later. With the awkward silence in the car, the drive feels like it's taken years.

As I pull into the parking lot, Jack runs his hand through his slightly messy hair, taming it from the ride. I wonder if he's going to be shining that smile of his at another girl inside the shop.

Suddenly, he says, "Win a contest, any contest."

What in the world is he talking about?

Jack continues, "Revenge on Jack Yasuda. Oh, you should cross that one out."

"Huh?"

"Fall in love."

Oh, hell no.

I screech to a stop, throwing us both forward, the seat belts snapping against our chests. *"Jack!"*

It's like he's read my phone's notes, but my phone is still on the dashboard clip, the navigation chiming in that the Garlic Hut is forty feet ahead to our left. Or maybe he's cast some sort of curse to read my mind, but that's impossible, unless he wants to get kicked out of magical society—

Shock fills my veins as Jack points at a piece of paper taped onto the sun visor above the passenger seat. "I was trying to use the mirror and found . . . that."

It's my list.

Lia and I had taped our lists to the sun visor, with the idea that whoever wasn't driving would be able to cross items off or check on what was left. Hers is gone, like every other trace of her in the car . . . but my list is still taped up there.

In full, embarrassing glory.

From the driver's seat, my handwritten title, *The Anti-Wallflower List*, is in blaring red pen. Before he can recite another line out loud, I zip into an empty space, throw the car into park, and yank the list off the visor.

Jack protests, "But—wait—"

I tear the paper into tiny, indecipherable bits. Even with Cam's vial of luck, I wouldn't be able to puzzle this shredded mess back together.

"Don't. Read. Any. Further," I grit out, tearing the list up even more. "Wipe it from your memory. Or I will leave you here in Gilroy to become a freaking garlic, don't test me—"

"I don't want to become garlic jam," Jack says solemnly, even though there's a twinkle in his eye that I want to grind out with my heel. And then he adds, "It was tough enough being on your list the first time. I don't think I'd survive a second mention."

My jaw clamps together so hard I'm going to crack a molar. "Let's keep it at one mention, then." I hook my finger over my shoulder. "Don't you have a job to do?"

Jack pauses, as if he wants to say something.

"Go," I hiss.

"Ellie, I'm flattered I made it onto the list—"

"Just *go*."

The passenger door opens and closes, and then Jack grabs his boxes from the back seat.

Pretend everything is normal, just disappear into the seat . . . Everything is normal . . . everything is normal . . .

Breathing in deep, I turn around, even though my fists are curled up against my legs. "Need help?"

He raises an eyebrow from where he's stacking up his pile of boxes. "Let me drive and I'll let you help. Or we can talk about the—"

His voice dies as I level a fiery glare. Instead of getting out, I enjoy watching him struggle under the weight of the cardboard boxes as he makes his way up the steps and into the quirky, garlic-bulb-shaped café. Because if I get out of the car, I really might try a dangerous memory-erasing charm to wipe out his memory.

"I'll be thirty minutes!" he calls over his shoulder. I squint. Is he smirking again?

I set a timer on my phone.

Then I pull up my messages and stare at the chat between me and Lia. She hasn't responded since before we met up for the prank. Slowly, I type out another message.

> **ME:** I'm really sorry, Lia. I wanted to tell you the truth so many times, but I wasn't allowed to. This road trip sucks without you. I miss you a lot, and I want to support you, in whatever way I can.

I stare at the update:

STATUS: Read

There's no response. She doesn't even try typing anything out. I stare at the screen until my eyes blur. How can I get Lia to forgive me? How can I get her to understand that I would've done anything, *anything* to chase away her pain if I could?

No matter how long I stare at it, she doesn't respond.

I try another chat, this one between me, Remy, and Cam.

> **ME:** Hey, have you heard anything from Lia?

> **REMY:** Give her some time. She'll come around. How's the drive with Jack dearest?

> **ME:** Oh, stop. I'm alive, he's alive, and we're at Gilroy already. So far, it's a success.

> **CAM:** Lia's been around your house to chat with your mom. I think she's still a little worn out from thinking things through, getting used to all the new stuff.

I lost Jack as my best friend years ago, and now it feels like I'm going to lose Lia. And the only plan I can think of—the one everyone else is convinced of—is to give her time.

The wait hurts. But I hope, more than anything, that it'll heal her.

It feels like hours later when I drag myself out of my self-induced misery and check my timer. If Jack is a minute late, I'm going to drive around the café and pretend I've left without him. Unfortunately, he gets back in exactly nineteen minutes and thirty seconds.

As he buckles his seat belt, my timer starts ringing. I scramble to turn it off.

"Were you . . . timing me?"

"No?"

He lets out a snort that sounds suspiciously like a laugh.

I'm about to make him swear to never mention the list again for the rest of his life when my stomach decides to make its running-on-empty status known. *Grrumble* . . . My cheeks flame as it echoes in the car. The delicate, soft mochi from this morning feels like it was really from days ago.

His lips quirk. "Want to eat? We've got that lunch from Cam and Remy."

I nod, certain that my cheeks are as red as a flamethrower. "Yeah. Cam told me about a park in the area, I'll take us there."

"Or we can eat here in the car, if you're too hungry. I mean, you sounded—"

"I'm totally fine!" I say, way too artificially cheery, and his shoulders jerk up.

I turn to look over at him. His eyes flash with amusement for a split second as they meet mine. Then everything shutters, and his face is solemn and still as usual.

I frown, certain about what I saw, even though . . .

No way. There's no way I actually made him laugh.

Chapter 14

I pull up to Las Animas, a spread-out park tucked away in one of Gilroy's neighborhoods. The tiny maple trees around the parking lot don't do much to shade the car from the toasty eight-five degree heat. I cut the engine, and before I realize it, Jack has already pulled the wicker basket from the trunk and is nodding toward the wood picnic tables to one side.

The complete silence that's settled between us isn't too bad; the breeze whisks the heat off my skin, and I can pretend I'm not shooting silent daggers at him. We walk down the path, stepping out of the way of a group of middle schoolers whooping as they run over to the skate park on the other end of Las Animas.

The park is full of families on summer vacation. Parents eat with their kids at the picnic tables that are spaced out in the shadows of the trees, and even more kids chase each other around the playgrounds and the grass field, shouting and laughing.

Under the cool shade of the tall evergreens, it's a little

quieter. Jack sets down the basket at one of the empty tables, about fifteen feet away from the others. "This one okay?"

"Yeah." I mean, all of the tan picnic tables are the same. It's not like I'm going to say, *Let's choose the one farthest away from the one you chose* or *I want to eat separately from you.* Even though that's a tempting thought. "Let's eat?"

"Sure, I'm starving." He flips open the top and pauses, blinking in surprise. "Uh, did you pack this?"

"No, why?" I step next to him and peek inside. "*Oh*, it's like . . ."

It's like *before.*

Onigiri, little triangular balls of rice, each with different seasonings, rest on one side of the basket next to packets of dried seaweed. And there's boxes of the best side dishes ever in the middle: everything from potato salad drizzled with tonkatsu sauce (Jack's favorite) to gomae spinach, boiled spinach with sesame seeds (my favorite). On the other side, there are tiny bottles of green tea and two boxes labeled *Dessert.*

The four of us—Jack, Remy, Cam, and I—used to picnic at Heritage Park in downtown Palo Alto. Our parents would cook in the morning, packing these same things in this very basket.

Jack starts trying to take the food out, but the instant his fingers close around an onigiri—*bzz.* A brief, sharp sound shrieks from the basket. We look around at the other picnickers, but no one else seems to hear. Is it an alarm for only magic-aware people?

His fingers waver above the food. He touches a metal canteen of tea. *Bzzzz.*

"I think Remy and Cam charmed our lunch," Jack says, in shock.

I reach out and poke an onigiri.

Bzz! Like a ringing alarm, it's a sudden sound that sends me reeling backward. It's louder this time.

He experimentally puts one finger on it. *BZZZ!*

Our eyes meet.

"I'm too hungry to deal with this," I groan, pulling my phone out and speed-dialing Remy.

Ringgg, ring . . .

"Hello?" Remy sounds way too cheerful for how hungry I am. Then, to whomever she's with, she says, "It's *them*."

I don't like the sound of this.

I poke one of the rice balls and it screeches. "Remy, what in the world did you do to the basket? Is it some sort of anti-theft thing? How do I disable this?"

"Is Jack there?" another voice says. Remy has put me on speakerphone, for her and Cam.

I sigh, pressing a few buttons. "Okay, you two are on speakerphone. So, what's up?"

"So . . ." Remy says. "The picnic basket is meant for the two of you . . . but you have to work on something first. You two have a problem . . ."

". . . It's communication," Cam finishes.

Thanks, Remy and Cam. Thanks for rubbing in how the two of you are perfectly in sync.

From across the table, Jack frowns and tries to pick up the box of potato salad. It shrieks at him, and he grumbles. "This is ridiculous. Things are fine the way they are now."

Wow. Straight-out say how unnecessary I am in your life, dearest childhood friend.

"Look," Remy says. "You two are on a road trip together, and I'd like to see you make it down to Huntington Beach all in one piece. And, better yet, be getting along like you used to. This is *way* overdue."

It's absolutely embarrassing that my younger sister is berating me for my lack of communication skills. Then again, when it comes to Jack, it's not just that I can't talk to him normally. We've got an ocean—no, the whole Milky Way separating us, like he and I are shouting at each other from different galaxies.

"Today, you two only have three goals," Cam says. "All are meant to fix your communication issues. And after you get them done, you can eat."

"We're *starving*." Jack's frown deepens.

"It's been hours since breakfast," I groan. "Can you *hear* my stomach rumbling?"

"It's so loud it makes my ears hurt," Jack says, and I chuck a bottle of tea at his head. It merrily screeches as he catches it easily with one hand and shoots me a cocky grin. *Nice try.* Damn him and his stupid tennis reflexes.

"More motivation to get this done fast, then," Cam says happily. He's probably high-fiving Remy.

"Look, the whole reason why you two got stuck together in the first place is because you both have too many misunderstandings," Remy says.

They're not wrong. I'd rather have Lia here with me any day. We'd be lying out on the grass, gobbling down the onigiri and laughing about everything and nothing at all. But now she's not even talking to me.

I sigh. "Fine, give us your goals."

"Perfect," Cam says. "Goal One is for Ellie. First, you've got to listen to whatever Jack says in the next hour."

Jack meets my eyes from across the picnic table, as if trying to read my reaction. *Listen to him? Why?*

I press my lips in a thin line as I check the clock. It's past noon and my stomach is screaming almost as loud as the food with its desperate hunger pains. I could drive us to a nearby fast-food stop, but this ridiculously tasty-looking picnic would go to waste. "Fine."

"Goal Two is for Jack," Remy says. "Jack, you've got to properly explain things, starting with that Santa Cruz mess."

Jack blinks with surprise. "Wait, what? How did you know—" He cuts off, glancing at me.

"Know what?" I ask.

"He'll tell you," Remy says quickly.

Jack pauses, as if he wants to say no. Then he chews his lip, which surprises me. I haven't seen him do that in ages. What's he nervous about?

"C'mon, Jack," Cam says. "You said you wanted to change things—"

"Okay. Fine." His tanned cheeks look slightly red. Is he *blushing*? What does Cam mean?

"Great!" Remy says. "Now, Goal Three. I know this is on your summer wish list, Ellie. Go on, enjoy your picnic!"

Jack raises an eyebrow at that, and I glare at him. *Number 5: Go on a picnic date.* I thought my bucket list was causing me trouble before. Now I know that my Anti-Wallflower List is seriously the Cursed List.

After I cut off the phone, Jack and I stare at the delicious, but currently off-limits, pile of food.

"They're unbelievable," I groan. "They sent us all the way here with food we can't eat, knowing we're hungry. They're mini pains in the ass."

Jack shakes his head, and to my surprise, he lets out a laugh. I freeze, watching his eyes crinkle, just a little bit.

Did I—make him laugh? Again? No, it was our siblings' trick on the food.

I move the basket to the side so we can be face-to-face. "I guess that means . . ."

He swallows, lacing his fingers together. "That we . . . should talk first."

∽ ∽

Oh. This is torture.

We sit in a stiff silence. I'm so hungry that I want to tear into the food, no matter if alarms ring, but knowing Cam and Remy and their ways with puzzles, it's probably not just an alarm. They've likely charmed the food to disappear if there's still a trace of annoyance buzzing through us or something like that. With their clever minds, they always think these sorts of things out way too thoroughly.

I settle my chin on my hands and stare at him.

He glances off at the grass field, maybe thinking of some of the birthday parties we spent at Palo Alto's parks back when we were little kids.

In this silence, I take a moment to study Jack. The last time we had a picnic together, he still had those same light brown eyes, that same muddy-brown hair, and the tanned skin from long days out under·the summer sun. But his face is more chiseled, grown up. He still has those same full lips. *Dammit, Ellie. Don't let him catch you staring at his lips.*

"So," I say, and he blinks as I draw him away from whatever thoughts are making him drift off. "You've got this hour."

"Right. Your goal. The hour of listening to me." He checks his phone, sliding it out of his pocket. "It's more like twenty minutes now."

"Good, because I'm starving. Go on, then."

He pauses, chews on his lip. And there it is again. That childish habit his mom broke him of. Why is it back? Or did he never really stop?

"Well." Jack pauses. "It has something to do with what . . . what Remy and Cam are forcing me to tell you."

"You seriously don't have to tell me they're *forcing* you to be this vague." In other words: *I don't really care.*

He shakes his head. "I . . . It might make you mad."

More annoyed with him than I am already, especially since *he's* the obstacle separating me from my lunchtime feast? Mmm, not possible.

But I just say, "Go for it."

His hands look slightly damp when he pulls his phone out again, checks the time, and then nervously sets it next to him. But he puts it down too hard, and the plastic clacks loudly against the table. I wince.

"So?" I prod, glancing over at the basket. Darn Remy and

Cam. I'll have to have a word when I see them at the convention. Keeping me from lunch is unnecessarily cruel.

Jack takes a deep breath, his eyes flicking up to meet mine. "It's about that guy . . ."

"What guy?" I don't have any guys in my life. And no girls either, after Lia stopped talking to me.

"Ezra at Santa Cruz," he says. "He . . . I may have told him to stay away from you. And I'm sorry for that—"

"Sorry?" I hiss sharply. "When did *sorry* ever change anything?"

Sorry doesn't even *cover* how embarrassed I felt watching my could-be summer romance skitter away from me like I'd suddenly caught the flu. "What does it matter to you who I'm dating—"

"You would've ended up as another picture on his account," he snaps. He scans his finger on his phone and pushes it over.

My jaw drops.

I take in the picture on the screen. That halo of golden-brown curls, those green-brown eyes . . . It's Ezra.

But Ezra, with a girl. And the date on it—the date on it was the day before we went to Santa Cruz. The tagline?

Exotic beauty and some summer fun.

I scroll down. And down. And down.

His Instagram is filled with pictures of him and countless girls . . . Girls kissing his cheek, arms wrapped around him like he's amazing—like he was something special to them.

They probably each thought they were something special, until he posted a picture of them on his Instagram account like some bro-trophy.

"I . . ."

"I've heard of his reputation from tennis friends." Jack's voice is softer this time. "I tried to tell you, but you didn't want to talk with me. I'm sorry, I should've let you know first, and let you decide. But it was all in the moment—then Ezra was into you, holding you . . ."

My skin is cold and clammy. I've lost my appetite.

"This is disgusting," I finally breathe out. And Jack's shoulders go slack, as if he's been rigid with tension.

"I'm sorry." His voice is sincere.

But I stare down at my lap, thoughts of *could've beens* and *should've beens* whizzing through my head.

I'd been so mad at Jack for getting in the way of my so-called summer romance that I'd tried to get revenge on him. Were Cam and Remy right? If he and I had talked it out, would this summer have been totally different? Totally better?

"I wish I'd known . . . I wouldn't have pranked you. This is all my fault, Lia not talking to me—"

"Whoa, Ellie. You can't change what happened with Lia—"

"I could've. I should have," I say bitterly.

"It was surprising that she'd never found out about magic, what with being around you and Remy and Cam so much. Plus, it's my fault. I cast that protection charm. Blame me."

"I do," I say, and he stares with surprise. Then I crack a tiny grin, and he gives me a faint smile back, even though he still seems worried.

His eyes linger on mine, as if studying my smile, but I turn away, poking at an onigiri. The alarm is finally silent. Grabbing two—salmon and umeboshi, Jack's old favorites—I pass them over to him. "Here. I think we did it. We can eat."

He sets down the onigiri and glances up. "Wait, there's one more thing." He grabs the bottles of tea, setting one in front of me. His voice lowers, with a surprising gentleness. "Your list . . . I think it's cool, Ellie, I—"

"Let's—not—talk—about—that." My face is going to burst into flames in this summer heat. "*Ever.*"

"Then what *can* we talk about?"

"Rules for this road trip." Ever the planner, I've been thinking about this on the drive down.

"Rules?" he echoes. "Like what?"

"For the sake of the next few days, let's get along."

His hands freeze on the way to picking up his rice ball, as if I've asked him if I can have all his food. "A treaty? Just the next few days?"

"That's the limit of my trust." I mean it as a joke, but the words hit sharp as an arrow, a bull's-eye on our past.

He swallows. "You don't trust me at all, is what you're saying."

"What reason would I have to, Jack?" His name is fire and ice on my tongue, but this truth burns through my body worse than flames, flaring as strong as the torment he's put me through. "You've changed, and you damn well know it."

Jack's eyes grow shadowed as he takes this in. "Ellie, I didn't— I'm sorry—"

Then he cuts himself off. Has he . . . has he never realized how he's acted after his mom passed away? How much he's closed himself off?

I watch him breathe in, breathe out. He stares back, watching me do the same, but there's a trace of pain in his eyes. No quick apology will smooth things over. He swallows, maybe to speak, but just as quickly returns to chewing on his lip again. If he has some stupid excuse for his behavior, he knows I'll give him hell in return.

Jack says quietly, "Let's do that. A pact for the rest of the trip."

"Yeah," I say. "And once we make it to Huntington Beach and set up the booth, I'll see if I can convince my parents that I can drive home alone."

He chews his lip once, twice. Then: "Fine."

I blink, looking at him. I didn't expect him to agree so quickly.

"Anything else?" he asks.

I shake my head. "No. Anything you want to say?"

He's silent as he starts unwrapping his salmon rice ball, as if considering what he *can* say. But then he takes a bite, the crackle of the seaweed making my stomach growl.

I clear my throat. "Jack? Was there something on your mind?"

Jack is midbite, but at my words, he freezes. After a long moment's pause, seeing me ready to demolish the pile of food, he says, "No. A temporary pact sounds fine. Temporary is good."

I frown at him, but he's too busy stuffing his face to respond. That's weird. It almost sounds like he's trying to convince himself. For a second, I thought he was going to say something else, that he wanted to tell me something more.

❧   ❧

About thirty minutes later, we've polished off all the food and are back on the road again, our stomachs stuffed and happy.

This time, the silence is peaceful, like we're two friends who had a picnic, not mortal enemies who were forced to make temporary amends.

As Jack dozes off next to me, I touch my hand to my heart. It's still beating rapidly. I can't believe he saw my list. But most of all, I wonder . . .

Earlier today, I looked straight into his face, and saw his light brown eyes, his tanned skin, the familiar features I've seen throughout all these years. But, today, I also got a glimpse of sorrow and regret, and even a hint of an apology.

I wonder, over these past years, have I really been seeing him at all?

Chapter 15

Along our three-hour drive to San Luis Obispo, Jack points out the window. "Look, do you see that?"

I glance over. The scenery is beautiful—rolling golden hills, the dried grass glinting under the sunlight. There's even a tiny cottage set into the hills. "What am I supposed to look at?"

"The magic-aware map on my phone says that's a magical cottage. You've heard about them before, right?"

"Not really. The last time we drove this way was like ten years ago, for the convention. I slept most of the way."

"Oh." He pauses, maybe remembering that trip, too. We'd gone together, now that I think about it. It was for the ninetieth anniversary of CMRC. His mom and Mr. Yasuda had driven the car with the exhibit booth and goods, and my parents had brought down the kids. We'd played our car games and napped after our lunchtime picnic. But after Mrs. Yasuda got sick, Mr. Yasuda and my parents switched off duties, and all the kids stayed home with Mrs. Yasuda, trying not to cause trouble for her.

"What are they used for, again?" I ask.

"Magical cottages are like rest houses. Back when magicals didn't fit into 'normal' society as well, it was a place for people like us to stay in times of need. Non-magicals see a fenced-off power station or sometimes a rundown, uninhabitable cottage. It depends on the person; whatever it takes to make them stay away. But the magic-aware see it as the cottage that it actually is."

"That's neat. I want to check one out sometime."

"Right?" Jack says. "I've never been, either."

As we drive on, the tiny cottage disappears into the hills, and Jack and I lapse into a somewhat peaceful silence. This feels so *strange*. It's weird trying to be friendly. It was almost easier to ignore him.

When we finally make it to San Luis Obispo, my brain is frazzled from the drive, this odd state of not bickering with Jack, and not having internal arguments with myself. Still, we've got one more stop in Paso Robles until our overnight stop in Pixley. Jack goes to a gift shop on Higuera Street, balancing his boxes in his arms, and I yawn, wondering if I can catch a quick nap while he does his sales pitch.

Then he gets to the door and starts trying to pull at the handle with one of the hands he's curled around the boxes.

C'mon, I think, *make those tennis muscles work for—*

One of the boxes wavers at the top of the pile.

I sigh. And before I know it, I'm at the door, squeezing past him to grab at the handle.

"Here." I hold the door open. "Would it kill you to ask for help?"

"I thought you looked like you needed rest. But thanks, Ellie."

"Oh, thanks for commenting on my appearance."

But he doesn't walk in quite yet. He studies me. Those damn eyes of his look weirdly soft, like he's seeing something different from what I see when I look at the reflection of us in the glass front of the store, like he's not really seeing the way my hair's getting frizzy or my rumpled clothes. It's as if there's something he *wants* to say, but he doesn't know how to say it. Maybe this temporary pact was a bad idea. I frown, opening my mouth—

"Ah, if it isn't Jack Yasuda!" a voice cries, and the shop owner grabs one of the boxes from Jack's pile. "Welcome, welcome!"

"I'll be at the café next door," I say to Jack, hooking my thumb toward a cozy coffee shop to our right.

"I won't be long, maybe thirty minutes," he says. "Thanks, Ellie, for the help."

"Come in, Jack! We've been looking forward to seeing you!" The shop owner is motioning him in, and he follows her lead.

The door swings shut after him. And then the moment's gone. Whatever that moment was.

Through the glass, I can see him pile his boxes on the shop's counter and begin to open them up to display the latest CharmWorks wares, another one of those way-too-charming smiles lighting up his face.

In front of the coffee shop, I groan. It's past four, and the shop's closed for the day. But I need *something* to keep me going. The drive has been so long that I want to curl up with a book and take a little nap. I'm looking longingly at the shiny mugs through the glass pane when I sniff the air.

Tea. Somewhere. There's a spring in my step when I see a little indie bookstore down the way, with a tea mug carved out of wood hanging in the window. Another wooden sign declares its cute and utterly perfect name: Books and Boba.

Oh, this is *heaven.* Round bean bags are scattered among the long shelves, crammed with everything from picture books to young adult novels to coffee table books. The tea is forgotten as I pick up a graphic novel I've been looking forward to and start flipping through the pages. And then there's another new release that I want—I add it to my pile. Then another, then—

I've got a stack of ten books by the time I make it to one of the bean bags, this one in a funky electric-blue daisy pattern. My muscles start to unknot as I relax into the soft back. *"Ahh."*

"This place is the best, isn't it?"

Jack? Is he done already?

I look over to the end of the row, where there's a guy lounging in another bean bag. He's maybe a few years older, wearing a Cal Poly San Luis Obispo T-shirt, a just-as-tall pile of books next to him. His brownish eyes look almost bronze in the warm bookstore lighting, and his skin is dark. A college boy.

It's not Jack. A hot blush burns up my neck; why did my neighbor even come to mind?

The college boy is smiling in a way that's kind and sweet. He nods at my book. "I've read *Wild Beauty* by Anna-Marie McLemore, I've been looking forward to their latest release." Then he smiles down at the mound of books next to his bean bag. "There's so many books to read, and never enough time."

I laugh. "My to-read list would reach the moon if I stacked it up."

He takes a sip of his boba tea and nods. "I know that feeling."

Oh no. Conversations are like a tennis game, and I'm supposed to say something. He's cute, I *need* to say something! And . . .

I give him an awkward smile and wave at my book—*why am I* waving *at my book, oh crap, I don't know what to say.* Shy-girl mode is full-on activated. My cheeks burn as I nearly hit my nose with the pages as I try to hide behind the cover.

My palms are all sweaty. What can I say? Or is it too late?

Why can't this guy be like Jack? I can always find something to say around Jack, even though we never get along.

I sweat as I awkwardly sort through my stack, trying to decide what to buy. But when College Boy glances back my way, I scramble to grab the top book and begin to read like I've been in a word drought (which, technically, it seems like I'm still in).

And then books do what they always do so well—*Jade Fire Gold* sweeps me away into a world where I'm not too hesitant to take risks, I'm hell-bent on revenge. And with the first few pages, the book convinces me it's an insta-buy. I put it down and then pick up a recent romance novel release that I've been looking forward to, but I yawn, the words blurring in front of my eyes . . .

Suddenly the warmth of the bookstore and the long drive get to me, and I'm nodding off . . . I blink, focusing on the page again and flip it, but . . .

Before I know it, I'm drifting off.

૭   ૭

"Ellie!"

"Mmm?" I'm so warm and comfy here. My body feels cocooned.

More urgently. *"Ellie!"*

"Hey," another voice cuts in. "She's sleeping, let her rest. Who are you, anyway?"

"I'm with her. And we have to get back on the road," that familiar voice growls.

Then my eyelids fly open.

I stare at the person in front of me, the last person I'd ever expect to say my name with any sort of worry. Jack Yasuda's eyebrows are knitted together. As if he actually *is* concerned.

I sleepily wave at him. "What's wrong, Jack?"

College Boy drops his eyes back to his novel. "Sorry, I didn't realize you two were together."

"Oh! We're not, he's my neighbor . . ."

But the boy smiles a little differently, as if he thinks I'm trying to be nice. He gets up, tucking his stack of books under his arm, and waves his empty boba cup. "Got to go check out. See you around."

He walks away to the register, clearly never expecting to

see me again. And definitely not in that semiflirty way from before.

Dammit, what's with Jack being a boy repellent? First Ezra (even though that may have been for a good reason), and now Cute College Boy?

I stare at Jack. "Really, did you have to yell to wake me up?"

It's then I realize he looks a little pale.

"Ellie," he says, "I tried going to the coffee shop you'd mentioned, but it was closed. And then I tried calling you, and it was like your phone was turned off or something."

"Please don't tell me you're worried about me, because that's like five years too late," I snap.

"What?" He looks genuinely confused.

"Never mind," I groan, rubbing my eyes. "Anyway, you found me, that's good."

"Yeah, but I thought something had happened to you! Why didn't you pick up your phone?"

Oh. Well . . . about that . . . I look down.

"Did you *block* my number?"

My eyes shift toward the register, where Cute Bookstore Guy is checking out.

"What the hell, you did, didn't you, Ellie?"

I shrug. "It's not like we ever talked." It was too painful, too strange to see his number show up in my contacts when I scrolled through to call Lia—their names were right next to each other. It was easier to block his number and have him disappear from my life, in every way possible.

Jack breathes in deep, pinching the bridge of his nose. "Okay, but, if we're going on a road trip together . . . can we have some way to communicate if we get separated again?"

I yawn, pulling my phone out of my pocket. I've missed a text from Remy: *Jack's looking for you. He sounds really worried. Are you okay?*

Quickly, I shoot back a message so she doesn't freak out and alert my parents: *We met up, it's fine. He's dramatic. Thanks, Remy.*

Then I unblock Jack—deleting the contact photo I have of him and me at eight years old, making funny faces at the camera—and wave my phone. "There. You can reach me anytime."

He sighs, shaking his head. "Want to head out?"

Back at the car, with my shiny new copy of *Jade Fire Gold* in hand, I fumble through my pockets, finally finding my keys. Then I use my free hand to stifle another yawn. Ugh. It's going to be a thirty-minute drive to Paso Robles, so it's not too bad. I can manage . . .

A hand wraps lightly around mine, closing in on the car keys. I jolt from the sudden warmth.

Jack's holding my hand, tugging me back a bit.

But that's not what's strange. It's the unexpected softness in his eyes.

"W—what is it?" I look away, and he drops my hand.

"I know you can drive," he says. "But, please, won't you let me take a turn? You're tired, you've driven me around all day to all these stops. At least let me take us to Paso Robles. You need some rest, Ellie."

I frown at him. "I can drive."

"But you're also tired, and you've driven all day." There's something about his voice that's almost a plea. "Take this chance to rest. Please."

That last *please* melts my iron resolve. It's so un-Jack-like, nothing like the Jack of the past five years, and everything like the Jack from before.

I breathe in. "Okay, fine. But if I hate your driving, you're going to pull over and switch."

He cracks a grin. "Deal."

I slide the keys into his hand, a strange static buzzing up my fingers when I brush against his calluses from the electric guitar. An odd thought weaves through my mind: *I wish I could hear him play again.*

He and I used to spend afternoons in his room, after school. The moment we'd finished our fourth-grade homework, we'd sprawl out, me drawing my heart out, lying flat on the floor, and him plinking away on the secondhand electric guitar that was way too big for him. Those were some of the best memories of my childhood—a freshly made cupcake from Ana's with a dash of courage, Jack's music drifting around the room, and being in the company of someone I once trusted with all my heart.

When I slide into the passenger seat, I can't seem to find anything to say. I study the way Jack's hands hold the wheel so steadily, and my fingers itch to draw them. Sometimes, it feels like he holds my words in his hands, so delicately, like he's that same Jack from years ago. And it's that part of Jack—the part that I never see anymore—that I miss.

I tilt my phone screen toward the window, so he can't see it if he glances over, pick up my stylus, and start sketching.

Chapter 16

Paso Robles is known as one of the top wine areas of Central California, and the endless vineyards glowing in the slowly setting sun make it seem like an ocean of tangling, golden vines. Jack's still inside the winery, finishing up another sales pitch. I'd lingered in the gift shop, but hadn't found anything for Lia or my family or Cam, so when I caught a glimpse of the patio, I slipped out.

I've just stepped outside when a voice calls from behind me, "Wait, Ellie. Won't you try this?"

It's Mrs. Garcia, one of Mrs. Yasuda's old friends, and the owner of this beautiful, Tuscan-style winery. She's hurrying over, holding a glass with a thin pour of rosé, and Jack's trailing behind her. "It's our newest product, made with beautiful black grapes."

I shouldn't drink. I've got to—

"I can drive," Jack offers immediately.

I stare at the frosty, perfectly chilled, pink-tinged glass in her hand. Back when I was ten, my parents let me try their red wine during one of our family picnics. I spat it out and immediately dove for ramune, my favorite soda.

But I'm not a kid anymore. I take the glass, thanking her as she and Jack head back inside to talk about orders.

On the patio, all alone, I stare down at the glass, trying to hide my apprehension and the conflicting thoughts.

I'm technically *underage.*

But my parents let me drink before.

Well, you do have another whole day with Jack.

I tip the glass over, and the chilled wine coats my mouth, sweet and fruity. I crack a grin. It's the adult version of ramune.

"Wow," I whisper. I snap a photo holding out the glass in front of the vines to try sketching later. I want to capture the streaks of sunset through the glass, even though it'll be like trying to capture sand before it sifts out of my fingers. This would look good on my Instagram, too. If I ever make it public.

The door creaks open from behind me.

"Ready to head out?" Jack steps out onto the patio.

I blink, pulled away from my dreamland of art and paintbrushes. "Done already?"

He nods. "The Garcias loved the private line; our stuff always goes fast in their gift shop."

We have to go. We've got to head to Pixley, a two-hour drive. But I can't help soaking in the glow of the sunset, and the way it makes it seem like the world has been dusted with gold, cast under a spell. My fingers trace the patio railing longingly. I want to capture this sunlight in a bottle and create an elixir to bring up this feeling of eternal sunshine someday in the future. If I put on a pair of spectacles, I bet I'd see that even the raw magic dust is floating around gentle and lazy and beautiful.

Jack clears his throat. "Want to stay a little longer? We can take a few pictures. Or you can even draw, if you want."

"It's going to get dark soon." I hesitate. We have plans, another long drive to our next place, and—

"You're making another mental list, aren't you?" Jack leans against the railing. "Reasons why not to enjoy this sunset, or something like that."

"So what if I am?" My retort comes out stronger than ever, maybe because of my liquid courage. "What's wrong with lists?"

"Lists are great." A dangerous smile tugs at his lips. "Anti—"

Quickly, I set down the glass and cover my ears, running down the stairs that lead off the patio and down to solid ground before he can finish what he's saying. *Hell no.* Not listening to him repeat my list.

And face-to-face with the lush vineyard, I feel my worries melt away. The grapes glow with that magical golden sunlight, but from here, it feels far more real. I turn and turn, drinking in the sights of the green vines, thick with plump grapes, the same sage green as the broad leaves fluttering in the breeze. Dusty paths stretch between the rows, and I want to walk through them forever, listening to the almost-quiet of this strange, beautiful world.

"It's enchanting," I whisper.

The stairs creak under Jack's weight, and he says, "A perfect time to have a fake model shoot to use as a senior yearbook photo."

What he's saying doesn't make sense. Why does Jack want to model—

"Dammit," I curse. "Did you memorize my list?"

He blinks innocently when I swing around to glare at him. Jack has always had amazing recall. I could mention I liked a song at California Pizza Kitchen or wherever our families were eating out together, back when his mom was alive. And then later that day, he'd be picking away at his strings, re-creating the song that I'd mentioned. Or when it came to homework, he'd always remember what our teacher had typed out on the screen without having to check the classroom website. It was a blessing and a curse.

But right now, it's definitely a curse.

"It was only thirteen items?" he offers, and I groan.

I can't believe he read all of it . . . and *memorized* it, too. *Number 11: The perfect first kiss? Number 13: Fall in love?*

If embarrassment was a sword, it'd impale me right now.

"Seriously, though," Jack says. "You should fulfill your list."

"I tore it up," I shoot back.

He taps the side of his head with a knowing look. "I can write it out again for you—"

"No! Thank! You!" I blurt out. Then I sigh. "What will it take for you to stop bothering me about it?"

He holds up his phone and motions at the vineyard. "Go on, try it, Ellie."

"No. Hell no."

"I thought you didn't want to be a wallflower," he says.

And that's it. I explode into a million embarrassed pieces. I bury myself underneath the vineyard to be remembered forever, I—

"I like your list," he says, breaking me out of my thoughts of complete and utter mortification.

"Don't—don't you *dare* tell anyone about it!"

He frowns as if I've said something stupid.

No way. Is it too late? Has he posted an Instagram Story about my list, laughing about the weird things his once-childhood best friend does?

Then he says, "Why would I do that?"

As if it's simple. As if he hasn't spent the last five years ignoring my existence. As if he has some sort of loyalty to me, though I know he never did. We were friends once upon a time, like a twisted fairy tale, until it was more convenient to drop me and focus on CharmWorks instead. To be liked and popular, to become somebody who people remember at school, to no longer be invisible.

I grit my teeth. "Because . . . because . . ." *Bringing up the past is too painful.* I have to try a different angle. "We can't trespass—"

"Isn't that on your wish list?"

Damn Jack and his photographic memory.

I close my eyes, blaming the hot flush on my neck on the setting sun and wishing I could curse Jack to the other end of the continent. I guess that's what college is for—to get away from the people you've always known.

"Mrs. Garcia won't mind if we go in."

"This is way too embarrassing, still."

"One picture."

"Not with *your* phone."

He holds out his hand. "With your phone, sure."

I toss my phone at him, and with his stupid-clever coordination from tennis, he manages to catch it, even though I've kind of sort of thrown it wildly to his right.

Then I stalk down the path.

"Turn around," he calls after me, his voice mock-wounded. "Don't leave me all lonely here."

I stifle a laugh and turn around. But when he points the camera lens at me, I stand ramrod straight, as if I've just gotten my driver's license and I'm taking my picture at the DMV.

"Smile," he says. "Pretend you're looking at a giant tub of Marini's taffy."

I glare at him even more.

"Okay, maybe pretend I'm Mochi?"

"I always knew you were a dog—"

"Pretend whatever you want, as long as you stop glaring, Ellie," he interrupts, shaking his head as he laughs. "C'mon. What would make you smile?"

Then I think of the one thing that could possibly make me smile at him again.

In a perfect little world, we're friends again, Jack. I'm going to pretend that you never ditched me in middle school. I'll pretend the impossible, that we've stayed best friends up until this day . . . That this isn't just a temporary pact. That Lia isn't mad, and the three of us are best friends taking this road trip together, that things are different . . .

Then the realization jolts through me . . .

Would it make me that happy to be friends with him again?

"There!" Jack crows. He hands me my phone, and I scroll through a mess of pictures of me looking completely dorky—most with my eyes closed (typical)—and then . . .

The last of the photos that he's taken are of me smiling vaguely and looking off into the sunset. Somehow, I look slightly ethereal and at peace. And these pictures—they're totally senior picture–worthy.

"Not bad," I admit.

"You made it easy," he deadpans. "After the first hundred outtakes."

I roll my eyes at him, but then my lips curve up. "Your turn."

He blinks innocently. "Me?"

I take a step forward. "See anyone else?" I gesture at the spot I've vacated.

"I don't know." He's got a devilish look in his eyes. "I don't think I'm model-worthy. Should we even go in? What if we disturb the grapes, and the wine gets all weird tasting?"

"I heard this was a friend of a friend's vineyard. They won't mind if we trespass. And please, you know you're cute."

Jack raises an eyebrow, his eyes seeing only me, not looking anywhere else.

And, somehow, I don't feel like a wallflower, not with the way he looks at me. The rest of the world might not know I'm here, but he does.

He *does*.

We're so close it feels like each breath alone is a dare, an impossible hurdle we're both overcoming. *In, out. In, out.*

"Me, cute?" He steps closer, eyes glittering. His hand brushes against my fingers, leaving a blazing trail of gooseflesh. And it's like I've forgotten how to breathe. *In, in, hold, hold, hold—*

His phone rings. We jolt away from each other, and he scrambles to pull his phone out of his pocket.

A name flashes on the screen. *Minami Vu.*

"Mind if I take this call?" he asks.

I nod, waving him away. He doesn't notice—he's too busy frowning at the screen—so I have to say, "Go for it."

He heads back up the stairs, his voice unbearably and perfectly husky. "Sorry, Minami, I forgot about the time. So—"

Jack disappears inside. I can't hear what he's saying, but it's not like I need to know.

He's got a girlfriend. Of course he does.

I walk fast down the vines, my fingers tracing the leaves the way his hand brushed against mine. And I pretend I'm frowning because the sunset is bright, straight in my eyes, and not because this strange, confusing feeling tugging at my chest.

Chapter 17

My white Toyota Camry rumbles into the quaint town of Pixley around 10:30 P.M. It isn't unusually late for me—nights are my favorite time to curl up with a good book to help me drift off to sleep. But with the long drive, even Jack looks weary as he turns down a road, following his phone's navigation.

Despite my protests, Jack's at the wheel because of another damn, soft *please* that I just wasn't able to reject. Plus, even though I only drank a sip of wine, I hadn't been planning to drive anyway.

But that *please*—the gentleness of his voice still wraps around me, comforting and warm and lingering far longer than I ever expected.

"Where exactly are we supposed to stay?" I ask as I scroll through Instagram.

"It's only a little farther," Jack says, but I don't really hear what he's saying.

Lia has posted a picture.

It's a vague, blurred shot of a few people from our school, hanging out next to a sleek pool. No caption. I'm guessing Minami's invited everyone to her summer party except me. I sigh, wishing I could talk to my best friend. I haven't even seen any "Close Friends" Instagram Stories—and Lia usually posts at least ten a day. I wonder if she's taken me off her list. I exit out of Instagram; it's got no answers for the questions tumbling around in my mind, dark as the night around us.

The headlights sweep across the gravel road weaving through heavy oak trees, and I peer out the window. This is a strange place, far from paved roads. "Is this the start of a horror movie?"

Jack snorts. "Yeah, because being stuck in the car with me for anything more than an hour is torture? Is that what you're going to say?"

"Dammit, you stole my thunder."

He laughs as he takes a right off the main road, following his phone's navigation.

"Wait, this really does look like we're going the wrong way," I protest as the road gets bumpier. "Where are we—"

Lights flare all around us, and I blink in shock.

We're in a village that wasn't here a second ago, driving on a smoothly paved road, cheery, bright lampposts with sparkling fairy lights strung between them lining our way.

"*Oh*," I whisper. "A magical village?"

We pass under a sign that declares WELCOME TO PIXLEY'S HIDDEN MAGICAL VILLAGE, ESTABLISHED IN 1875.

I roll down the window, staring at this new world.

At this hour, only a few people are strolling on the sidewalks. It's a typical small town, with one main road that runs through, with shops and quaint restaurants. But it's *magical*. Each shop looks like a world of its own, with stately brick fronts or sleek glass minimalistic buildings or quirky cottages in a rainbow of colors. And the signs take my breath away:

ELIXIRS OF EUPHORIA

MYSTIC HAHN'S HAVEN FOR THE OCCULT

SARAH AND SUE-O'S SCONES AND SWEETS

QUILL TREE FOX ART GALLERY

LEON THE LION'S TOY EMPORIUM

I've never been to a magical village before, not with Magizon being able to ship anything charmed straight to my doorstep, but I've always wanted to go to one.

Magical villages were once tucked away all around the world, similar to the magical cottage we'd spotted along the road. In these special villages, conclaves of magic-users stuck together in solidarity. Only certain people—like the Town Leader, similar to Mom's role now—would go out into the greater world as peddlers, selling enchanted items here and there to those who needed them. The magic world stayed hidden in these secret villages until about a hundred years ago, when a movement came for magic-users to live among the non-magic-aware, where we'd learn more about the people we'd sworn to help. The internet boom and the start of Magizon didn't hurt, either. Now they exist as tourist destinations for the magic-aware.

"I'd always known there were a few in Central California," I murmur. "I didn't realize we'd get to stop in one."

I hadn't even looked up any magical villages for the road

trip. After all, I'd been planning on going with Lia, who hadn't been magic-aware, so a place like this wasn't even on my wish list. Guilt ripples through me, thinking of how she never answered the door.

"I wish Lia could see this," I whisper.

"Next road trip," Jack says, "you can take her here. And she'll love it, too."

"I dunno . . ."

Jack pulls into a parking spot in front of a squat brick three-story building with a hand-painted wood sign labeled DAN'S MAGICAL INN.

A tall set of wooden stairs leads up to the inn's doorway, draped in fairy lights. It feels like we're in an enchanted story-land instead of in the middle of Nowhere, California.

"It's got to be tough for her right now," Jack says, cutting the engine. "There's a lot for her to process. A lot of wishes that she thinks magic could've granted, even though she's learning it can't. That's the hardest part of knowing there's magic—knowing the limits, too."

There's a darkness in his eyes that isn't from the night.

His mother. . . . It's as if I can hear her light, cheery voice, laughing and chatting with me and Jack after we've come back from school, and she's filling us up with plates of bunny-shaped cheddar crackers. Cam and Remy were so young back then, so usually they were taking a nap in Jack and Cam's room. There was no magic in Mrs. Yasuda's food, but those afternoons had a special kind of charm.

"Isn't there something I can do for her?" I ask, wishing I knew the right words to chase the shadows away for Lia . . . and . . . even for him, too. It makes my chest clench to see him like this. Like the way he stood with his father and brother next to Mrs. Yasuda's casket, in a suit that was too big for him, as if even the suit knew how big of a role he had to grow into, to help fill the missing hole his mother left.

He presses his lips together. And with a jolt of surprise, I realize that this is another, deeper way he hasn't changed after all these years.

Jack has always been the type to think things through. On reality shows, men always blurt things out, not caring about the impact of their words. Mr. Yasuda's like that, but Jack has never been. When there's something he wants to say but he knows it's incredibly important, he kind of looks like that Rodin statue, *The Thinker*, but human flesh and blood instead of bronze. Also, thankfully, he's not naked.

The way he spends time considering things instead of rushing to a conclusion is one of the things I used to respect so much about him.

Until he started ignoring me.

Then, I knew it wasn't just a misunderstanding. He'd thought it through, in the same quiet way he's thinking things through now.

Jack breathes out, a heavy sigh. "Let her set the pace of things," he says finally. "Try to show you're around to support her as much as you can, without overwhelming her. That'll show her how much you care."

"But . . . I want to do more."

He rubs his chin, thinking. "Ellie . . . maybe she can't see beyond her grief. You've got to give her time to let her process magic, and also work through mourning, again."

I pinch my forehead, trying to ease the building headache.

"Cheer up," he says, elbowing me. "Time. Give Lia time."

The corners of my lips crook up. "How can *you* give such good advice?"

"Hey, now," Jack says warningly, with a teasing smile.

And, in a sudden realization, I'm actually grateful for Remy and Cam's stupid picnic basket that led to our temporary pact. "You're not as—"

Boom. Boom.

I startle, staring at the outline of a huge shadow that's fallen over Jack's side, knocking ominously on the glass. "Holy curses, this *is* a horror movie."

"Dan!" Jack says brightly, opening the door, waving for me to get out, too. My face burns.

Moments later, Jack introduces me to Dan Wright, owner of Dan's Inn. The burly, middle-aged guy, who looks like a wild mountain man with his dark shaggy beard, green plaid shirt, and well-worn jeans, shakes my hand with gusto. "Ah, the Elissa of Elissa's Tea Shop! I went to your parents' tea shop years ago, when I drove through Palo Alto on my way up to Eureka. I didn't get to meet you then, but your family's matcha is delicious."

His booming voice has drawn the attention of the few folks walking around, and I'm sure that my ears are bright as fairy lights. "Oh, everyone calls me Ellie," I say, embarrassed.

Jack stifles a yawn, and Dan turns to him. "Let's get you inside. My staff has set up two rooms on the second floor, and they're made up for you to hop straight into bed. Ready?"

"Never been more ready," I say gratefully, and Dan grins back.

After a blissful but quick shower, my head hits the goose-down pillow, wet hair and all. I barely remember to send a message to my parents to tell them I've made it to Pixley.

But instead of turning off my phone screen, I pull up my drawings from today.

My stomach flips as I upload my latest drawing of Paso Robles' vineyards onto my private Instagram account. Then, my stomach flipping even more, I also add in the sketch of Jack's hands, scar and all.

I scroll through my uploads. Oddly, these additions feel more *me* than my older art.

When I check my profile—232 posts uploaded, 0 followers—my heart flips when my fingers accidentally graze against the Settings button. A prompt pops up: *Do you want to make your account public?*

Sweat instantly forms on my fingertips and I quickly jab *Cancel.*

I'm not ready. My drawings aren't good enough.

I can't make my art public, not yet. I put my phone on the nightstand, my heart thumping so loudly that it feels like it echoes in the dark room.

Chapter 18

B last it!" A sudden roar pulls me from my restful, cozy dream of living in a magical cottage on a hilltop, surrounded by golden, sun-dried grass waving in the breeze.

I sit up straight, blankly looking around. I'm in a tiny bedroom with all-white wood-slat walls, a round mirror above a small vanity, and gentle morning light shining through the frilly white curtains. I scratch at my nose, and then at my neck, like there's an itch I can't ease, trying to think things through. *Where am I, where am I . . .*

Dan's Inn, I finally remember, breathing out. The road trip with Jack, the magical village—

Which means that sudden *bang!* from downstairs isn't a pan dropping on the floor. It's probably a spell gone awry.

I race to get into my denim shorts and a clean V-neck from my duffel bag, and head out the door. The room opposite mine opens, and Jack stumbles out, rubbing the sleep from his eyes. His hair is an absolute mess, his brown, slight waves sticking up like he was shocked in his deep slumber.

And he's also shirtless.

His body is . . . *ripped*.

Jack's got a six-pack that disappears under his low-hanging shorts and every muscle looks like it was sculpted out of earthenware clay and baked to perfection. I thought it was fun to draw his hands, but why draw just his hands when his whole body should be cast into a bronze sculpture?

I don't blame him for playing tennis all these years.

In fact, I thank tennis—

He clears his throat and, unfortunately, I have to drag my eyes up. "Are you okay?"

I splutter. I'm okay, are his *abs* okay from looking that good? Is the way he looks even *legal*?

Oh. He wasn't asking about my strange reaction to his body. "Yeah. The sound came from downstairs, it wasn't from me—"

"No, I mean, *you*." Jack motions at my face.

I want to say, *Rude. Your abs are the issue here!* But then that itchiness from earlier comes back two-fold. I scratch at my cheeks and realize there are bumps all over my skin.

"Wait, what?" I spin on my heel and dart back into my room. At the circular mirror tacked onto the wall, I stare into my reflection.

Mirror, mirror, who's the fairest of them all . . .

Jack's abs, maybe.

Because, whoa. Definitely not me.

My face looks like pepperoni pizza gone wrong. Tiny red welts cover my entire face and extend down to my neck. And the need to scratch at them only increases when I see how patchy and awful they look.

"It has to be something new you've been exposed to . . .

The towel?" Jack glances at the white towel hanging next to the shower. "We can't let you touch it again, I don't want to see your skin get worse. It looks painful."

"Don't worry, I'll survive. I'm not allergic to a towel," I say dryly.

He crosses my room and pokes at the pillow I used. "Are you allergic to goose down?"

"No?" *But I am allergic to your shirtlessness.*

He frowns. "Did you start using any new face products?"

Do I have to go through my beauty routine with him? "My normal micellar water . . . then a foam cleanser . . ."

"What's micellar water?" Jack sounds suspicious. "And what's a foam cleanser?"

"I've used that routine for a year," I say defensively. "This reaction is *not* the micellar water or my cleanser." Then I stare at the pillow again, the comfy, soft pillow that helped me have sweet, restful dreams after a long day with Jack. How can a plush, soft bed like this betray me? "Maybe I *am* allergic to goose down. Or did you curse me?"

"I wish," Jack says.

"Thanks, I think I'll say it's the goose down, then."

"At least if I had cursed you, I would know how to fix it."

"Curses aren't that easy to lift," I argue back, scratching at my chin.

"Why, have you cursed someone before?" he asks. "Other than me, of course."

"I haven't cursed you." Then I add, with wide-eyed innocence, "Why would I ever want to?"

Jack snorts and motions out the door. "Let's go see if Dan

has a healing elixir . . . and check out what he was doing earlier. It sounded like some sort of magic misfired."

Unfortunately, he grabs a shirt before we head downstairs.
I sigh, scratching at my itchy face again. I've decided what I'd
want to curse, and it's that shirt.

On the first floor, Jack weaves his way through a few
rooms—a sitting room that looks like it's from a different
century or maybe a different world, with high-backed, velvet upholstered chairs and an intricately carved wood table
with such delicate work it could've been made by fairies. Then
there's a dining area, where a few other patrons of Dan's Inn
are tucking into piles of pancakes and waffles, the heady scent
of maple syrup and blueberry jam piquing my interest.

Jack stops in front of a set of swinging metal doors. "Hey,
Dan, it's Jack, can we—"

"Come in, come in." Dan's faint, gravelly voice echoes
through the thin crack between the doors.

Jack pushes one of the metal doors and whisks us into a
beautiful, state-of-the-art kitchen, all stainless steel and big,
bright windows that overlook an orange orchard. It's a square
room, with countertops on one side and a set of burners on the
other, where Dan's busily stirring a pot. A few other workers
are cooking up more fluffy stacks of pancakes or pulling trays
of hash browns and sausage links from the oven. But despite the
other smells, the heavenly scent of blackberries from whatever
Dan's working on swirls around me, tugging at my taste buds
and making me salivate. I rub at my cheek, the hot rash nagging.

Jack leans against the counter, sniffing appreciatively.
"Wow, what're you making?"

The inn owner smiles proudly at his bubbling pot. "A new creation. A creamy blackberry spread with a hint of milk powder and, of course, infused with a spark of confidence. My favorite charm from the *Two Cooks in a Kitchen* magical cookbook."

"A creamy blackberry spread? That sounds amazing," I say.

"Well, gotta keep my guests on their toes." Dan grins. "Got to change it up sometime."

"Speaking of change . . ." Jack glances over at me, and Dan follows his gaze. "Got any salve?"

Dan blinks. "Ouch, Ellie, are you all right? Did you fight with the pixies in the attic?"

My eyes widen in horror. "Pixies?"

"There're no pixies in the attic," Jack informs me dryly. To Dan, he adds, "I think it was the goose-down pillow."

"Drat!" The chef groans. "I forgot to apply the pillow charm to the room you're staying in. Customizes the pillow to the guest, you know. A helpful bit of magic. But I can get you fixed up in no time . . ." He shuts off the burner and bustles to a pantry, waving at us to follow him.

Dan runs his hand over the line of glass bottles and picks up a small jar covered in hand-painted flowers labeled *Healing Salve*. "Ah, here it is. This will fix you up in a jiffy."

When he opens the jar, the smell of piña colada fills the room, and then dies out. I lean over to look at the bare traces of ointment at the bottom. Dan stares down at the empty glass, neatly scraped down to the rim, and bellows, "Who used the rest of the salve?"

"Sorry, Dan!" A pink-faced boy pokes his head into the pantry, hefting a tray of waffles. "I got a burn on a pan; I'll go get some—"

"Nah, keep on serving, but stay away from the oven." Dan waves the boy off. To me, he says apologetically, "I'll have to nip out to the Enchanted Forest." Noting my confused look, he clarifies. "It's not an actual enchanted forest. Well, kind of but not really . . . It's an apothecary."

All of a sudden, there's a loud *BANG!* from the kitchen. Dan scurries off, his face paling under his beard as he sees splatters of blackberry jam all over the counter and even coating some of the pancakes next to it. "Blast it," he groans. "I must've added too much raw magic. The jam's gotten *too* confident." He waves away an incoming worker with a rag. "I'll clean it after I get back from the apothecary."

"I can go," I say quickly. I've been meaning to check out the village anyway.

"And I can guide her," Jack volunteers. He glances over when I frown. "It's difficult to find the Enchanted Forest."

"Would you?" Dan says, glancing over at his seething pot. "Tell Fleurie to put it on my account; it's the least I owe you." The inn owner stuffs a sugar-dusted waffle, wrapped in wax paper, into each of our hands, and winks. "Come back whenever you get hungry. And don't get bitten by the wolves in the forest."

I laugh, thinking he's joking, but Dan only nods and goes back to work.

❧   ❧

Jack and I stroll down the main street of Pixley's magical village, my eyes drinking in the sights, the world around me soothing away the constant itch.

"Don't forget your breakfast," Jack says. "It's getting cold."

I pause at the window display of a magical toy emporium, watching a toy plush tiger open its mouth in a silent roar. A hand-sewn bunny rabbit hops over and bats at it with a paw. A kid runs up to the window next to me, pressing her face so close that it looks like she wants to fall right through the glass. "Mom!" she calls. "Can we get that tiger?"

I bite down on the crispy waffle, and the soft, fluffy inside melts like butter in my mouth. "This is amazing."

Jack grins as we continue to walk down the street. "Wait until you get to—"

I take another bite, and blackberry jam dances along my tongue. "*Whoa.*"

Jack nods. "He gave us some of his newest creation, that courage-enhancing blackberry jam. We're lucky we got an early taste. Dan's Inn is popular as a getaway vacation for the magic-aware, and his food is really something else, right?"

"For the first time ever, I think you're right." I stick my tongue out at him teasingly. Then I blink. "Is that . . . is *that* the Enchanted Forest?"

The airy, beautiful shop on the edge of the magical village looks like a forest that's growing within four wood walls. The opened display window is as charming as a scene out of *Bambi,* with birds twittering as they flutter in and out and vines winding glass bottles filled with jewel-tone liquids.

Jack pulls the door open for me, and I peek inside, catching a glimpse of white wire racks covered with more vines and topped with countless bottles of ointments and elixirs.

As I walk through, I glance up at him to say thanks, and pause. A smile tugs at my lips. "Wait a second, you've got something on you." I reach up and brush a faint dusting of the white confectioners' sugar off his jaw.

His eyes flash, widening with surprise. After all, we're only pretending to get along for our pact. We're oil and water, or chemicals that are sure to erupt. But he doesn't move, not like I expected, or push my hand away.

Instead, he has the least reasonable reaction. Jack sucks in a breath, holding it like I've pulled him underwater.

And it's in this moment that I notice impossible, magical things.

His skin is soft, softer than his calloused hands.

His pupils are big and dark, like he's drinking in the sight of me. There's a strange look to his eyes that doesn't make sense.

I can't breathe. Somehow, I can't breathe with the way he looks at me.

His hand reaches up, maybe, impossibly, to cup mine, just as an ethereal twinkle of chimes ring all around us.

"Hello, hello," a soft voice says, and we jump apart. A breeze blows through the doorway and I suck in air, sending oxygen back into my lungs.

A beautiful woman steps forward out of the shelves. She's outfitted in a loose, emerald-green dress that accentuates her curves. The light filtering through the skylights makes her dark skin shine, as if she glows from within. A woven band of peonies crowns her forehead. She looks like a fairy who was hidden in the forest, saving me from making a bad, bad move.

"Oh." Jack blinks, startled. "Hello, Fleurie."

"It's been too long since you were here last," Fleurie says. There's a hint of mischief to her voice. "But now, you've brought someone in need?"

Jack nods. "This is Ellie Kobata, my neighbor back in Palo Alto. We're looking for your healing salve, for an allergic reaction to goose down."

Fleurie's eyes scan my cheeks, still mottled with the red spots and now probably burning red from this latest interaction with Jack. She nods, waving her hand out toward the forest. "Go ahead. The solution will always present itself."

I blink, and then she's disappeared.

There's the vine-covered racks, the jars of ointments . . . "Where did she go?"

"Typical Fleurie," Jack says with a smile. "She's probably in her back room that looks out on her orange orchard, sipping on her rosehip tea. She likes to keep people guessing. C'mon, let's find your salve."

He moves forward through the shelves. "I think it's toward the right side, but if we really can't find it, we can call her for help, using one of those." Jack points at a silver bell hanging from one of the shelves; when I look through the store, I realize there're bells hanging here and there, all different sizes and shapes, most rusted over as if she's picked them up over time rather than ordering a box set from Magizon. It's beautiful.

"How do you know so much about Pixley? About this shop?"

"I interned here last summer, with their magical village government. I thought you'd heard about that?" He frowns, as if I should've known this already.

I shake my head with surprise. Honestly, I'd assumed

he'd worked at PricewaterhouseCoopers or some fancy, suit-required accounting firm, not a magical village. But maybe this is my fault; I'd been so bitter and uninterested that all I cared about was knowing Jack was away for the summer, and hadn't even asked Cam where his brother had gone.

"I'm interested in magical societies," he explains. "I'd thought of interning at Google or Facebook but . . . I want to help those with magic. I want to help those without magic, too. So I was thinking of taking a year at Foothill Community College and then transferring to a magical college to major in biology. And working in healthcare within a magical society, or maybe even in a magical government, and finding out ways to best distribute healing magic to those who need it, through stores like CharmWorks."

My jaw feels like it's hit the shop floor. This is a part of Jack that I never knew about . . . a Jack who's grown and changed. The Jack I knew in middle school hadn't yet thought of these things, of what he could do as someone magic-aware. I mean, *I* don't even know what I want to do, other than aiming to go to college. I'd been planning on majoring in business adminis-tration or something generic like that, but even though senior year and college apps are just months away, I hadn't thought about magical colleges.

Maybe . . . maybe I'm not seeing all of Jack if I compare him to the boy he was in middle school.

"I think it's over here," Jack calls. He's been searching through the glass jars. "This looks like the right section."

I hurry through the Enchanted Forest. A sign at the top of the shelf reads HEALING. The glass clinks as we look through the jars of creams and vials of oils for burns and scrapes, with beautifully hand-drawn designs from frolicking foxes to majestic flowers, but nothing for my hives.

Then I turn one of the jars, and a warm flush flows through my hand like a ray of sunlight. The label, with flowery vines painted all over, states *Allergic Reactions.*

"You found it," Jack says, leaning over to look. "Let's pay and you can put it on."

He leads me to the front of the Enchanted Forest. At a table that looks like a modern register—with an iPad tablet for checkout—he rings a clunky bronze bell.

"You found what you need?" Fleurie stands in front of us in an instant, though I hadn't heard her footsteps.

Jack nods, pushing forward two jars. "Ellie's ointment and another jar of the all-purpose Healing Salve for Dan."

Fleurie rings them up. She motions at a small bench next to the door. "Go ahead, you should use it right away. It's all been paid for; Dan messaged me and said that he wanted the purchases applied to his account."

"I should pay," Jack tries to protest, and I nod, pulling my debit card out of my phone case.

But Fleurie waves us away. "No, Ellie, you should get the ointment on your skin, no time for delay." To Jack, she says, "Put it on for your girlfriend, would you? I don't have a mirror by that bench."

Jack and I freeze.

"She's . . . she's not my girlfriend," Jack says. I frown. Is *his* face red?

I'm definitely not . . . But I'm too chicken to ask—is *Minami* his girlfriend?

Fleurie leans her head to the side, her dark eyes widening

with surprise. "My apologies! It was poor judgment of me to assume. I simply thought—it feels like there's a strong connection between the two of you. I'm usually never wrong about these things."

"Er . . . we're just friends," I squeak out. My eyes meet Jack's as I wonder, *Is that even the truth? We're only talking to each other because of our pact.*

Fleurie smiles. "Friendship can always change over time. Here, try this." She places a small bronze coin in my hand and another in Jack's. "Fold your hands around it, just for a second or two. Go on, Jack, you can show us now."

With his brow wrinkled, he opens up his hand. In a split second, it has turned into a cerulean blue, bright as the sky we've been driving under together.

"What's this do?" he asks, flipping it over. It's the same blue on the back, with the emblem of an olive tree branch embossed on it.

She nods. "If you two have matching colors, it shows compatibility as friends—and as lovers."

I peek down at my hand, opening my fingers just a crack. Enough for me to see . . . *oh, hell no.*

That's robin's-egg blue. Not cerulean blue, not . . . the exact color as Jack's.

"Ellie?" Fleurie prompts me.

I jam my coin into my pocket. I'll burn it before I let anyone see what color it is.

"Um, that's neat," I say. "But I should get the medicine on. Itchy face, you know?"

The store owner blinks. "Of course. But check the color of the coin later. It might be informative."

Oh, it's already been *too* informative. Maybe the spell's broken or something.

I drag Jack over to the bench and busy myself with the ointment. And thankfully, Fleurie, in her typical fashion, seems to vanish among the shelves.

The salve is buttery smooth, and I scoop out a palmful to spread it over my face. An instant coolness soothes the constant itchiness. "Oh, this *is* magical."

"Er, you're getting it all over your eyebrows," Jack says.

I groan, trying to rub it off with the back of my hand. I use a darkening powder on my short, barely-there eyebrows or else it looks like I've got only a dot of hair as an eyebrow, and if I get the creamy salve on it, then the powder is totally going to smear.

I glance at the nearest shelf of jars, trying to use their reflection to guide me. *There, I think that's right . . . Some more on my chin . . . I wish I had a mirror. I should do this back at Dan's Inn, but it's way too itchy . . . At least the ointment leaves my face matte, so I won't feel silly walking back through town.*

Then, in the reflection of the glass, I see Jack settle on the bench next to me. "Let me help."

I freeze as he reaches out. His fingers, despite the tough, calloused spots, are so tender as he turns my face toward him. He smooths the clumps of ointment, his hands skimming gently over my cheeks, my jawline.

My throat is dry. I can't breathe.

If this was someone other than Jack Yasuda, I would say they're being caring.

The blue coin burns in my pocket, but that can't be right.

There's no way that he'd . . . he'd care about me anymore. After all, we haven't really talked at all since middle school.

And this is the boy who ditched me to find new friends, leaving me alone day after day, until Lia came into my life and rescued me from complete loner status in the cafeteria.

Still—there's something about the way he's taking care of me, even though my bumps probably look chicken-pox-awful, that makes something in my chest feel tight.

"Finished," he says, turning away to screw the cap back onto the jar. And I feel like I can finally inhale the sweet, floral-scented air again.

My phone buzzes noisily, and I have no choice but to pull it out and check. My heart lifts—is it Lia, maybe? Finally responding?

But it's only Dad, checking in on me through my group chat with him and Mom.

> **DAD:** Hope all is well?

> **ME:** Yeah, we're still in Pixley and Jack's got a sales visit later. After that, we'll head over to Huntington Beach and should be able to start the exhibition booth setup later today or early tomorrow.

> **DAD:** Okay. We'll be flying into Huntington Beach tomorrow around 1 pm. Mr. Yasuda's getting a rental car to drive us from the airport. See you soon.

> **ME:** Got it. How are things?

DAD: Doing fine. Mom's been busy with the paperwork and certification classes for Lia. A lot for her to get done before we leave tomorrow.

ME: I'm sorry, Mom and Dad.

STATUS: Read.

I swallow. My parents aren't as enthusiastic as they usually are, and I'm the only one to blame. I sigh, glancing around the forest, wondering if there's some sort of salve called *Fix Your Relationship with Disapproving Parents*.

Out of the Enchanted Forest and back on the main street, Jack and I weave our way through the noontime crowd.

I sniff at the air. "Tea?" Now that the ointment has soothed away that furious itch, I can focus on getting some caffeine into my system, and maybe more of those tasty waffles.

Jack pauses, hooks his thumb toward a glass and metal building on the corner. "Want some? When I stayed here, Tea-riffic kind of reminded me of being back at your parents' shop. It's a nice spot."

"Tea-riffic?" I echo.

He grins. "It's pretty tea-sty."

I groan, but then I let out a laugh. "Well, you had me at tea."

Chapter 19

Tea-riffic Café turns out to be the perfect place to load up on caffeine. I go for a milky hojicha with brown sugar boba, and Jack chooses a winter melon green tea with bits of aloe.

I try to hand over my debit card, but Jack is faster. "This one's on me."

"But . . . no way, we can pay for ourselves." I don't like the idea of being in debt to *him*.

Jack pauses, as if searching for an excuse. Finally, he says, "You've been paying for the gas. It's the least I can do."

I squint. "Did you just make that up?"

"No?" But he motions for me to grab a table that has just opened, while he waits for the drinks. I beeline over before he can elaborate.

While the drinks are being made, I immerse myself in sketching on my phone, tapping my stylus against the corner when I'm thinking through my design. I love the way there's direction and guidance for something as wild and emotional as art, so some of my favorite books to read are on art theory.

But the best learning comes from practice, after being guided by the lessons in the books. I sketch all sorts of hands around me—knobby hands, coffee-stained hands, ink-smeared hands, soft hands. But despite all the inspiration around me, I keep drawing this one set of hands that I know too well, with a scar on the thumb.

"Hey," Jack says a bit loudly, and I have a feeling he's been trying to catch my attention. He's got both of our drinks in hand, and he's already sitting across from me. I hadn't even noticed. "Is that me?"

I glance at the scar on his thumb wrapped around my drink and then down at my drawing. "Oh! No. Of course not." I start trying to close the drawing app on my phone, but he gestures at it.

"Could I . . . see your drawing?" His eyes are curious. Then he looks a little contrite. "You were in your own world, so you didn't hear when I walked up to you. I promise I wasn't trying to sneak around."

"Hmm." I'm too embarrassed to say much.

"I promise. Can I see your drawings, please?"

"I'm not showing you. You're going to think I'm a freak."

"No," he laughs. "I doubt that."

I frown. I don't believe him for a moment.

Then I check myself. Since when did I get so cynical toward him?

I peek at my first drawing. It's that mysterious set of hands. No way I'm showing him these. Quickly, I swipe to another sketch.

"What was wrong with that first picture?" he asks, craning to see the screen. I tilt it away as I keep swiping through my rough, unpolished drawings.

Finally, I show him the first set of hands I'd drawn today; it was a boy sitting in the corner, who'd been gripping his tea mug as he talked to his boyfriend.

Jack studies the drawing, as if he can see something within the quick pencil lines, as if it's more than just any set of hands.

"This person, they look nervous," Jack mused, his nails tracing the tense lines of the boy's hands.

"It was a warm-up, before I start applying my drawing theory to the sketches." When I begin, I draw rougher, more jagged lines to get out my excess energy before I can focus on what I see before me. Before I can study the angles and get them right, before my practice and proper theory sets in.

"I like it," he announces, and I breathe out. *Why do I care about his approval? It doesn't matter.*

Quickly, I grab my hojicha latte. I'm so desperate for caffeine or *anything* that will make sense of how nice he's being that I shove my drink in my face. I can't look at him, not now. Not with this.

I take a deep swallow, and the spark of peace in the smoothly roasted tea melts some of my worries away. I can still feel my concern about Lia and my parents tugging at my attention. Or the way that being around Jack feels different during this trip—is it just our pact?

"Can I see one more drawing?" he asks. "It's been so long . . . your art has improved so much."

Nervously, I swipe to the next drawing.

He frowns, studying my messy scribbles of the barista's hands making a shot of espresso.

A flush of heat runs up my neck. The way he stares at my sketch is unnerving. It's like he's unpeeling something away from me, maybe that barrier between him and me, and for once, he's seeing me as I am. Not the girl he used to be friends with, but the messy Ellie I am now.

And I don't know what to think about this.

He turns his head to the side, thoughtfully. "I like studying music theory, especially for my electric guitar. Neo-soul's my favorite. It's a little funky, but it's got soul, a touch of R & B . . ."

I frown. What does this have to do with my art?

"And I think it's like that. My music theory studies shape the way I play songs on my electric guitar. And it's the same as your art—the barista, isn't it?"

I nod, surprised. I hadn't even drawn the espresso tamper that the barista had been holding.

"You drew the hands in exact, very barista-like motions," Jack says, mimicking the movements of the barista prepping a shot of espresso for an affogato. Then he pauses. "How about you draw something for CharmWorks?"

I laugh. "No way! I should erase your memory, honestly. I never share my drawings with anyone."

His eyes flash with surprise. "You used to . . . Never mind."

Jack used to see all my art. Mrs. Yasuda even taped a drawing I got an award for as a fourth grader right on their fridge. There's a lot that's changed since we were friends. The silence stretches out like a wall; our shared past separating the two of us.

"Never mind to never mind," he says suddenly. "You should share your drawings with the world. It's such a big part of you, and I love seeing them. The rest of the world would want to see them, too."

I don't know what to say. How does Jack know what it feels like to be me, to hide away so many parts of me—magic, my art—and expect that everyone will accept me, as I am?

"I know I like seeing them," he says softly. Then, even softer, he says, "Even though someone like me doesn't deserve to see your art."

I rub at my ear with one hand. Clearly, I've misheard things.

He takes a swallow of his green tea and sets down the cup. "Can you show me the next drawing?"

I'm too shocked to do anything but swipe to the next picture, the hands of two new acquaintances sitting across the table from each other, nervously chatting as they clutch their cups of tea. I'm pulled into describing what I thought they were thinking, though I know I could completely be wrong.

Too soon, we get to the end of my drawings—I've been skipping all the sketches of those mysterious hands. He frowns at the last one, the hands of a young mom pushing a stroller.

"They're getting more structured," he says. "More exact."

I nod. "I apply more and more techniques as I continue sketching. More theory, you know. I like looking at art theory. Perspective tips, things like that."

"There was a freedom in that first drawing I liked," he said. "You've already practiced for years and years. You can draw perspectives and things like that properly. I like those first drawings, because they have your own flair in them." He pauses. "Before you edit it out."

I recoil, and he backpedals. "Not that it's bad. I can see why it's great to be precise. But it's beautiful as is, too."

Is Jack complimenting me or making fun of me? I don't understand him at all.

He studies me; maybe he realizes I need him to translate his own words. Jack says plainly, but with an extraordinary gentleness I haven't heard in years, "Your drawings are all beautiful, Ellie. I like the way you draw, no matter what style it's in."

Oh. My throat closes up. It was a compliment; it was all a compliment. A surprising warmth fills my belly, like Mochi's curled up in my lap. I search for something to say, but my usual acidic retorts to Jack have somehow evaporated.

I stare down at my last drawing. What do I say? What can I even say to that?

Clack. I flip my phone on the table, hiding the screen; it's louder than I expected.

"Want to get something to eat?" I desperately need fresh air. "I'm . . . I'm hungry."

He looks up, a trace of confusion on his face, but he nods, following me down the steps and out the glass doors.

Next up is paper bags of popcorn chicken at the Taiwanese shop down the street. The cashier explains that the pink Himalayan salt will fill us with a sprinkle of gratitude. The air smells so heavenly that I'm already grateful. When it comes time to pay, I've got my debit card out before the cashier can say the total.

"My turn." I raise an eyebrow at him.

To my surprise, Jack doesn't argue. He just smiles and says, "Thanks, Ellie."

⁓　　⁓

After we've polished off our popcorn chicken and cram in some cleverness-charmed blueberry pastries from the magical scone shop, we begin heading back to Dan's Inn. It's already three o'clock; getting the ointment and snacks took way longer than I expected. But every step through Pixley's magical village makes me want to stay, even though I know we have to make that three-hour drive down to the convention center in Huntington Beach and begin setting up our booth. We don't have much time but—

"Oh, *wow*," I gasp, staring into the window of a drugstore. "Is that *magical* lipstick?"

I read the sign quickly. ALL-NEW, COLOR-SORCERY LIP STAIN. PRESS THE BOTTOM OF THE LIPSTICK CASE TO THE COLOR OF YOUR CHOICE, WATCH OUR EXACT-MATCHING MAGIC GO TO WORK, AND ENJOY 12 HOURS OF THIS NONSTOP, NON-TRANSFERABLE LIP STAIN!

> BUT BEWARE: LIKE CINDERELLA'S CARRIAGE, THE
> STAIN WILL DISAPPEAR IN EXACTLY 12 HOURS AFTER
> THE FIRST APPLICATION! LIMITED APPLICATION:
> TURNS INTO CLEAR LIP GLOSS AFTER FIVE USES.

Lia's always been looking for a vampy red lipstick to match her favorite scarlet dress, a gorgeous retro number that she found a year ago at a thrift shop. But no matter what she tries, she's been unable to find the perfect shade, even when she's mixed colors together.

"Lia would *love* this." Then I glance at my phone. "Dammit, we spent too much time in the Enchanted Forest."

"We can go inside," Jack offers.

I rock on the balls of my feet. This might show Lia that magic can be fun, something that she might enjoy. "But . . . we have to get back to the inn. You need to do that sales pitch, right?"

"Dan's free anytime, but he invited us to eat dinner with him and chat over a meal," Jack says, checking the clock on his phone. "We can spend a few hours here, eat an early dinner, then drive out. As long as we make it into Huntington Beach tonight, there's enough time to set up the booth tomorrow morning."

"But . . ."

"When's the next time you'll be in a magical village like this, really?"

I bite my lip. He's right. My parents are expecting me to drive straight home after the convention, no pit stops. And they're so furious with me they'll likely go through with their threat to ground me for the rest of summer vacation, if not until the moment I graduate high school. There's no more time for me to explore Pixley, not after this road trip with Jack. Still . . .

He nods at the other side of the road. "There's a puzzle shop over there. You could pick something up for Remy; she still likes those puzzles, right? Some of the prizes are pretty epic—an elixir that's almost like a genie in a bottle, a custom-made candy that's always the flavor you want and never gives you cavities—but you have to finish the puzzle to receive the prize. And I can show you a shop with cooking supplies, so you can look for a souvenir for your parents."

That spark of peace from Tea-riffic's drink is becoming reality. It's only a small gesture, but if I get gifts that show my gratitude, then my parents and Lia will realize how much I appreciate them.

"Thanks, Jack. You're awesome."

He blinks at those words, as if I've said something weird. Because, typical me, I have. *"You're awesome"? Am I in sixth grade again? What's next, "Cool beans"?*

My cheeks burn up as I hurry into the drugstore. "Um, well, first stop, then? Let's go."

৩৩   ৩৩

It's nearly four o'clock by the time Jack and I've explored Pixley, oohing over the magical fountain (the mist turns into shimmering bubbles when someone throws in a penny and makes a wish), the twisting and moving alleys with hidden art exhibits and sculptures, and the stores that have the perfect souvenirs. I've even found a magical stud for my new piercing that can change shapes with two twists to its base.

A charming touch is that we're not weighed down by shopping bags. At the drugstore, the cashier had asked me if my recipient was magic-aware. And once I confirmed Lia was, she offered to send it directly to her, free same-day delivery, even with gift wrapping and a card.

"*All* of that is included for free?"

"Shop local," the cashier had said with a wink.

"I agree." Jack grinned back at her. To me, he explained, "It's these small touches that keep magical villages like these—or stores like our parents'—in the running against magical conglomerates like Magizon. I've been starting initiatives like this for Dad's shop."

Oh. I'd heard about how CharmWorks has some of the best customer service and loyalty programs, but I'd never really believed it. And with Jack and I having our falling-out, I'd stopped going by their shop.

There's been so much I've missed.

As Jack and I make our way up the creaking wooden stairs of Dan's Inn, I sniff at the air. The popcorn chicken, scones, and boba tea feels like a distant memory as I breathe in the scent of roasted salmon with a hint of dill.

"Okay," I admit, "you were right. It was a good idea to stay for dinner."

Minutes later, Dan's staff seats us in a cozy, private room off the main dining area that's bustling with the inn's guests and some local folks who come in for a hearty meal. Like the rest of the inn, this room is also unique—grandfather clocks line the walls, the pendulums swinging in unison, and all the plates have hand-crocheted lace doilies underneath.

Jack and I sit across from each other, my stomach growling. The ceramic plates in front of us are piled with everything from buttery biscuits to a whole roasted salmon with crackling skin to bowls of garlicky green beans.

Moments later, Dan strides in, taking the seat next to Jack. "So, how was Pixley? Did you get a good sense of the town?"

"It's *amazing*. I want to move here," I say.

Dan lets out a belly laugh. "Ah, I knew I'd like you. Anyone who sees the magic in this town is welcome in my inn. Dig in, you two!"

He doesn't have to ask us twice. Before I know it, I've tasted nearly everything within arm's reach, and I still have so much left to try.

Jack swallows his mouthful and carefully wipes his lips. There's something about him in this moment; he's buzzing with so much energy.

"So," he says, and I realize that he's ready for his sales pitch.

Dan takes a big bite of a buttered biscuit. "Tell me about what you've got in mind. The spot next to my inn's register is looking mighty lonely, and it's the perfect chance to get in some new products. But I've been approached by a few distributors, which is why it's perfect we got to meet in person."

"I think what CharmWorks can offer your inn will fit perfectly with your clientele," Jack says. He pulls out the boxes he'd retrieved from my car before dinner. "We've got a new special line of bullet journals and notepads through CharmWorks, and a very limited distribution channel—hopefully including your inn. Like our previous private label launches, CharmWorks has been working with our contracted social media influencers to distribute these, and they're likely to sell out fast."

He begins taking out the bullet journals, offering them to Dan. The inn owner runs his hands over the smooth covers, murmuring about how an ex once swore by bullet journals for productivity.

As Jack explains the details of the strong, magic-reinforced materials of his products, his eyes brighten with a passion I've only seen when he plays electric guitar. Like this, he *glows*.

"How do I know you won't list these on Magizon?" Dan asks, pursing his lips. "Or that someone else won't buy a load of stock and do that?"

"These won't be offered in our online store *or* Magizon *or* to any third-party vendors," Jack says smoothly. "All part of the contract."

Dan frowns, shaking his head, and my heart rises in my throat. Is that a no?

"Let me get dessert," Dan says gruffly. Then his lips split in a grin. "I've a feeling that if I stay around too long, you'll be able to convince me to sign away my inn. I need a moment to think this through."

Dan collects our dishes on a tray, waving us back in our seats when we try to help, and whisks himself out the door.

"That went well!" I say.

But Jack's pinching his forehead, shaking his head. "Dan would agree upfront if he really wanted this. He's not the type to hold back like that. This private label idea . . . it's not enough."

"I think it's pretty neat, though." I run my fingers along the stitching of the bullet journal. "These are so popular, I don't see why he would say no."

"But that's it," Jack says, sitting up. "That's it. It's *too* popular for Dan." He waves around at the room, decorated with lace doilies and grandfather clocks. "He's popular because he doesn't *do* popular. He's learned to do his own thing. And this isn't good enough for him."

"But you've signed up all of the other shops we went by. It's been pretty amazing, your success."

"Dan's Inn has the most foot traffic for magicals, being

that it's in this village," Jack says. "I want CharmWorks to succeed in the 'normal' world, so we need support and brand awareness in the magical world, too. I've got to figure out how to get Dan to agree."

I chew on my lip. Jack runs his hand through his hair, making it even more of a mess. "Without the sales I calculated from this inn, Dad will think this private line is a lost cause. It was my idea, and I promised him this would turn a fast profit."

"Not every business venture will be in the black from the beginning," I say. I know this from my parents' shop, from helping them plan which new teas or products to try out. More often than not, it takes time for customers to start adding in our new items—even if they're as tasty as our matcha macarons or hojicha sugar cookies—to their regular order.

"We can't afford to wait—Dad won't agree—"

He shakes his head, cutting off his own words, and I frown. There's something that feels so unjust about the way Jack's eyes are downcast. He's working so hard for Charm-Works, and his dad won't acknowledge that? I mean, I was never really close with Mr. Yasuda, but this is another facet to him I can't agree with.

Jack puts his forehead in his hands. There's an edge of worry in his voice—close to panic—as he mutters to himself about how to convince Dan that CharmWorks' goods are better than all the other distributors that have tried to claim that valuable retail space. "I could do a heavy discount, but Dad would be upset . . . or maybe I can offer a different set of products, but if Dan doesn't like this one—"

"You could do custom stationery just for Pixley," I blurt out. "There's no stationery shop here. Make it a souvenir . . ."

I pull out my phone to draw a few designs. The boba tea from earlier today, clusters of trees like the Enchanted Forest . . . the front of the drugstore that I'd found Lia's lipstick in.

Then I slide my phone in front of Jack. "Look—notepads and bullet journals with Pixley-themed items. It combines the magical village with CharmWorks."

He rubs his chin.

"There's one condition," he says, his eyes meeting mine. "I can only propose this to Dan if you agree to be the artist on this project."

"Me?" I stammer. "My art's no good." I'm a wallflower, but my drawings aren't wall-worthy. "Don't say this to be nice."

"It's not about being nice. Your drawings are good. Better than good. And I can't use your idea without giving you proper credit," he says. "It's okay if you don't want to draw it, no pressure. I don't feel right without you being a part of it."

From across the table, his eyes meet mine, earnest and true.

Just then, Dan walks back in, carrying a long tray with crystal-clear bowls. "Ready for dessert?"

But Jack's still watching me. "It's okay, Ellie, don't worry about it. I'll use what I have."

"No." This admission comes out so fast, so true, that it surprises me. "I'm in."

"In?" Dan asks. "I hope by 'in' you mean you're in for some of my homemade ice cream!"

But Jack's smiling back at me with a level of gratitude I haven't seen in years. And I want to feast on this instead of ice cream or biscuits, and revel in this strange warmth.

I drag my gaze away from Jack as Dan sets the bowls in

front of us. Mine is filled with a generous scoop of ice cream, but it's surprisingly crystal clear like ice.

Dan digs in immediately. "Mm, coffee. I guess I've been putting off sending in my order for too long." He laughs. "What about you two, what'd you get?"

"Each bite will have a different flavor, depending on what's on your mind," Jack explains. "One of Dan's specialties. Beware of some of the unexpected flavors."

I scoop up a generous mouthful, thankful for something cool to take away the sudden heat flushing up my neck. *I can't believe I agreed to this. . . . My drawings aren't good enough.*

Then the flavor of the ice cream bursts through my mouth. And it isn't vanilla or chocolate or any ordinary flavor like that.

Honeysuckle.

Our favorite activity during third-grade recess was to hide behind the classroom, lying under the window so Ms. King wouldn't see us and ask what we were doing. Jack and I would lie out among the clover and honeysuckle, holding hands and just staring up at the impossibly huge sky.

Some days, I'd bring my sketch pad so we could draw the clouds, and we made those little pictures into stories. A cloud-bunny would go on adventures with the cloud-dragon, and they'd find gleaming treasures and hidden magical lands, always together. When we got bored, we'd suck on the stems of the honeysuckle for a drop of sweetness.

Those honeysuckle days are some of the sweetest moments I ever had growing up.

Jack's forehead creases when he takes a bite of his first scoop. "That's strange," he says.

"Ah, blueberry," Dan says after another spoonful, with a blissful sigh. "I always get that, at least once. Reminds me of my first boyfriend. First love . . . they always stay in your memories, don't they?"

I have the bizarre urge to say, *What if your first love never left?* And then, *thankfully,* instead of saying something downright stupid like that, I just nod and smile.

"I got honeysuckle," Jack says, frowning down at his bowl. "I haven't thought of honeysuckle in years . . . What'd you get, Ellie?"

Don't say it, don't say it . . .

But I'm paralyzed by both Dan and Jack looking over curiously. "I . . . I got honeysuckle, too."

Dan's lips twitch. "Well, I wonder why that is. Unusual for folks to get the same flavor."

"Er," I stammer, my face feeling like I've gone and stuck it into Mount Vesuvius. "It's because we've got a partnership."

Oh crap. It sounds like we got married.

"I mean, like a business partnership." I quickly turn my phone screen back on and show it to Dan. "Jack and I discussed a custom line of bullet journals and stationery, just for your inn. What do you think?"

Dan sets down his spoon and studies my sketches.

"These are rough drawings," I explain, my face burning.

"But Ellie would be the artist," Jack says firmly, and my face goes into full-on volcano mode. I wonder if anyone will notice if I crawl under the table with my bowl of ice cream.

"Clever," Dan says, a bushy eyebrow quirking as he studies my sketch of the Enchanted Forest, zooming in on the baskets filled with Fleurie's ointments.

"It's a great design, perfect for Pixley," Jack says. "So, what do you think?"

There's a heavy pause as Jack and I study Dan.

The inn owner knits his eyebrows together. "My verdict . . ." He takes a bite of ice cream. "Mmm, now I'm tasting the brown sugar boba from Tea-riffic."

Is that a yes? Let that be a yes. I cross my fingers in my lap.

"The verdict . . ." Dan flattens his lips.

Oh, no. Jack and I exchange worried glances.

But then Dan bursts into a grin. "Okay, I guess it's time to celebrate. I'm in!"

Jack cheers and gives me a high five. When his hand meets mine, sparks tingle my fingertips, like some sort of strange magic is shimmering between us.

Chapter 20

Jack and I walk up the stairs to the second floor, my blood pumping fast from this victory. Who would've ever thought I'd be cheering for CharmWorks' success?

Feeling Jack's immediate trust when I came up with the idea, compounded with seeing Dan's eyes light up when he saw my drawings—that's never happened before.

Maybe because I've never put my art out there. But I'd never thought my simple sketches were worthy.

"You were amazing," Jack says, grinning. I think I might be grinning stupidly back, but I'm not willing to examine that too closely. We stop in the middle of the hallway; our doors are across from each other.

"It was a group effort. Ready to head out?" I ask. "I just need to pack my bag."

"Sure," Jack says. "But . . . Ellie, seriously." He pauses, searching for words. His voice lowers an octave, sending shivers up my arms. "You *are*—"

Rinnggg. Ringg.

"Ah, shoot," Jack groans, pulling out his phone. I glance down at the screen. *Minami Vu.*

The ice cream feels like it's frozen into a solid lump in my stomach.

"Mind if I take this call?" Jack asks, rubbing his forehead. "I'd forgotten about it . . . I might take up to an hour, though. She and I have a lot to catch up on."

I want to snap, *No, we've got to get to Huntington Beach. We're already late in our plans to get on the road.*

But I smile and say, "Sure."

The only reasons why I don't say what I really mean are because 1) Hello, My Name Is Doormat and 2) a little inkling tells me I don't care about the travel time, but I do care about . . . something else I refuse to think about in detail.

So I wave Jack off; he's already halfway through the door. "Hey, Minami," he says, his voice light.

I try to ignore how my jaw clenches as Minami cheerily responds so loud that I can hear it. "Jack! I wish you made it to my start-of-summer party, it just wasn't the same without you!"

Jack laughs. "I'm sorry I'm late—"

His door shuts with a solid click, leaving me alone in the hallway, my heart thumping with feelings I don't understand.

෴   ෴

Back in my room, I throw a mutinous glare at the goose down pillow.

If not for that damn pillow, we might not have gone into town. If only we hadn't gone into town, Jack's talk with Dan wouldn't have been delayed. Maybe I would've been doing my own thing, and Jack wouldn't have looped me into a project with that practiced, impossible-to-resist smile of his.

If only . . .

The walls are a little thin, and I can hear the rumble of Jack's husky voice reverberating through the wood.

My heart clenches strangely and I glare at that damn pillow again.

I need to wash out the sound of his voice. Quickly, I pull out my phone and start playing my favorite playlist, but even music falls flat in my ears. So I check my speed-dial contacts. I have two options I can call.

Lia . . . or Remy . . .

Remy . . . or Lia . . .

Ring . . . Ring . . .

The dial tone is shrill, even over speakerphone. But, finally, there's a click and a face pops onto the screen.

"Hello? Ellie?" My sister stifles a yawn. "What's up?"

I show her the cute room Dan's put me in. "Packing up before we head out. And I wanted to check in," I say as Remy moves the phone so I can see what's around her. I wave at Cam; the two of them are hanging out in the kitchen, working on another puzzle. This time, it's a puzzle of a peaceful-looking town tucked into the cliffs and overlooking a bay.

"Check in?" Remy's face fills the screen. "Check what?"

I bite my lip, my hand resting on the bottle of micellar water I'm putting back into my toiletries bag. "How . . . how's . . . Lia doing?"

"Um . . ." My sister's eyes slide over to the other side of the table, probably to glance at Cam.

"C'mon, tell me."

Remy grimaces. "She doesn't want to talk to you yet. At least for right now."

The words hit me like a heavy blow to my chest. I slump against the wall and sigh. "What a summer." From the other side of the line, Mochi whines in commiseration. "I wish she was on this road trip." My chest aches as I look over at my otherwise-empty room. With Lia, we'd be hanging out at one of the drive-in theaters she'd wanted to visit during our journey, or if we were stuck at home, Lia would be sprawled out on the rug, playing with Mochi as we complained about how annoying Jack is.

"I wish I hadn't screwed up!" I want to shout, but my voice is weak and hollow, like saying the truth has knocked all the strength out of me. "I never thought—I never thought that revenge on Jack would go *that* wrong."

"Oh, Ellie . . . Don't blame yourself." Remy is so kind that it hurts even more. "Lia needs time to process things. And you never would've known that Jack was going to use his omamori. We're lucky—seriously, we are—that we grew up near Cam and Jack. We didn't have to worry about explaining magic, and it always felt *real* to us."

"But I want to help her—"

"It's about more than just magic," Remy says, speaking the words that have been on my mind throughout the drive.

"I know," I whisper. "And that's what hurts."

I know she's burning mad about me keeping secrets from her, but her anger and frustration is about more than that.

It's about her parents.

It's about Lia wondering what she could've done, if she'd known about magic then.

But these spells we can do—clean things up, give a hint of joy or courage to someone's day—it's never enough to save someone's life or truly change the world. That's what's so bittersweet about the powers that we have. It's like the chance to get everything we ever hoped for is *just* within reach, but knowing that hope, sometimes, just isn't enough. The magic we have isn't powerful enough.

Hope is bright and earnest and beautiful; but it's also dangerous and cruel.

"For Lia, learning about magic is almost like she's trying to believe aliens exist," Remy says with a half laugh, trying to steer the conversation away from adding to my desolation. I miss my best friend.

"But I could—"

"She's got help." Remy takes a deep breath. "Mom is giving her tutoring sessions on magic, Ana's been talking her through things, and there's a new girl in her classes who she's been hanging out with. And Lia did mention that she's okay with you knowing that she's still going to therapy, and she's started up with a magic-aware therapist, too, someone who learned about magic when they were around Lia's age."

My heart aches, wishing I could be around Lia to help her through this. But . . . if . . . if she's telling Remy that I can get some updates, maybe she'll find a way to forgive me eventually. "That's . . . that's great. Thanks, Remy."

"She's always had a bit of a crush on Ana, so that probably

helps ease things, too." Remy winks. Then she sobers, seeing the bittersweet look on my face. "It's a huge shift, and it probably helps her come to terms with things, to hear from someone who isn't you or Mom or the Yasudas."

"Hmm . . ." I always knew Lia had a thing for Ana, but— I'm her *best* friend. It still stings. But, if this is what Lia chose, and this is what makes Lia happy . . . I *have* to accept it, at least for now, until my once-best friend will let me back into her life. Because I miss her terribly, and just the thought of the rest of the summer without her makes me feel so empty. Because whether I'm by her side or not, I want her to be happy.

"Anyway, how's the road trip going?" Remy asks, changing the subject, as if she can guess I'm going to get stuck thinking about Lia.

"As you can tell," I say, waving my hand around me, "we're currently not driving. Jack's taking a call from some girl."

Remy raises an eyebrow, looking over at Cam again. "Wow, he's got someone in his life? I always thought . . ."

Cam clears his throat quickly. "I haven't heard of him dating anyone."

It's not my place to tell Cam about Minami if his own brother hasn't said anything. "Oh, I must've mixed it up— maybe it was a supplier calling about CharmWorks."

Yeah, not likely. Minami's got nothing to do with stationery, unless it has to do with a certain neighbor.

"I mean, it's not like you two have to be around each other after this road trip," Remy says.

Her words are meant to be comforting.

But it feels strange.

After this, our pact is over and the peace ends. I won't need talk to Jack again. I won't have a reason to, really.

And that feels stranger than I ever thought it would.

⁓   ⁓

"We're pretty behind." I hunch behind the wheel, peering out at the dark night. "We won't make it to Huntington Beach until eleven o'clock."

Even though the highway is empty at this time of night, there's still a long way to drive. Right now, we're chugging through the Grapevine, an isolated winding mountain pass, and then we have to get through Los Angeles, and finally down into Orange County, where Huntington Beach is.

"I'm sorry," Jack says for the twentieth time. He's apologized twenty more times in the past ten minutes than he has in the past five years that we've been avoiding each other. "Chatting with Minami took a lot longer than I expected."

That's because your girlfriend is probably wondering why you're on a road trip with another girl. I wonder what he's told Minami about me. Maybe he says I'm weird, or he laughed about how splotchy my face got from the goose-down pillow or . . .

He crosses his arms. "It's not . . . it's not what you think."

Silence.

"You don't owe me any explanations," I say, my voice as smooth as I can make it. "It doesn't matter to me."

Now the silence is downright *cold.*

From the corner of my eyes, I can see him rubbing his chin. It's his *Thinker* pose. What is he going to say next?

Ugh, why do I even care?

I concentrate on the highway that weaves through the dark, empty hills of the Grapevine. *Keep focused on the road, keep focused on the road . . .*

The silence makes my head throb, so I have to turn on my music. But even my favorite song—"Let Me Know" by BTS—isn't enough to keep my mind off things or take away the frosty air between me and Jack.

And that's when I see it. My headlights flash against something shiny up ahead. My heart jumps into my throat when I realize it's a broken glass bottle, scattered all over the far-right lane. The very lane I'm driving in. There're no other cars around—

Magic—a spell—

But there's no time. I slam on the brakes, swerving to the left—

It's not enough.

Crunch.

The tires on the car's right side flatten immediately. *Flop, flop.*

Jack swears as I move the car to the side of the road, putting my hazard lights on.

"Are you okay?" he asks when I turn the engine off and lean my forehead on the wheel, trying to slow my racing heart.

I nod, looking over at him. "Just a little shocked. I'm hoping we can fix things."

His lips flatten. "I sure as hell hope so, too."

I take a deep breath as we clamber out, using our phones as flashlights. The damage is obvious: the Camry's already slanted to the right.

The occasional car whizzes by, but no one stops to help. Which should be fine; I mean, we've got magic on our side.

As I lean down to look at the tire, my phone beeps and turns off. *Dammit.* It's been playing music and navigating us, and I'd forgotten to charge it. "Ahh, shoot. My phone ran out of battery."

"Want to use mine?"

"Nah, I've got a flashlight. I'll check the tires." I pull the car repair kit from its spot under the driver's seat and toss Jack a bottle of Spill Clean, by a magical company called CarCharms and grabbing a flashlight. "Can you sweep up the rest of the glass on the road? I don't want anyone to get hurt. This should help with the glass, just pour it on."

Jack sends a fleeting look at the glass embedded in the tires before nodding. "Stay safe. Be careful of the cars driving by."

I dig through the car repair kit, sifting through air freshener strips, GasPellets, and bottles of Window Repair Glue. "C'mon, c'mon, where are you . . ." I'd restocked this before heading out, but I've forgotten how many spare tire spells I've included.

I shine my flashlight at the bottom. "There it is!" Relief eases the stiffness in my shoulders as I snatch up the handful of black rubber rectangles.

The tire repair charms are the size of a credit card but made of tire rubber instead of plastic. I peel off the paper label that says *"Instructions: After ensuring your car is in a safe place and away from the general public, place the charm on the tire. Our handy charm will fix your tire by repairing the rubber. This may take 1 to 5 hours, depending on the severity of the issue. Note: Please take your car in for a new tire within one week, as this charm is only temporary. Also! After removing this label, please plant it. It will turn into wildflowers."*

"Clever," Jack says. "Except . . . how long did it say it'll take?"

I take another look at the label. "*'May take 1 to 5 hours, depending on the severity of the issue.'*"

We stare at the completely deflated tires.

"It looks more like a five-hour fix," Jack says with a sigh. "We're going to be stuck for a while."

"Time for a nap in the car?" I look reluctantly at my Camry. While it's comfortable enough to drive in, I'm not sure I'll get a good night's sleep.

Jack frowns, looking at his phone. "Let me see if I can pull up a map." Then he groans. "I don't have reception."

"This sounds promising. I've always wanted to be stranded with you."

Jack laughs despite the heavy atmosphere, and it feels like even the darkness of the sky has lightened, the stars above shining a little brighter. Then he turns his head to the side, in his *Thinker* pose. "Wait, my magic-aware map app is set to download the routes that I search. Let me see . . ."

I look over his shoulder as he scrolls through the app. "Let me guess . . . we're in the middle of nowhere?"

"Yep." His dry tone makes me laugh.

But then he frowns down at his phone again. "Wait . . . there's . . . My map shows *something* ahead."

All around us, there's only the empty road and hills, as far as I can see. About a hundred feet ahead, a narrow paved road just big enough for one car splits off from the highway, passing by a small building and then disappearing behind one of the hills. But that can't be a normal exit; we're in the middle of the mountain pass.

I squint at the shadowy building in the distance. "Is that a magical cottage?"

Jack's eyebrows knit together as he studies the dark shape and looks down at his map. "You're right . . . I think that *is* a magical cottage."

Chapter 21

A gravel path twists through dry grass, leading up to the small, shadowy building. Jack flashes his phone light at the front. It's a one-story house made of gray-painted wood slats, but it looks surprisingly well maintained. Wildflowers line the walls, adding a splash of color in the dark night.

There's a sign, too, made of polished wood. Jack reads it out loud: "The Grapevine Cottage: a safe place to rest for magical travelers in need. Open to all magic-aware."

I knock; there's no answer.

But the letters on the wood sign wiggle and change: WELCOME, TRAVELERS. ENTER FREELY.

"I guess that's an invite." I turn the doorknob, and the door swings open.

Jack presses one of five switches on the wall immediately inside, and lights flare all around.

It's a cozy little place. Slightly dusty, but comfortable, in sleek grays with a stained-white wood floor. It's a small living area with a dining table with chairs for two, and a tiny gray love seat next to a bookshelf crammed with gilded covers.

"I want to *live* here," I declare.

Jack laughs. "Love at first look. Or should I say, love at first book?"

I elbow him. "C'mon, I mean, look at this!" I grab him around the wrist and pull him forward, so that we can explore the rest of the rooms. There's a tiny bedroom, a bathroom, and a kitchen. When I poke my head in the fridge, it's filled with staples like a carton of eggs and butter.

"Wow," I whisper. "I seriously could live here."

"I've heard of some magic-aware folks living in the cottages long term," Jack says. "But the magic runs out if they don't take care of it. This kind of magic requires loads of people to apply charms over time. Before we leave, we'll have to add a few charms of our own in thanks."

I nod, trying to think of what I could contribute to an already amazing place like this. But then a yawn overtakes me, so big that my eyes tear up.

"It's midnight, we should sleep." Jack glances at his phone. "I can set an alarm for five o'clock, and that should be enough time for the tire to patch up. Then we can switch off driving and napping to make it to Huntington Beach by seven."

"So enough time to set up the booth before our families come in." I nod. "Sounds good, let's sleep."

Jack and I return to the first door we went through, to the bedroom.

But once we're inside, we both freeze, staring at the bed pushed against the wall, next to a big window looking out on a hill.

Then I blink. *Oh.*

There's two of us.

And one bed. I mean, it's not a tiny bed.

But Jack and I stare at it wordlessly.

"I can sleep on the floor," I offer immediately. "Take the bed."

"No, no way," Jack says. "I'll sleep on the love seat."

Before I can protest, Jack goes out to the living room and lies down on the tiny couch. But it's meant for a cuddling couple, not a nearly six-foot-tall guy. His head and legs stick out awkwardly. Even when he curls on his side, he doesn't fit.

"I can take the love seat," I say. "I'm shorter."

He sits up, rubbing his neck. "No, the floor is better than this."

But we both stare down at the hardwood planks. It doesn't look particularly comfortable.

I bite my lip. "We can share?"

He blinks. "The floor?"

Oh my gosh, he's dense.

"The bed." I hope my face isn't burning as red as it feels.

His jaw drops. I wish my phone wasn't dead so I could snap a photo of this. I've never seen Jack so taken aback.

"It'll be a sleepover." My mouth feels oddly dry. "Like old times. Remember when we snuck into your kitchen and tried to make Cup Noodles that one night?"

Jack and I used to have sleepovers all the way up until middle school. We'd spend the afternoon creating a blanket fort in his living room, and we'd fall asleep looking at the plastic glow-in-the-dark stars that his mom had put up on the ceiling for us. After a late-night snack, of course.

"We almost burnt the noodles putting them in the toaster, until my mom ran in." Jack laughs but then bites his lip, and I have to drag my eyes away from the way his lips are so red. "Are you sure you don't mind sharing?"

"Yeah, if you take the first driving shift, if you don't mind," I say. "It takes me a while to fall asleep."

Jack pauses, looking between the tiny love seat, the floor, and the bed. "Deal."

⤳   ⤳

The bed is bigger than the love seat. But not by much.

I feel like we're frozen icicles, laying side by side. I've never been so aware of anything—*anyone*—as I am at this moment.

Jack is as still as a statue, too. I don't dare look at him. Instead, I squint at the faintly dusty light bulb overhead, the glow burning into my eyes.

"Um, let me turn off the lights." I shift, rolling off the bed. My loose shorts and T-shirt make me feel so naked, even though I'm wearing a sports bra and underwear underneath. It's an outfit that I'd wear to Ana's for some cupcakes with Lia, or to run errands around Palo Alto. So why does it feel so weird now?

There are two switches by the doorway. I hit the one on the left and nothing seems to happen. I try the other one, and the light turns off.

"Um . . ." Jack says. "Ellie . . ."

"Do you need the light back on?"

"No, look up . . ."

I tilt my head toward the ceiling and gasp. Because, some-how, there *is* no more ceiling. No roof, nothing. It's the night sky, brilliant with shimmering stars, the rare cloud pale against the darkness, and the full moon that glows so big it feels like I can reach up and brush my fingers against it. Here, by this highway that's nearly deserted at night, there are so few lights and no cities for miles around so the stars can glow bright.

Awe fills my heart, like a breath of clean, pure air.

The bed creaks, and Jack stands up, walking toward me.

In the faint light, I can see his eyes are dead set on me, like I'm all he sees.

My heartbeat races. "J—Jack?"

His voice is a husky whisper, like he, too, doesn't want to break this enchantment. "Number seven?"

He can't actually want to . . .

Slowly, he holds his hand out, his intentions clear.

Oh . . .

My heart thumps. *Number 7 of the Anti-Wallflower List: Dance under the stars with someone.*

"I . . . I . . ."

He hesitates. "I mean, if I count as 'someone' to you. It's okay if you were saving that for someone special . . ."

Am I someone special to you? Like Minami?

No, wait. It doesn't matter if I'm someone special to him. Right. This is just to tick off another item on my list.

I try to push down that swelling nervousness that prickles over my skin as I step closer to Jack.

His eyes widen in surprise, as if he'd expected me to run off. And if anything, that steels me. This is *Jack*. He was the only one who saw me cry when I sparked my finger on a spell. The boy who held my hand during doctor visits when we were kids, wiping my tears away as I cried from getting a shot. The same Jack who nearly burned his kitchen down for me, because I'd said that food was better than flowers, and so instead of just a bouquet of handpicked daisies, he baked me lumpy, burnt cookies for Valentine's Day in fifth grade.

It's like I'm at a middle school dance. He slides his hands around my waist, and I loop my arms around his so-broad-they-should-be-illegal shoulders. Oh, *tennis*. Damn.

He shifts, and we begin to sway side to side. There's no music, but the natural world outside is like a magical, real-life orchestra. The rustling grass sounds like the soft keys of a piano; the faraway cars thrum like the beat of a drum.

Jack and I study each other for a bare second before we both look away; it's too intense to stare into each other's eyes.

He clears his throat. "I knew magical cottages were cool, but this is a whole new level of sorcery."

"Seriously," I agree, trying to keep my voice light and airy, even though *what are words* right now? "I kind of want to visit all the magical cottages around the world and see what each of them are like."

"I can see so many constellations," he says in awe.

Ever so slightly, I turn my face up to drink him in. I hope, in the darkness, that he can't see my burning cheeks from our close proximity. But I can see his outline, and I study him, trying to remember every detail. His head is tilted up like he's breathing in the sights of the sky, or maybe so absorbed in the world above him that he could almost fall into it. Maybe it's been too long since he's had a quiet moment like this.

It feels like I'm seeing parts of Jack that I've forgotten about. Or parts no one ever gets to see anymore. Because, somehow, he's hiding it behind that facade of Jack, the heir of

CharmWorks—not Jack, the living, breathing boy who was once my best friend.

Jack points to my right. "Hey, see that set of stars above Orion's Belt? It kind of looks like Mochi."

"I adore Mochi more than anyone, but I don't see it."

"No way!" Jack moves in a little closer, motioning as he tries to show me where I should be seeing it. "There and there. Her eyes. The star in the middle is her nose, and those two are the points of her ears."

"I dunno . . ." I laugh.

Then he tries to convince me of other just-as-impossible constellations, tracing shapes in the stars. "Look, look, I think that's a cupcake there. I think that should be called . . . hmm . . ."

"Ana's Amazing Cinnamon Cupcake," I say, with reverence, and he laughs.

"I like that. Aren't her cinnamon cupcakes the best? And there, that looks like Cam and Remy, two peas in a pod. I think I'll name it RemyCam. I should register that."

"No one would accept it." I laugh. "I bet all those stars have names already."

"We can make our own names for things." Suddenly, he sounds more serious than ever. "We can, can't we? Just because something had one name for a while, it doesn't mean the stars can't move, that things can't change."

I press my lips together. Because it doesn't seem like he's talking about the stars anymore. And there's a rawness to his words that makes me breathe in sharply, with an overwhelming confusion.

If I put on a pair of magical spectacles right now, I know

I'd see emotions sparking into raw magic dust, gentle yet bright, shimmering around us with unsaid hopes.

"Remember when . . . when we were in third grade?" Jack looks back down at me, his voice dipping. "We'd search for shapes in the clouds, and you'd sketch them out for us. And we'd make up silly stories, but they were the best stories, I swear."

He remembers, too. I swallow; it feels like my heart is caught in my throat. "I called them honeysuckle days," I whisper. I long to reach down and hold his hand, like when we were kids. But I curl my hands into fists. I don't dare.

"Like . . . like the ice cream we had tonight," Jack says quietly.

"Like the ice cream," I agree.

The sound of our breaths float into the night air. Through the open roof, chirping crickets, with the occasional car zipping past. It's perfect, so impossibly perfect.

There's so much left unsaid as we dance under the stars. Yet, at the same time, the stark truth doesn't need to be said at all. Together, we share a recognition of the past we had and the beauty in those all-too fleeting moments.

My heart feels full, to every corner, with memories we've shared, our past that is only known to the two of us. It's a world all our own, just like this cottage.

Chapter 22

Ringg! Ring!

    I'm still in the *perfect* dream. Lying in a field, surrounded by honeysuckle flowers, and Jack's holding my hand like when we were kids, and—

Jack's phone alarm blares louder. *Wait—Jack's here . . . I'm sleeping in the* same *bed as him.* And that thought pulls me fully awake.

It's still so early that the sun has barely risen over the horizon.

I'm on my side, facing Jack, who's still asleep. My heart is in my throat as I look down.

At my hand, entwined with Jack's.

Our fingers fit perfectly together, our tanned skin a perfect match of gold and bronze under the faint rays of the sun.

Just the way our bodies melded together perfectly last night as we danced.

My stomach flips. I thought I'd be running away with shock if this were to ever happen . . .

But this feels comfortable. This, strangely, feels *right*.

Until his eyelids flutter, and he mumbles sleepily, "I've missed you, Ellie."

And I pull my hand out of his as quickly as I can, sliding off the bed. I quickly switch off his phone's alarm.

He blinks awake, rubbing his face into the pillow in a way that's too cute for this early in the morning. His eyes are sleepy, like he's still half in dreamland. "What? 'Larmz go off?"

"Oh, I turned it off."

He frowns, rubbing his hand over his face, and then looks at it strangely. "I feel like I'm missing something."

I push his phone over on the bed. "This?"

He rubs his hand over his eyes again. "It felt like something different . . . Never mind." Jack shoots me a sleepy grin that makes my knees almost buckle. "I must've been dreaming."

That's my *line.* "Right. Um, well, I have to get ready." I motion at the bathroom. And before he can say anything else, I grab my duffel bag and dart for safety.

❧   ❧

Five minutes later, with my teeth brushed, sunscreen on, and a fresh change of clothes, I feel a little more ready to start the day, even though questions still tumble over and over in my mind.

Jack's sitting on the love seat when I get out of the bathroom. He's changed, too. "There was a laundry machine in the closet. I threw the sheets in there, and they were finished a moment later and back on the bed before I could blink."

"Wow," I say. "This only reaffirms my decision to live in a magical cottage later in life."

He grins. "Same."

My heart thumps. He doesn't mean that he wants to live with me. *Don't be stupid, Ellie.*

Jack gets up, and my veins thrum with blood as he steps closer. I can't breathe.

Oh, oh, oh.

And then he passes by me. "I'll brush my teeth really quickly and then we can head out? I grabbed some breakfast bars from the pantry."

"Sure," I say, my shoulders dropping. *Duh, he wanted to brush his teeth.*

"Is there something else?" he asks, pausing to turn back.

I thought you were going to hug me or something. Or kiss me or—

I smile sweetly at him, squashing my very misguided thoughts. "I need to make a cup of tea. Want one?"

He waves for me to help myself. "No, go for it."

I find a box filled with single-serve, non-magical tea bags and a ceramic mug (infused with magic dust and a spell to keep a drink always warm) in the pantry. As the kettle boils, I wander around the cottage. On the bookshelf, Jack's already put two of his red omamori charms as his way of repaying the cottage for our night's stay. That's sweet of him to think about protecting the future inhabitants of this magical cottage. Even though I secretly want to live here and stay until I'm old.

I fish through the pocket of my duffel bag. I've got the vial of good luck from Cam, but this doesn't feel like the right place

for it somehow. I dig deeper and pull out a tin of my parents'
matcha that I like to keep for travels. Like in the way that Lia
needs her coffee to get up, I always want my tea.

But it's still unopened, and maybe whoever stays here next
might enjoy some green tea with a spark of contentment. So, as
my gift to the cottage, I stick the tin next to the box of tea bags.

With my mug of hot tea, I wander back into the bedroom
and check on the ceiling. "Oh." Jack's switched it back. The
rooftop is solid again, all white rafters, even with a spider scuttling along a silky-thin web.

It's like our night of constellation watching never happened. But I glance down at my hand. My fingers can still
feel the imprint of his, like they can recognize that he has a
warmth I've missed for a long, long time.

For a moment, I'm tempted to click the switch again, to
see the morning sky.

But it won't be the starry night sky and it won't be with
Jack, on the bed. So there's no use, really.

"Are you ready to go?"

I spin around and smile at Jack, who looks a little more
awake. I'm hoping I've hidden this weird feeling somewhere
deep inside me, so he can't see my emotions on my face.
"Ready. Let's get to our show."

Chapter 23

The Huntington Beach Convention Center is only a few miles away from stretches of golden sand, and as we set up our booth in the atrium of the convention center, an ocean breeze wafts in through the open doors.

For a second, the salty-bitter scent reminds me of the Santa Cruz Boardwalk. I glance over at Jack; sweat gleams on his forehead as he wrenches down the last pole for our booth. This isn't the time to daydream about the beach and a shirtless Jack.

I brush off my hands and take a step back to admire our booth. As Jack had set up the signage, declaring PALO ALTO's SORCERER SQUARE, I'd arranged the goods on our three tables—to the left, center, and right—for shoppers to browse through.

We've got an awesome display. Since Mr. Yasuda and my parents are attending in person, the other stores gave them more space in the booth: CharmWorks' standard stationery lines are on the long table on the left; tins of my parents' magical green tea are on the long table to the right; and I've saved the center for the other shops: Ana's cupcake mix, in adorable mason jars; charmed magical clothing; sparkling crystals; enchanted spice packets; and even cases of magical dragon fruit from the other shops in Sorcerer Square.

Jack pauses next to me, studying the cardinal-red sign fluttering in the slight breeze, and then his eyes drop to look at the products I've lined up. I suck in my breath, waiting for him to say, *CharmWorks should be front and center* or *I know of a better way to rearrange this.*

But he only says, "Want to go around the rest of the convention? I think there are some exhibitor-only events soon that might be fun to check out."

I haven't been to a convention in the longest time, since that drive down ten years ago. "Really? What's it like?"

Jack's eyes study me as he throws a black sheet over our goods, signaling we're closed for now. Here, among the other magic-aware, no one dares to steal goods; the convention staff has antitheft charms laid out all over.

"You'll have to see for yourself," he says, and it sounds like a challenge. "Are you ready?"

I meet his gaze evenly, though my stomach flips. "Ready if *you* are."

❧   ❧

Since the California Magical Retailers' Convention is a fully magical event, security rings the outside of the convention center. The non-magicals think it's a boring old retail gathering, and no one without a proper convention badge is allowed close. So that means, inside these walls, lots of the booths are decked out in enchantments, to the point of nearly bursting with spells.

Our booth is in the atrium, by the front door, so we hadn't had a chance to get to the main floor. The security guard scans our exhibitor badges and waves me and Jack inside.

A cool breeze whisks over my skin as we take our first steps. "Wow," I whisper. "It's a magical *city*."

Seemingly endless rows of booths line the rectangular convention center that's longer than a football field. Light shines down through the skylights, making it truly seem like an indoor city. There's a symphony of sound, a rainbow of color, and so much to explore—it's like a book I've been waiting and waiting to read.

The booths are selling everything under the sun. This stock is for use by the magic-aware only; a change from our usual slightly magical goods that can be shared with the non-magic-aware and sold widely.

A voice announces over loudspeakers, drawing me out of my state of wonder, "The first sellers' contest starts on the main stage in thirty minutes. See you there for some thrilling fun!"

"C'mon," Jack says, nudging me, his voice teasing. "We're not going to explore if we sit here and stare."

"I could be content just staring." *No, no, that's a wallflower move.* "But, yeah, checking out the booths is even better."

Jack and I wander through the aisles, and I try to keep my jaw connected to my body.

But *oh my charms*, I've been missing out by not going to these conventions.

The closest booth, with rippling purple cloth partitions, reminds me of a fortune-teller's hut. There are signs warning passersby that a sniff of their incense might sweep the users away (*"Relive the pleasant past, all with one whiff!"*), and I can't seem to resist.

I take a step forward, breathing in the cotton-candy scent. And in a moment, it's like a magical carpet is under my feet, pulling me into a memory of the elementary school Halloween parade.

Jack and I are sitting in his bedroom, trying to think of costumes. In previous years, Jack's mom made costumes for the both of us. As babies, she did costumes like "two peas in a pod" or "ketchup and mustard" or "two boba teas." But Jack just told me she's getting sick, and she won't be able to make a costume this year.

Jack's been quiet all week during class. And I know it's because he's been trying to think of a way to make a costume on his own, because he doesn't want to burden his mom. But as talented as he is with music, he's got two left hands when it comes to making his Power Rangers costume.

So I run back to my house and pull out two raggedy sheets from the cupboard and bring them back over. And with a few hacks of our scissors, we're ghosts, dashing through the halls of the Yasudas' house, making Cam and Remy shriek with laughter.

"I could've made a costume for you two!" Mrs. Yasuda protests when she sees us.

"Boo!" Jack jokingly jeers. "We're the best ghosts!"

"You are," Mrs. Yasuda agrees. She snaps a photo with her phone as we run around, and she laughs and laughs. "You should go show Ellie's parents, too."

Jack grins, giving me a high five as we race out the door. As our hands meet, I want to take a photo, too, and capture the way his eyes shine in this moment. Jack has been quiet because he's been so scared of asking for help. Because he feels alone in trying to deal with his mother's illness and taking care of himself and his brother. But I'm here for him. I'll always be here for him.

"Ellie?" Someone's shaking my arm.

I blink. I'm sitting on a plush purple stool at the front of the incense stand, still reeling in the aftermath of that memory.

"That pulled you away, didn't it?" A dark-skinned man smiles kindly. "Happens with those particularly meaningful ones."

I shake my head in awe. "It did. What *was* that?"

The shopkeeper waves his hand at a nearby shelf of incense boxes. One set is on display, slightly smoking with that sweet cotton-candy scent. "It's part of our therapy series, to help users reflect. Sometimes, it helps to relive things to process the past. But because of the intensity of these visions, there're spells that limit usage to once a month."

I buy a box of incense. And, to my surprise, Jack buys two boxes.

"For me and Dad," Jack says quietly, without me asking. "I think this would be helpful for us . . ."

He doesn't explain further, but it makes me wonder.

Apparently, the next stand over is already calling to him. And there's no time for me to nudge him to talk about his mom, something he's never done with me. It's like there's a complete wall. Over the last few days, though, he's been mentioning the past more than ever.

Jack waves me over. "Look, Ellie. Wouldn't Cam and Remy like this?"

It's an intimidating stand next to the main stage. They're selling plain-looking black boxes about the size of a board game container, but judging by the crowd that's gathering, it's nothing ordinary.

"Escape Room in a Box," Jack reads the sign, and then turns to me. "Isn't that cool? All it takes is a six-by-six-foot room. Apparently, you just open up the box and go inside. As soon as you close the door, the room starts. There's three difficulty levels and boxes range from thirty minutes to two hours."

"This sounds awesome." And then I see the price tag. "A hundred and twenty-five dollars?!" I regret the incense I bought earlier. This would be the *perfect* gift for Remy, and her birthday is coming up at the beginning of July.

Jack chews on his lip. "That's like the average price of an escape room for the non-magic-aware, but you can take this one on the go. But, yeah, it's pricey. I guess that's why people are looking instead of buying."

"Recruiting volunteers!" calls a tall woman who reminds me of a sleek, elegant Abyssinian cat, as she adjusts her tortoiseshell glasses. "Entrants for our Escape-and-Win contest! Winners get a free box . . . if you can make it out alive!"

The rest of the crowd takes a step back.

A warm hand with tough calluses tugs at my wrist. I look up at Jack, who's grinning at me. "I think it's time."

"Time for what?" I ask, confused.

"Lucky number six: *Win a contest, any contest.* Your list," Jack says.

I groan. "You seriously memorized it, didn't you?"

He winks. "Maybe? Anyway, if you enter the contest, you could win a box for them."

I take one look at Jack's hand around my wrist, soft yet strong. And I shoot a smile back at him. "Shall we?"

"*We?*" he echoes in confusion.

"Oh, oops! How'd this happen? Your hand is raised, too," I say innocently. He instantly drops my hand, but I'm not going to let him get away.

"C'mon!" the host calls over her microphone. "The both of you, get your magical selves up here!"

"See?" I grab him, my fingers lacing perfectly into his, like the way we woke up this morning. A thrilling shock runs up my skin at the touch, as my cheeks burn. I can't look back without him seeing me all red.

We make our way up to the long table on the stage and stand at the edge of the line of eight other participants.

"It's time for our annual Escape-and-Win contest! It's a team contest, so everyone on stage, find a partner!" The host winks. "And here's a hint—find someone who's *brave.*"

Jack and I stare at each other. *Us, a team?* But four people swarm Jack, pushing me out of the way. He backs up to the other end of the stage as he tries to fend off the enthusiastic contestants.

There's a tap on my shoulder. I turn to a boy about my age, with stick-straight black hair. He's cute in a dorky sort of way. "Hey, want to partner up?"

"Oh," I say, surprised.

But then I glance over at Jack just as he looks over. A split second later, he shakes off the people around him and strides toward me, his intentions clear.

"Sorry," I say to the boy. "I, um, I'm already on a team."

The boy nods, shuffling somewhere else. But I barely

notice him, because Jack's at my side, and he nudges me with his shoulder. "C'mon, you weren't going to ditch me, were you?"

"Me? Ditch the person who got me into this contest in the first place?" I raise an eyebrow. "Now, why would I want to do that?"

He laughs. I don't want to read into things, but he looks kind of glad.

"Great! Everyone's teamed up," the host says, scanning the other groups. "Now, here's the challenge . . ." She snaps her fingers and a shimmering mist fills the stage. "You'll have to make it out of a quick-play room! These rooms come in a set of ten, and each are thirty minutes. Or"—her sharp eyes narrow at the crowd, and she grins ferociously—"less, if you can't make it out alive."

One of the host's assistants hands out blindfolds. Jack stares down at the black cloth with confusion.

"All right, one partner will have to be blindfolded," the host calls. "Whoever got the blindfold is the lucky one. Other partners help them put it on. I wasn't joking when I said you needed someone brave to be blindfolded."

Jack and I stare at each other. This is an escape room, but it's also a game of *trust*. And unlike most of the other people on stage, we know each other. We should be able to win because of our history . . . or maybe that's a reason why we *won't* win.

Slowly, he holds out the blindfold. He bends down slightly.

"I'm not that short," I growl.

He laughs. "Hey, just trying to help." A second later, he adds, "Shorty."

I reach down to his side and give him a *helpful* tickle.

"Hey!" He doubles over, choking on his laughter. "That was a low blow. After I get this mask off, I'm going to get you back."

"Try me," I say, sweetly. "But you'll never be a match for me."

"Want to try?" His voice is low and husky, shooting shivers straight through my body.

Thankfully, thankfully, he can't see my burning red face. Or the way I breathe his scent in, the aroma of mint and just-washed laundry that swirls around us. It's like the incense from the shop, but a million times more extreme. There are so many memories of him and me, him and that damn delicious scent of his.

I step away. My palms are sweaty.

Jack turns left and right. "What am I supposed to do like this?" Then he wraps his arms around his sides protectively. "Don't you dare try tickling me again, Ellie."

The assistants come out again, this time each holding a box. One slides a box into my hands, and I look down at the label in shock: *Locked in the Library—Escape Before* YOU *Get Checked Out!*

"Don't worry," I say as confidently as I can. "The next time, it won't be me tickling you. It'll be the murderer in our escape room. You can be the bait."

Jack nearly gurgles in shock. "Murderer? What? Wait a minute—"

"Ready?" the host calls. She raises an eyebrow as if saying, *Do you all really think you're up for this challenge?* "First group back wins the grand prize, our full deluxe set of Escape Rooms. Ready, set, go!"

"Grab my arm!" I say to Jack. "Hold on to me."

As quickly as I can, I peel off the sticker sealing the black box and open it up. It's like a treasure chest made of cardboard. The moment I pop the lid, the box tumbles out of my hand and falls to the ground, rising into a bloodred door that stretches up from the stage.

I look to the left and right. The other contestants stand in front of doors, too, though theirs range from a gate covered with ivy to a stone archway glowing with light. When I look overhead, I realize that there are screens around the convention center that are now broadcasting the contest. The screen flickers briefly to show me and Jack, who's latched onto my forearm.

The other pairs push into their rooms. I stare at the door, my hand hovering above the bronze doorknob.

It's time to take a risk, I tell myself.

My hands shake as I open the door, and it screeches ominously as it swings open.

Chapter 24

We step into a dimly lit, rectangular library, lined with shelves of old books with gold-embossed leather covers and coated in a layer of dust. Plush, just-as-dusty armchairs are scattered next to small, round tables, with spiders scuttling up thick cobwebs around them, like they'd trap us if we sit down. There's a dark red door at the other end, but my guess is that it's locked, and that's what we need to find a key for.

The sound of rain pounds on the roof. I look up; it's a pitch-black void above. There are curtained windows that break up the shelves; maybe there's a way to escape from there, if the door doesn't work.

It should be impossible for a room like this to appear out of thin air, but then, that's the power of magic. I wonder how many complex charms were used. Remy and Cam would be awesome working at a company like this in the future—it's right up their alley.

I take a step forward, and Jack stumbles behind me, still

holding on to my arm. That's right. I'm stuck with him, literally.

"So, can I take off the blindfold now?" Jack says, his warm grip tight around my arm.

"Let me try." I lean around him, tugging at the knot in the cloth.

A loud *zap!* resonates around the room, and Jack yelps. "Okay, I'll take that as a no. *Ow.*"

I peer at the back of his blindfold. "There's a message on it. Stay still, let me read it. *Take this off before you leave, or your head will pay a fee. CLUE: Uncover the view.*"

"That's comfortingly vague," Jack comments. "So, what's the room like?"

I describe the narrow room, the creepy atmosphere, the walls of books. Jack shudders as I get to the part about the cobwebs.

"Twenty-nine minutes remaining, contestants!" a cheery voice calls, and we both jump. That's right. Even though this place is downright creepy, this is still a thirty-minute game.

"Okay, let's look around," I say, even though I'd really like to curl up in a corner with a book and pretend like I'm not in a disturbingly scary escape room. "I wish Remy and Cam were here."

"What am I supposed to do?" Jack asks, his forehead wrinkling. "Sniff around? It smells musty here."

Despite the nerve-racking tension that this room gives me, I let out a small laugh. "Sure, sniff. Just don't get caught by the murderer. Maybe keep close to me?"

His hand stays firm around my arm, and his voice turns smooth. "You're the only anchor in my world right now."

I laugh awkwardly as my stomach flips. I'm sure he didn't mean it in a romantic way, though.

Jack and I make our way through the long room in one piece, and I jostle the doorknob on the bloodred door. I explain to Jack, "Yep, the door's locked, and there's a big bronze keyhole above it; we need to find the key for this. There's a crooked sign nailed to the door that says, 'Exit if you can . . . while you can.'"

"Sounds promising."

I rub my hand against my pocket and feel the outline of a tiny glass vial inside. Is this the time to use that bottle of good luck from Cam? I should probably wait to see if we can make it through, though. Luck like that is hard to find.

The rain continues pounding on the ceiling, with the echoey sound of tin. Even though I know that the world outside is sunny Southern California, this feels way too real.

"Let me check the windows," I say. "Maybe there's another exit out?"

"Sure," Jack says, shuffling behind me to the nearest set of emerald-green and gold brocade curtains.

I draw the curtains; it's too dark out to see anything, but I lean closer. Maybe there's a clue to how we can escape here. Maybe—

Lightning cracks, illuminating the view.

A skull swings in the air, eye sockets dark and empty, but the jaw twists up into a malicious smile.

"*AHH!*" I scream.

Jack grabs me, pulling me behind him. "What is it? Ellie! Are you okay?"

His body is unnervingly close to mine, with one arm

shielding me. I can feel his warming heat through his back. Even though he's blindfolded, he turns his head, listening closely.

"Sorry. I just . . . There's a skull dangling in the window. I think it's fake, thankfully."

I expect Jack to laugh, but he only nods.

"As long as you're okay. We've got this," he says earnestly, unable to see the way my eyes are tracing over the broad stretch of his shoulders, the curves of his strong jaw, the way his body is tense, trying to protect me from this strange, scary game.

"Yeah, I hope so." Before I get more distracted, I spin on my heel and turn toward the center of the room. "Let's check over here."

This time, I grab his hand, tugging him forward. And his fingers lace into mine, like they did this morning. A perfect fit.

"Here!" I pick up a dusty piece of paper from the table closest to the locked door. "It's a puzzle! *Find the book with the hidden key; and then you'll be able to leave willingly.*"

"So it's in one of the books?" Jack says. "That should be easy, right?"

"*Twenty-five minutes remaining!*" The host's voice calls. "And it looks like some of our contestants are getting close . . . and some are close to never leaving!"

I think we're the latter. "Jack, there's like . . . a thousand books in this library. There's got to be some sort of meaning. And you still have that blindfold."

"Can we get this off first?" Jack asks, tugging at the cloth with his free hand. There's an angry zap, and he groans. "Ouch!"

I reread the clue on his blindfold. *"Uncover the view.* The view? Like, the windows?"

I wrench the curtains off the nearest window, muffling my scream when a disembodied hand slams against the glass.

In a flash, Jack's pressing close to my side.

I take a huge, jagged breath, trying to laugh. "Just, you know, a hand without its body."

Jack follows close behind me, our fingers still laced together. When I draw the other curtains, I let out a huge sigh of relief. Just rain splattering the window, the droplets flowing down in rivulets.

"No skulls?" Jack asks.

"Not this one."

We advance toward the next window. Again, empty.

After I've drawn the curtains on the remaining three windows, I spin around, looking at Jack expectantly. "Okay, we've 'uncovered' the view."

Jack tugs at his blindfold, and there's another angry zap. "Ouch! Apparently, it's the wrong view?"

I scan the windows, the hanging skull leering at me, and the disembodied hand still slapping at the window. "Let me try covering up all the windows except the freaky ones."

"I'm kind of glad I'm blindfolded," Jack mutters as I draw the curtains closed on the rain-only windows.

"Okay, go for it." My stomach flips. What happens if we *don't* make it out in time?

Jack tugs tentatively at the cloth. No zapping sound this time. He tears it off, and the black cloth bursts into a cloud of smoke. His eyes shine through the gloom. "You did it!"

"I've never been so glad to see your face," I say dryly.

"I'll take that as the compliment I deserve," Jack says. Then his voice lowers as he studies me, and he takes a step forward. "What next?"

Creak.

We spin around. The walls are crumbling. And a furry, gigantic spider's leg reaches in through the gaps, pincers clacking.

Jack yelps. "No one said anything about *spiders*." He's always hated spiders as much as he's hated mice; he can't stand scuttling things in the way I can't stand needles and blood.

"Well," I say. "I'm not a fortune-teller, but this feels like how we die . . ."

"We've got to get out." Jack looks positively green.

"We can make it out, Jack. I'll get us out." I spin around, trying to figure out the clue for the door. This is supposed to be a short escape room, which means fewer puzzles. So if we've been able to clear the blindfold puzzle, there must be something inside this room that leads to the key to get out.

I scan the room again. Same books, same tables and armchairs. I take a step closer, reading the book titles, trying to look for some sort of pattern, the way Remy and Cam might. Because puzzles are a lot about logic, right?

The titles are all legendary books, with fancy leather-bound covers. Haruki Murakami, Angie Thomas, Fonda Lee, Aisha Saeed, Tae Keller . . . But what do these authors have in common?

I try to run my hands on the bookshelves, but my fingers go straight through.

"Whoa!" Jack says from behind me. He dashes to the shelf

on the other side, and his hands go through the books, too. "I feel the wall, but I can't grab any of the books."

I go on to the next shelf, running my hands through the spines. Then—

Thump!

My palm slams against a solid book. Quickly, I yank it open, and instead of pages, there's a fragment of brass.

"It's part of a key!" I exclaim. "Jack, we've got to find the rest of the key and put it together!"

Jack and I hurry up and down the shelves, pulling out books and gathering the bits of the bronze keys. Finally, we've cleared out the shelves, and pool our finds on the floor in front of the dark red door.

Our fingers bump into each other as we maneuver the puzzle pieces together. But it's a familiar comfort, compared to the spiders hacking away at the walls.

Finally, twenty-some pieces later, Jack and I cradle our hands together, holding a hefty bronze key the size of his palm. There are cracks all over from how it's puzzled together, but it's in the proper shape of a key, and most of all, even if it was once broken, it looks whole again.

Maybe like me and Jack. But I push that thought aside.

The question is—will the key work?

Jack helps me up and we step toward the door together, pressed close together to avoid the spiders. With our hands in sync, we push the key into the hole and turn it.

My heart pounds so loud I can barely hear, but then there's a *click!*

And the door swings open as Jack and I cheer. But it's

leading into a void of darkness that looks anything but invit-
ing. We pause, looking at each other.

"Um . . ." Jack chews on his lip. "I can go first." He holds
his hand out. "Hold on."

We lace our fingers again. Because of this room, he's somehow become a source of comfort.

Suddenly, the floor shifts under us, forming into a slide
that pushes us out the door, and we yelp in shock. I stumble
forward, losing my footing.

I cry out with surprise. And I'm falling into the darkness,
but—

Jack catches me, my momentum so strong that I land hard
against his chest. His arms wrap tight around me, not letting
me fall.

His body is firm but oh-so-soft, his shirt comforting with
that scent of just-washed laundry. And from the way my body
is cradled in his, I can feel his heart beating fast.

I look up. *Oh.*

His eyes are so close to mine. Our faces are mere inches
away from each other. I can't breathe. If he dipped his head a
little closer, our lips would brush.

I'm so grateful for this semidarkness, so he doesn't have to
see my burning-red cheeks as his arms wrap around me.

My heart is racing; I don't know if it's adrenaline from the
escape room or because he's holding me, but my heart pounds
so hard I can't think—

Then light bursts all around us, and the darkness falls
away like a tug of a curtain.

We're standing back in the convention center, the empty

black box on the ground next to us; it's shimmering with a golden light.

The crowd cheers as they see us; someone at the front calls, "Cute couple."

He drops his arms and even though it's the middle of June, I somehow feel cold. I breathe in deep, steadying myself.

"Are you okay?" Jack's voice is soft and gentle.

For a second, it felt like Jack and I were the only ones in the world.

"I thought we weren't going to get out," I say with a shaky laugh.

"It felt so real, didn't it?" Jack says, shaking his head.

The host strides over to us, adjusting her tortoiseshell glasses. "And our third-place contestants have made it back. What a thrilling escape you two had—and may I say the cutest escape of all? Congratulations, and enjoy the prize pack!"

One of the assistants pushes a small black box into my hands. In a surprised haze, Jack and I make our way down the stairs leading offstage, my heart still pounding.

"Wow, I can't believe we won a prize!" I laugh, clutching our box. "Although I don't want to try another escape room soon. I'll leave it to Remy and Cam."

My arms are still a little wobbly, and my fingers slip on the box. I stumble on the last step.

Jack reaches out to steady me, his arms sliding around mine. "You were awesome."

Slowly, I steady myself, the fear of the escape room fading with the strange comfort of his touch.

His arms loosen. But I don't step away. Jack's eyes darken,

drinking me in. It's like we're back inside the escape room, but this time there's no game-over countdown.

And I shift forward, just a little closer.

His hand runs up my back, cupping my neck. His touch is gentle yet firm, sparking like magic.

I can't breathe. I can't breathe. I clutch at the box in my arms, wishing we'd never won this, because then there would be less space between the two of us.

We should talk about this. I should bring up reasons that this, whatever it is, won't work. But I can't seem to move away from his electrifying gaze, from the thrilling feel of his fingers weaving into my hair, the way our legs, our bodies, are pressing against each other.

I tilt my head up, and he breathes in, ever so slightly, like he's surprised. But there's a deep *want* in his eyes. Something that seems to speak the truth, drawing me closer.

And—

"What are you two doing here?" an angry voice snaps. "Why aren't you two at the booth?"

We slowly turn.

Mr. Yasuda stands in front of the crowd, his arms crossed and his eyes narrowed at us.

And behind him, my parents, Remy, and Cam stare at us in complete shock.

Chapter 25

I jump away from Jack. My face probably looks like I've drunk ghost pepper hot sauce; it feels like I did.

"Oh, you made it," Jack says. I glance over at him. He looks as composed as ever, as if he wasn't just holding me close.

As if he wasn't just looking at me like he wanted to kiss me.

I want to curse. Did he not feel anything in that moment? Was it all physical to him? Because it felt like something different, like his shields had finally dropped, like he was letting me in to see a part of him that he'd locked away for so long.

"I, uh, we entered a contest," I explained hurriedly. I shove the Escape Room box into Cam's arms.

"We knew this would be perfect for the two of you, so we couldn't pass up a chance to win this," Jack says with a grin. *That's right. It's for our siblings . . . not for us.*

"Whoa, is that really a full set of the thirty-minute escape rooms?" Remy squeals. I swear, I adore my sister. Her bubbly enthusiasm is putting a damper on the death-glare Mr. Yasuda is sending me and Jack.

"Yeah, I heard it was a limited-edition set," Jack says. "Better than wasting money on it, right? So Ellie and I had to work together. To get it for you two."

Had to work together . . . He makes those moments of him holding my hand sound like torture, doesn't he?

He'd told me he wanted to enter the contest to knock an item off my list. He made it seem like he was doing something for me.

Funny how his words change in front of his father.

Mr. Yasuda glances down at the box derisively and lets out a loud *harrumph.* "Well, Jack and I will take the first three hours at the booth. Then your family can take over."

My mom nods. "I've got a Lead Sorcerer meeting for a few hours, but I'll have Remy and Ellie take the next shift, and then we'll take the dinner shift," she says, motioning between herself and Dad.

"I can help during Remy's shift," Cam volunteers. "It's going to be busy around then."

"Fine," Mr. Yasuda barks. Then he turns on his heel. "Let's go, Jack."

Jack glances over at me, but it's another of his unreadable gazes. And before I know it, he heads off after his father. My parents disappear to their meeting, leaving me, Remy, and Cam on our own.

But I barely notice as my parents leave.

Instead, I watch Jack's broad shoulders disappear into the crowd, my heart feeling like it's dropping to the ground.

"The pact is over," I whisper. *And it didn't take him much time to change back to the Jack I don't know anymore.*

Then an elbow bumps into my side. "So?" Remy says. "*What* was that?"

I blink, my face ghost-pepper hot again. "Hmm?"

"The whole in-each-other's-arms thing?" Cam says, gesturing with his arms as if I've forgotten the name of that limb.

There's no way I'd ever forget his arms. The comfort, the sudden security of being with him, when everything else felt like chaos . . .

"Earth to Ellie?" Remy calls.

"Um, I had stumbled on the stairs." I motion at the stairway that's about fifteen feet away.

Cam frowns, looking concerned. "That was really a big stumble, then. Are you hurt?" To my shock, it sounds like he genuinely believes me. Which would explain a bit about why he and Remy have never been able to get together.

"*Oh my gosh*, it was not a stumble! Don't be so clueless," Remy groans. Cam only looks more confused.

"Well, I'm okay now," I say quickly. "Want to walk around the convention center more before we have to pick up our shift at the booth?"

Remy grins, momentarily distracted. "Sure! Let's go."

Remy, Cam, and I wander back to the booth, our hands heavy with samples and purchases. This retailers-only time slot has wrecked our wallets. Remy and Cam loaded up on more puzzles, including a 3D magical version that they spent nearly thirty minutes drooling over before they pooled their money together. I've got a tote bag filled with makeup samples and purchases for Lia, and a second bag of treats and magical toys for Mochi, who's back at the hotel, waiting for us to return.

There's a lull in foot traffic right now at the entrance, as the other retailers are heading back to their booths. It's right before the gates open to the public, so there aren't any customers at our booth, and Jack and his father have their backs to us as they rearrange the boxes to restock the front.

"You're spending time with *her* again?" Mr. Yasuda snaps in a low voice.

But, only five feet away, Remy, Cam, and I are close enough to hear. We freeze in confusion. We don't want to interrupt—

"It's not like that," Jack says, sounding weary. "We wouldn't be hanging out if it weren't for this punishment *you* came up with."

"This *punishment* is for you to remember that Charm-Works is our top priority," Mr. Yasuda growls. "She's no good for you. Not a good match. Spend too much time around poor folks like them, and it rubs off on you. We can't afford any distractions, especially not any like her."

"I know, I know. The Kobatas are too poor, and we need to do better than the competition," Jack says, a strange edge to his voice as he talks about *my* family. "I should spend time with someone richer, like Minami, right?"

"*What?*" I say, my voice shaky but loud, louder than I mean it to be.

I'm not good enough, I was never good enough . . . Nothing has changed. I really am a nobody, aren't I?

Jack spins around, eyes wide. He pales. "Ellie—"

I shake my head wordlessly, too shocked to speak. Remy and Cam gape between me and Jack.

"Too poor?" Remy echoes, her voice small.

Cam growls, "What the hell—"

"There's nothing you need to worry about," Mr. Yasuda says with an edge of panic; there's no magic to erase what we've overheard. "I'm taking care of it."

Then recognition flashes in Cam's eyes. "Wait, are we having money issues? Why haven't you told me?"

But Jack is only looking at me. He tries again, taking a step forward. "Ellie—wait, no—you misheard—"

"I think I heard clearly." My voice is a sharp whisper. "I'm not good enough like Minami, am I? My mom isn't a loaded venture capitalist, willing to invest in CharmWorks."

"That wasn't—"

"*My family* is not worthy enough for you. We don't meet the *income minimum*. I heard you, loud and clear. I *knew* better than to trust you again."

He rears back. Before he can utter another word—or another lie—I turn on my heels.

"You never told me," Cam is saying as I pass, looking stunned. "It isn't Mom's medical bills, is it?"

"You didn't need to know!" Mr. Yasuda is panicking, not that I care anymore.

"Why did you never tell me?" Cam's voice rises.

Jack pleads with his younger brother, "Wait, Cam, hear him out—"

My eyes are blinded with hot tears as I slip out of the convention center, leaving the Yasudas and their rising argument.

Jack's trying to talk down Cam, who's getting angrier by the second—and I've never seen levelheaded Cam upset.

I'm not the only one who Jack and his father have kept secrets from.

Remy catches up, wrapping her arm around me, and silently keeps me company as I walk out to my car, where I sit and cry.

Chapter 26

Am I supposed to feel this empty?

I should be glad. I should be glad that I know Jack is awful and deserving of every time I went the opposite direction of him, all throughout high school.

I should feel victorious, knowing I'm right. Knowing that I should've never trusted him again.

Instead, I stare up at the hotel ceiling, a slice of morning sunshine beaming through the crack in the curtains. I'm the shadow of that light, feeling like everything good has long since been forgotten or washed away.

There's a whine, and then Mochi pads over on her tiny paws. She leaps onto the bed, curling into a roll on the fluffy hotel blanket, her bright eyes gazing into mine.

"I thought things had changed," I whisper. "I thought he wasn't like his dad, not really. I thought I could believe in him—in *us*—again."

Mochi whines in commiseration and gnaws anxiously at her tail as if she wants to chew away all my bad feelings.

Jack had opened up from the quiet boy he'd become after his mother's death. The boy who'd ignored me, who'd acted as if my very presence had aggravated him. Talking, making amends over the road trip . . . It'd felt like I'd found one of my best friends again. But had it really been any different?

He hadn't let me in. He hadn't told me the truth.

Like he'd said, we'd been forced together as punishment, and he'd promised to see it through, so he had.

I had been a duty, a checklist item. Until he was sure he could keep his magic. Until he could go running back to Minami.

I groan, rolling over, and cover myself with the blanket. Mochi harrumphs from where I've displaced her and jumps off the bed.

Even my dog finds me too sad to be around.

I sigh, staring at the dark shadow world under my blanket, wishing I could fall asleep, wishing I could wipe away this past summer and start fresh, but there are some things even magic can't change.

~   ~

After hours of tossing and turning, someone sits on the edge of my bed. "Hey, sis."

I peek out. "Hey, Remy." My voice is gutted, raspy from crying.

She doesn't ask how I'm doing; with one look at my matted hair and puffy eyes, she can tell.

"I'm sick and tired of him. Isn't there some spell that will wipe him from my memory?"

"It would be easier, at least at first, but would it really be better if we forgot? Besides . . . I know you don't want to see him, but he wants to meet with you, to apologize."

"Why would he do that? I'm just some poor loser he was forced to hang out with," I growl. "Not that I care."

Remy widens her owlish eyes. "You should know . . . he talked to Cam. Told him everything."

"Everything?"

She nods, tipping her head down sadly. "You didn't hear it from me . . . but Mr. Yasuda didn't want Cam to know about their money issues."

"I don't want to hear about him." I've already heard too much. "I need your help," I say to Remy, switching the subject to something safer. "I need to get ready for my shift later. But I think I was on a shift with . . ."

I refrain from saying Jack's name.

"I'll take your shift," Remy says.

That's too tempting. "No, I need to work my hours. Or Mr. Yasuda will chew me out again. And the less I have to see him, too, the better. But it would be awesome if you or Cam switched with me."

"One of us can swap, and I'll get Cam to make sure Jack's not around when you head over," Remy says.

"Thanks," I manage a whisper. "You're the best sister."

"Your one and only," Remy shoots back with a grin. It hurts to see how much she's trying to cheer me up.

⁓ ⁓

During my shift with Remy, Cam sticks around. The two of them are monitoring me worriedly, which makes me feel bad. Out of anyone, Cam should be hurt.

During a lull between crowds, I turn to Cam, nudging him. "Are things okay between the two of you?"

Cam takes in a deep breath, rubbing his forehead with one hand. "We . . . Jack and I stayed up all night, talking things through. He's explained the situation—I was right, yesterday. Mom's bills still haven't been paid down." He shakes his head. "Expensive private insurance doesn't cover everything, apparently. I'd guessed and guessed, when Dad started pinching pennies here and there, but I'd never thought it was this bad. Dad took out a reverse mortgage on the shop and house, so . . . he's feeling the strain."

"Can I help?"

"No, don't worry," Cam says.

From my other side, Remy makes a sharp noise. "Don't worry? Of course we'd worry."

The wrinkle in Cam's forehead smooths out at that, and he shoots a sweet smile at my younger sister, so pure that it makes my heart ache. It's as if he only sees her in that moment. "Really, Remy. A year ago, I'd say let's worry together. But Jack's been helping Dad nearly every waking moment. He's pulled Dad almost completely out of the medical debt with his ways of streamlining the shop's profits, and his tennis lessons and tutoring."

"I didn't know he did tutoring, too," I say in surprise.

"Oh, yeah," Cam says, looking confused. "I thought you knew."

I shake my head. "Your brother's still a mystery to me."

"What's a mystery is how he's managed to secure talks with a venture capitalist," Cam says with a touch of awe.

Now that's a mystery I can solve. Cam doesn't need to

know about what a two-faced heartbreaker his brother is. But to me, it's obvious—because he strings Minami along like he did me, just so he can have an in with her venture capitalist mother.

Then I remember the truth. I'm the only one he's strung along.

To him, *Minami* is the real thing. She's Mr. Yasuda-approved, and her family has the funds to make a difference for the Yasudas' future.

"Jack doesn't want me to help him, even though I *want* to," Cam continues with a sigh. Then his face clears. "But he and I have agreed. I'll be helping with the shop more from now on, picking up shifts and helping Dad with inventory and things like that. And he and Dad will keep me in the loop about what's going on, especially with the possible investor. I should've been part of things earlier, but it's never too late to start."

"That's good," Remy says, echoing my thoughts. "And if you need help, I can pick up shifts, too, when the two of you are busy."

"Speaking of being busy . . . we should probably restock before our dads manage the booth," Cam says, patting the boxes of enchanted Indian spices. He grabs a heavy box on his own, but Remy stubbornly steps forward, lifting the other side, and he shoots her another grateful smile. This would be disgusting if they weren't so perfectly, awfully cute together.

It's nearing the end of my shift when I sigh in relief. No Jack. Perfect. I'll just have to figure out a way to avoid him for the next two days of the convention. Maybe Cam and Remy can swap shifts with me if I'm paired with him.

But as I hand a bag of CharmWorks stationery and my parents' green tea over to a customer, a husky voice calls, "Ellie?"

I freeze.

Cam swears under his breath. "Dammit, Ellie, I'm sorry, he wasn't supposed to come back."

"It's okay. I don't trust a word he says, so I'm not surprised he lied to you, either."

Jack appears through the crowd, his eyes stuck on me. "Ellie—"

Cam steps in front of me. "She doesn't want to talk to you."

"Please, let me talk to her." Jack nods toward the doors. "Ellie, can we go outside?"

Cam squares his shoulders, protectively standing between me and Jack, and Remy worriedly takes a step forward. I can't let the brothers fight because of me, and not in public. Already, a few people are glancing over curiously.

I study Jack.

I can see the bags under his eyes. The weight on his shoulders. A gaunt look to his flat lips, the way his fists clench at his sides. "I want to apologize—"

"There's nothing to apologize for. I'd have to be hurt, first." But my voice is stiff and harsh, a pure giveaway.

Jack's eyes are pained. "I'm really, really sorry—"

"You said that I—that my family is too poor for you."

Clearly, I'm doing a bad job of showing I'm not hurt. Anger and frustration seem to leak out of me; his fists may be clenched, but my nails cut into my palms sharply, leaving indents that will take time to fade.

"Please, Ellie, I . . . I have so much I need to explain to you, so much to make up to you. Come outside for a little bit?"

He gestures outside, where the sky is so blue and perfect, like nothing has ever broken.

A place that should be a whole different summer, a place that reminds me of how I was mending the pain of these past years, only to have my feelings explode again yesterday.

My logical, smart head screams, *Run*.

There's no reason for us to talk. No reason for excuses or explanations. I heard loud and clear: he's just near me for the convention, because it's his punishment. He doesn't want to be around me because my family's tea shop doesn't make enough money. Minami or the other well-off girls in Palo Alto are a better match.

There are a million reasons to turn away.

But my traitor heart won't let me leave.

Chapter 27

I lean against the railing of the convention center balcony. This area is tucked away from the main entrance, so it's empty.

Except for Jack and me.

I study the clouds forming in the sky behind him, feeling the sticky humidity of the air brush against my face. Peering at the surfers in the ocean, the security guard walking the perimeter, the trickle of people parking and heading into the convention center. Looking anywhere but directly at Jack.

Cam and Remy had been worried about me, but I'd told them I was fine. Even so, they'd shot pointed glares at Jack.

And I am fine. I'm a walking mess, but I'll be fine.

I think.

Jack hovers in front of me, five feet away, and then he shifts as if he wants to take a step closer.

I narrow my eyes at him, mentally threatening to bite his head off. He stays on his side of the balcony.

"Ellie," he says. He takes a deep breath. Then he pauses. Stops. Breathes again.

It's that damn thoughtful way he has of thinking things through before he blurts something out. But it just rags on my patience.

"Look, spit it out so we can get this over with. So I can go." That heavenly soft hotel blanket is calling me. Mochi will cuddle around my shoulders. Hiding away in my bed is the safest.

"I've missed you."

I stop breathing for a split second.

That's not what he's supposed to say.

He's supposed to tell the truth, how he agreed with his father about how I'm not worthy, how he's lied to me, how Minami is his girlfriend and he's going to have a family dinner with her venture capitalist mother, how—

"That's a little late," I whisper, my heart speaking before my mind can shut it down. Then I clamp my lips together.

"We used to be best friends . . . and I never explained why I disappeared."

I close my eyes. This isn't just about an argument with his father in front of me. It's about years past.

But hasn't it always been?

Hasn't the way we fell apart colored every interaction between us, like magnets that pushed each other away every time we drew near? "I've made a lot of mistakes," he says. "And I owe you a million apologies. Back then . . . after Mom passed away—Dad was hit with all those bills, and I was freaking out, thinking we'd lose him to depression, to being overwhelmed, if I didn't figure out a way to help him. I did all sorts of things to scrape together money. I started selling our store's inventory on Magizon, on Amazon, on eBay. I began tennis lessons and SAT tutoring in any free hour. . . . That was all I could focus on. We'd lost Mom. Cam and I couldn't lose Dad, too. But I lost something incredibly important in all of that."

He takes a deep breath. "I lost you."

My heart longs to hold him close again, but I can't give in. I can't give in, only to get hurt by him again.

"I was never yours to lose," I shoot back.

"You weren't," he agrees, his voice jagged. "No matter how much I wished you could be by my side. But it hurt back then, too. After Mom died, being with you reminded me of *her*. All those good memories . . . everything I've been remembering about our friendship throughout this trip—it was overwhelming to face when Mom wasn't there anymore. And my new friends, they didn't know much about Mom, they didn't know what I was really like . . . You didn't deserve that. You never deserved that. That's why I had to stop being friends with the one person who knew me the best. I couldn't hide my feelings from you."

"So it was easier to hurt me instead." My fingers curl into my palms, sharp and reminding me that his words are real, this pain is real, no matter how much I don't want it to be. "You couldn't have said something? *Anything* would have been better than ignoring me completely. Better than making me face everyone else as a loser, rejected by you, my best friend through all the years we'd grown up together."

"I know I messed up. I knew it every day we weren't together," he whispers.

I lean back against the railing of the balcony, feeling the

metal press into the thin fabric of my T-shirt. It hurts, but nothing close to the way my heart aches.

"I didn't want to take your high school life away from you, Ellie. I know you care, you care so much. I know you would've been at my side, supporting me as I tried to work through losing Mom. You didn't deserve to be bogged down with . . . with all of this." Jack takes a deep breath.

I can't speak. I close my eyes, trying to catch my breath that's gone jagged, sharp. I was expecting excuses and reasonings that wouldn't tell me anything real at all. Not this quiet softness. Not these barefaced truths.

My eyes fly open, digging for the painful reality. The reminders of why I want to be "lost" to him, forever. The reasons why I can't forgive him, no matter what sweet excuses he has for the past. "You told your father I wasn't good enough for you."

"I lied, Ellie," Jack says. "My dad . . . he makes comments all the time like that. He's never been the same after Mom passed. Mom was his light. His everything. And even though her passing doesn't mean that he—or I—get a free pass or anything, it really has hurt him, changed him. So sometimes I just have to pretend to agree, even though I know it's wrong. I would never think that."

I shake my head, making a noise of disbelief. "That's strong, coming after what you just said."

"Really," he says. "I know I've screwed up time and time again, but ever since the road trip brought us back together . . . things have been different. Better. Happier. I don't think I've laughed or smiled in these past five years as much as on this trip with you, Ellie."

"But you were the one who stopped talking to me, after your mom passed." My words are cold, but they're the truth.

Jack drags his hands over his eyes, takes a deep breath.

"I . . . I hate being a burden on anyone," he says, achingly quiet. "That's why I'm working on my own, outside of Dad's shop, to tutor and give tennis lessons. I'm trying to pay for my own way to college, because I don't want to burden my dad. So that he and I will be able to scrape together something to send Cam to college, later. CharmWorks is doing great . . . on the surface. Our margin of profit is thinner than an omamori charm, and that's why Dad is so happy Minami's mom is interested in investing in us. But I screwed up and pushed away the people—the person who had been by my side when I was younger, the person who accepted me as I was."

"You could have told me what was going on."

"I screwed up. I should've trusted you. I should've known better, but I was too tunnel-visioned on the next way to help Dad. It was easier to forget Mom, to forget . . . to forget everything that made me happy."

I close my eyes, his words too hard for me to bear looking at him. "Does Minami make you happy?"

"Minami?" He sounds confused. "Because of the investment?"

"Your phone calls. I mean, since you're dating."

Jack pauses. "That . . . Ellie . . . I'm *tutoring* her for the SATs at the end of August."

I blink in surprise. Suddenly, it clicks. Cam had mentioned Jack was busy tutoring . . . but I'd never realized his student was *Minami*.

"She's just a student," he says.

"A student whose mother is investing in CharmWorks? Seems like a little more than just a student to me." I stare him down, searching his face for the truth that I don't want to see. "Especially since your father wants you to date her."

"It's complicated." His voice is sharp and sad. "Ellie, is there . . . a chance? That, somehow, you can forgive me?"

I dig my nails into my palm. My eyes burn from unshed tears. But I won't let him see me cry. I refuse to let him see how much this really hurts me. Because, no matter how this tears me apart, I don't want to get hurt like this again.

Slowly, I shake my head. "I forgive you, but we can't go back to what we were. I honestly can't trust you again, Jack. You should date Minami. It's better for your future. Better for CharmWorks. Better for everyone. Better for me."

"It may be better for CharmWorks," he says, "but I don't think it's better for me."

I shake my head. I can't give in, not this time. I don't want to feel this same pain ever again.

"Please, Ellie, forgive me," he says, so earnest my chest throbs with a deep pain.

If I speak, my tears will fall. If I speak, my heart will never be able to recover.

The silence stretches out between us. *You could patch this up*, my heart cries. *You could fix this, if you weren't so scared of getting hurt. You could say the truth, if you just stopped hiding who you want to be.*

But I don't want to get hurt anymore.

Finally, he says, "I think we were supposed to break down

the booth together, at the end of the day tomorrow. You don't have to worry about that. I'll take care of it on my own. It's . . . the last thing I can do for you."

I jerk my head in a nod.

He doesn't move for a minute or two, as if studying me, as if seeing if there's some way I might forgive him. But I don't move, and eventually he breathes out, long and sad, and turns away.

I can hear each footstep, echoing in my ears as he walks away, back into the convention center, and out of my life.

And when he's finally gone, I press my forehead into my arms, and I cry in the deafening silence.

Chapter 28

I can stay in this hotel room for the rest of this trip. I'll be that weird aunt still living in her parents' attic, cackling and making weird magic to support my boring life. Only Remy, Cam, Mochi, and my parents will remember I exist.

I'll be nobody. A wallflower to the twentieth degree.

Exactly who I've always been.

Everything I've never wanted to be.

I wrap my blanket around my shoulders, but it's not enough to comfort me. So, even in the heat of summer, I burrito myself in the soft pillowy blanket. It's burning hot, but I desperately need its comfort.

There's a knock on the connecting door, and Dad pops his head in.

"How's my sunshine doing?" he says. "Want some barley tea?"

I feel nothing like sunshine. And I don't want a drop of Dad's special comfort-infused tea or whatever he and Mom have been trying to feed me. I doubt, really, that it would be enough magic to make me feel better.

I grunt, shaking my head, and my dad closes the door with the faintest of sighs.

I've been taking my shifts at the booth—none of them with Jack, thankfully. But after each shift, I walk the mile to our hotel and throw myself back into the bed, hanging out with Mochi.

From time to time, I pull out that bottle of luck from Cam. Should I use it?

My heart lifts at the idea of something that can just make things better, instantly.

But each time, I toss it back into my pocket. No amount of magic or luck will save me from being a mess. From being a wallflower. I'd need to bathe in the Pacific Ocean filled with luck to change things for me.

My parents and Remy have been trying, sweetly, to cheer me up. But I feel stuck, no matter how many mugs of comfort-tea they try to push onto me or how much they try to cajole me to go out into the world for a normal dinner.

Because nothing feels normal anymore, and I don't know how to fix things . . . or even what "fix" means anymore.

෨ ෨

That evening, I'm drifting into a restless sleep when my door rattles, like someone's shaking it. "Ellie, are you moping around in there?"

"No . . . way . . ." I blurt out, rubbing at my eyes and sitting up.

"Oh, good, you're awake," the familiar, smooth-as-velvet voice calls. The lock buzzes; whoever it is, they have the right card key. And then the door bursts open.

My mouth drops open as my best friend (or is Lia my ex–best friend now?) walks through the door, her eyes set on me, waggling the card key. She's dressed to kill, with shorts on her curvy legs, a ruby V-neck T-shirt, and lipstick that perfectly matches. Her eyeliner is in sharp, Lia-like daggers.

She slings off her mini backpack and crosses her arms. "So."

"Lia—what are you doing here?" I whisper. Is this a bad dream where all of my regrets from the summer come to torture me?

"The benefit of being magic-aware is that I got to come visit my cousins *and* check out this convention. But that's not why I'm here," Lia says. "We're going out."

"It's almost eight, Mom and Dad won't—"

"Your parents are okay with it."

"Really?"

Lia strides to the connecting door. "Mr. Kobata? Mrs. Kobata?" Then she disappears into the other room, and I hear a rumble of my dad's voice and my mom's higher-pitched murmurs.

Moments later, she pops back in, grinning. "Let's go. No curfew tonight."

I splutter. I want to stay in my sheets and wallow in my sorrows. Going outside sounds cold and uninviting and isn't Lia mad at me and what if I bump into Jack and—

Lia pokes me in the forehead. "Stop those shy-girl thoughts."

Ouch. That hurts.

She peels the blankets off of me, and I groan. Then she switches over to my duffel bag, pulls out a pair of denim shorts, a shirt, and a bra, and slings them over, with the bra landing square on my face.

"Get dressed by the time I get back," she says. I cover my head with the blanket as she smacks the night table with a loud thump, as if refusing to let me go back to sleep. "I'm going to give you five minutes, and if you're not dressed by then, I'll wrap you in a blanket and throw you over my shoulder, firewoman-style."

Before I can protest, she strides to the connecting door and shuts it behind her.

In the first minute, I stare up at the ceiling, longing for peace and quiet and solitude.

In the second minute, I swaddle myself tightly in my blanket, trying to burrito myself into oblivion. Maybe she won't notice me if I hide.

In the third minute, I grumble at Lia, who's chatting with my parents. Her voice rises, and I can hear, "Yeah, I want to take her out to get some fresh air."

And my traitor father says, "Great, great, she needs it. We've all missed you."

In the fourth minute, I'm peeking warily over the blanket at the door and at the pile of clothes that have slid onto the floor.

That's when I notice what Lia's stuck onto the nightstand: *The Anti-Wallflower List.*

It's a photocopied version of the list.

The dreams that I had for this summer. All because I didn't want to hide away anymore.

And what am I doing now?

Hiding.

In the fifth minute, I'm scrambling to change.

As I rummage through my duffel bag for my black hoodie, a small coin rolls out. Fleurie's charm.

The moment that my hand brushes the metal, I close my fingers so I don't have to see it flash with that certain shade of blue. What a hoax. As if a coin can really show compatibility.

The trash can is only a few feet away. . . .

There's a knock on the door. My time's up.

Quickly, I toss the coin back into the side pocket of my bag and throw on my shorts.

When the door opens again, framing Lia in the center, my parents hovering behind her shoulders, I stand up.

I can't ignore the flash of surprise in her face as she takes in the fact that I'm fully dressed. Then, her eyes widen further as she notices the new piercing in my ear. Despite the voice screaming inside of me that cuddling in blankets all by myself is better than going out, I take a step forward and give her a tiny smile. "I'm ready."

                                                              ∽   ∽

Lia and I walk down the road to the Huntington Beach Pier. At eight o'clock, most of the houses have turned off their lights. It's peaceful and quiet, but the air is stiflingly humid.

"I think it's going to rain," Lia says, frowning up at the night sky. "The weather forecast shows clear skies for tomorrow, but I still think there's going to be a summer storm, even if it's just a flash spot of rain."

"Um . . . are we—are you really . . ." I look down, and hastily zip the fly on my denim shorts. Maybe it's a smarter tactic to keep our conversation off me and how I'm a walking mess. "What have you been up to?"

"Classes, mostly," Lia says. "There are courses up in San Francisco that I've been taking, with other people that are just starting to learn about magic. It's cool, even though everyone else is basically in love, and I'm one of the few single ones. There's one other girl our age, though, from Menlo Park. Her mom is about to remarry, and her fiancé's magic-aware or whatever you call it, so she's being brought into the loop. And I've been talking to Ana about magic, and she's been a huge help, too."

We walk onto the pier, faint lamplights illuminating the concrete. At this time of night, especially with the dark clouds overhead, the pier's nearly empty except for a dad and his daughter, laughing as the dad shows her how to fish.

At the end of the pier, Lia stops and grins wickedly. "We're out beyond what's supposed to be your curfew, at a beach—and I think I have something that you might like, too."

"Wait . . ." I whisper as she slings her mini backpack off of her shoulders

She grins at me. "Don't tell me you've already knocked this off your list?"

I thought the weather was sticky, like going-to-rain humid. But maybe it's the moisture in my eyes.

Number 10: Sneak onto the beach for midnight s'mores.

She unfolds the blanket she's been carrying under one arm,

snaps it open with a flourish, and lets it float to the ground. Kicking off her sandals, she sits down, patting the spot next to her.

This feels like a dream I've magicked into reality, like our friendship breakup never happened. And so, like old times, I slide off my sandals and join her. Close, but not as close as before. But I've missed her so much, and this feels comfortingly good.

Familiar and strange, new and old, all at the same time.

But good.

Lia pulls a pastel-pink paper bag out of her backpack. "I brought some Honey & Butter."

"What is that?"

"The name of the best macaron shop in Orange County, California," Lia says. "All of California, if you ask me. My favorite are their giant s'mores macarons." She flashes the contents: two huge macarons, each filled with torched marshmallow, a layer of a spiced cookie, and a hint of chocolate cream. Aka, what dreams are made of.

Damn. It really feels way too humid now. My eyes sting.

"Watch this." She grabs a plastic box labeled *Instant Heat: Freshly Toasted* from her backpack. Then she puts the pink paper bag inside the plastic box and gives it a light shake.

A puff of white smoke fills the box. After it clears, she pulls out a macaron the size of my palm.

"Now, enjoy my favorite s'mores macaron, warm as if we'd just toasted the marshmallows over a fire. I can't start a bonfire on the pier, but now, with what you've given me, I can bring the flames to you." Lia winks, placing the macaron in my hand, and pulling out another for herself.

The giant macaron is toasty warm. My throat feels like I've swallowed it whole, though. Even though Lia had fought against the very idea of spells and enchantments the last time we'd talked . . . now, my magic-aware best friend has used a charm—willingly—for me.

"Try it," she says. "We have a hell of a lot to talk about, but macarons, *first*."

I nibble on a corner. The shell crumbles with just the right amount of sweetness, and the marshmallow melts in my mouth. "This is heaven on earth." As much as I would normally devour the macaron in one bite, this time, I can't stop glancing over at Lia. *Why is she here? Is she still angry?*

Lia laughs. "Right? Who knew that macarons could be this good? It's almost like magic."

Magic.

That word falls heavily between us.

It's out in the open now. The pier lights flicker, and I can't quite breathe. I set the macaron aside, twisting the napkin in my hands.

Then the words come tumbling out. "I'm sorry, Lia."

There's a million other things I want to blurt out. *I'm sorry. Please forgive me. I wish I could stop your pain. I want to give you a hug. I want to see you laugh and smile. I messed up, bad. Please tell me how to make things up to you—*

"I know."

Her response is so soft and gentle, so unlike her usual tone, that I startle.

Lia's dark eyes are studying me, looking at my ear piercing, how my hair is a mess, the tear tracks dried on my cheeks.

"I know," she repeats with a hint of her usual strength.

"I get it now, why you couldn't share this secret. I knew deep down that you wouldn't ever hurt me on purpose, but my denial and fear made me lash out."

She pauses, then adds, "I'm sorry that I disappeared on you. I needed time to think things through."

I breathe out. The weight on my chest shifts, like those worries are floating away into the sky.

"I'll always be around, even if you disappear," I say. "Even if you need more time."

We study each other tentatively, and for a split second, it's exactly like that moment in middle school, where she was deciding whether to sit next to me at lunch.

Then Lia's ruby lips tip into a wicked smile, and with a jolt, I realize she's using the lip stain that I sent her from the magical village, and I grin back at her.

"Me? Need more time?" she asks. "You know I'm not going to spend forever making a decision. Life moves too fast to wait around. I decided years ago that you're my best friend, and that's not changing. I stick by my decisions."

I lean into her shoulder. "And so do I."

This time, we've chosen—together—that we want to sit next to each other. That we want to be best friends, despite the ups and downs. No—*through* the ups and downs.

Then she grins. "So, what's this argument going on between you and Jack?" Lia asks, taking a bite of the macaron. She groans in delight. "Damn, these are the best, right? Anyway, Remy reached out to me because she was worrying about you, and that's why I came to find you."

My heart clenches.

"I'm mad at him." Below us, waves slap against the pier

as we devour our s'mores, and I explain to Lia about the road trip and how we'd been stuck together as a punishment. The unexpected—but maybe expected since it's *him*—things he said to me. And Minami, and how Mr. Yasuda only approves of her. "It makes me so *angry* whenever I think about him."

My explanation is messy, and that dad and daughter who were fishing are long since gone. It's me and Lia and the waves. She's been listening intently, nudging me to speak here and there, asking questions, but mostly just listening.

But now I want to hear from her. "What do you think? Stupid, right? I should forget about him."

"Forget about him?" She snorts.

"Yeah, like, there's no worth in worrying about him."

Her eyeliner is pointed and sharp as she narrows her eyes. "Did you forget about me when we fought and went our separate ways?"

"No way!" I say. "I've missed you every day, Lia."

She grins. "I've missed you, too."

I float in those words.

Then Lia adds, "But I think . . . he misses you, too. A lot."

"Ugh." I cover my eyes with my hand, blotting out the night sky above us. The world around me fades into black. "I hate thinking about him. Plus, if there's anyone he's missing, I bet it's Minami."

"It's not Minami," Lia says wryly. "She sent out an Instagram Story asking for SAT tutor recommendations last night. And her mom's company just announced they're investing in some other stationery chain. According to Cam, Mr. Yasuda's *pissed*, but he'll get over it."

Oh. All I see is the shadow from my hand, the darkness of everything broken.

Then she adds, "The fact that you feel so much about Jack—that it hurts so much—it means something, doesn't it?"

"But it *shouldn't* hurt, not like this." I fold both hands over my eyes, slipping into complete pitch-black.

"That's true. I don't want you to hurt, ever. But fights happen. If he has the ability to hurt you, doesn't it mean he's somehow, kind of . . . on your mind? In your heart? The depth of your friendship goes far beyond a summer road trip. Those years you two had together as the best of friends, I'm sure as hell gonna hope that means something. And the way you told me he used to act—that's how Remy and Cam say he's acting right now. I'd say trash him if he's acting like trash, but . . . I think the Jack you knew never really left.

"Some friends are here for a day, a weekend. And you learn something from those friends, for sure. Some friendships are toxic, and you have to walk away. But there's some friendships even if you've been away from each other for days, a few months—even if it's been years—when you two meet again, it's like you two never missed a step. *Those* are the friendships worth fighting for. Because a friendship that doesn't have some rough patches isn't really that real, it's just a suck-up contest."

I peek through my fingers at her. "Are you speaking from personal experience? Because you still adore me?"

"I think that's maybe like you and Jack."

I can't wrap my head around what that means about me and Jack. Even though . . . *Ugh.*

Lia gives me a knowing grin, as if she knows what I'm

thinking. "Like you and me, too, obviously. I'm always in your heart."

"Even if you try to wiggle away." I wrap my arms around her and squeeze her tight.

She laughs, but leans her head on my shoulder and goes still. "Really, though," she whispers, "isn't life too short to do anything but chase what you want?"

I nod, even though she can only feel me, not see me. "I know. That's why I made that cursed list of thirteen wishes."

"Cursed?"

"I mean, it made you and me drift apart, it made me stuck with damn Jack for an entire damn road trip . . ."

"It is *not* cursed," Lia says. "Okay, maybe those stinking mice were cursed, but not your list. Your list is full of dreams and hopes, and that's only full of charm—anything but curses. It's a charmed list, I swear."

"I dunno." I shake my head, trying to clear it.

"You'll see," Lia says confidently. "You'll change your mind. After all, even through the chaos, we're here, aren't we? Checking off another item on your list, back together?"

I look around, blinking at the blanket beneath us, the stars peeking out from behind the thick clouds, the faint sweetness of the s'mores macaron on my lips. My heart feels like she shook it in the warming box. I clear my throat. "You're the *best* of all best friends."

"Damn right, I am!" Lia laughs throatily, just as a few sprinkles of rain start misting our faces. She pushes off the blanket. "But we'll probably have to get back fast. This feels like it's going to be a summer storm, and we're going to get drenched if we stay here any longer."

She reaches out her hand to help me up, but I'm already standing, folding the blanket. Instead, she loops her arm into mine, like old times, and I laugh, a feeling of freedom and joy welling up in my chest. Lia's back at my side, finally.

This easiness between us feels right. Like we've never been apart—almost. But I've learned and she's learned in the time we've been away from each other, and we've both grown a little, on our own.

We stroll arm in arm, until the sprinkles turn into a full-out rain, and we end up dashing back to the hotel, laughing and catching up along the way.

Chapter 29

I stare out the window long after Lia leaves to head back to her cousins' house. Rain splatters the glass, and when I touch it, fog forms around my fingers.

Remy and Cam are huddled around the tiny desk, busily working on another puzzle they've bought from the convention. And Mochi's hanging out with my parents as they watch an action flick together in the room next door.

Neither of them notice when I slip out onto the balcony, the sound of rain thrumming harder than ever, the spray misting my face.

It's a lonely night. Back at home, I would be able to see if Jack was around if his light was on. . . . But here, I can't see where he is. And I've cut off all communication with him.

"What should I do?" I whisper, as if the stormy skies might help.

The rain keeps pouring down, without an answer.

Even though I already know.

Whether it would have been dry or raining, Jack wouldn't

have given up on breaking down the booth, not when he'd already committed himself to it.

Back in the hotel room, I rummage through the side pocket of my duffel bag when my hand brushes against a small, cold piece of metal, and I draw it out.

Fleurie's charmed coin. I'd laughed at it then, but . . .

I open my hand to see it blaze a cerulean blue as vivid as a cloudless sky. The same exact blue as Jack's coin. As bright as those mornings in recess, when we'd have our honeysuckle days. Back when life was simple, back when I thought I'd known him . . .

I do know Jack, after all. Some things haven't changed.

I'd hated him for his loyalty, but it's one of the things that makes Jack truly Jack. That he cares so much about the people around him. I remember the desperate look in his eyes as he did everything he could to get me to understand his father, his family's debts, his need to take care of his father in his mother's absence.

The logical part of me understood everything he was saying. The logical part agreed and wanted to give him another chance.

But I'd been too caught up in my emotions, too caught up in doubt and worries.

This, it's not just him.

That . . . maybe I have to trust what he says.

And if this is about us—I have to show I care, too.

I can't hide my secrets anymore. Not when it feels like they're stealing my breath, not when these truths feel like they're consuming me.

Realization fills me, certain as the rain pouring down. It's my time to stop being such a damn nobody. Hiding from what I really want.

Just because I can't talk about magic, it doesn't mean that I can't be *me*. Because there's more to me than a spell or charm. Because I'm more than that. I'm the girl who's Lia's best friend. I'm Remy's best—and only—sister. I had surgery at three damn weeks old and I'm a survivor. I'm calm and resilient when people comment about my scar. There's so much more to me than what any of them see, and they're not the kind of people whose opinions I care about.

But there is one person I do care about. The person who held my hand as I cried getting shots, the person I care about when he's calling someone else. The way it hurts when I think of the possibility that he might be better with someone else. Because I want to be the best me, for me. And for him, too.

Now, it's my time to step forward.

But I cling to my blankets, like they're my safety net. Like . . .

But if I stay stuck in my room, I'm going to still be the same shy girl that I was at the start of the summer, the same wallflower I made a whole list about, to change.

I'm so scared to move.

I have to break free of all the doubts swirling around in my head. I have to see him again. To fix things between us.

I have to break down the walls I've put up around myself— and step forward.

I look longingly at the sweet, soft comfort of my bed. "Hey, Remy, Cam . . . would you know where Jack is?"

My sister's jaw drops as if I've asked her if she's in love with Cam. "Jack? Why?"

"He's still loading up the car," Cam says. "So that you can drive back tomorrow. He wanted to get it done for you."

My heart wrenches. I grab my hoodie. "I've got to go. I'll be back soon."

෬ ෬

I walk down the empty street, the rain still sprinkling down. My cotton hoodie doesn't protect me, but I barely notice.

I turn the corner to the Huntington Beach Convention Center. I wave at the guard, flashing my exhibitor badge at her. She nods, letting me walk through, and I slide the badge back into my pocket. My hands are too shaky to hold it.

There're only a few trucks and cars loading up now; most are probably waiting for tomorrow, for the rain to let up.

I go into the atrium and pause. A lean, tall figure is working on the breakdown of our booth, the hood of his jacket long since fallen off, his hair already drenched, but there's something so detached about his motions, as if he just doesn't care.

Jack loads a set of boxes onto a hand truck and carts it out the exhibitor door toward my Camry.

But there's a bump, and he has to steady the cart, though the tower wavers.

My boots splash through a puddle and I'm there to catch the top box from falling. Carefully, I lift it into my arms. "I can take this one."

Jack freezes. His hands clench the metal poles. His messy hair covers his eyes.

"You don't have to help," he says, his voice low. "I can finish this."

"It takes one person at least five hours to break the booth

down on their own," I say. "It's past eleven. You'd finish at one, at the earliest. It's raining, it's—"

"I know it's not easier with just one person," he says. "But I don't want anyone . . . I don't want *you* to get hurt, Ellie."

The way he breathes out my name, like it's something special, makes my throat tight.

"I really am sorry," he says quietly. "And I understand that you don't . . . you don't believe in me."

The rain keeps pouring down on my hoodie, the fabric not thick enough to keep water off my face. I pull it off, letting the cold droplets splatter me, making me feel raw and new.

Then I set the box back down on the pile and take a step closer.

"I believe in you. I believed in you then, and I believe in you now." And then I take one last step forward, breaking that last wall and wrap my arms around him.

I can feel him let out a soft breath, as if he'd been holding too much in, too many worries, too many thoughts, all on his own. Maybe we're all boxed up by walls, caught up in untruths that hold us anchored to all the wrong things. But we need each other, we need other people to show us the light, and help us break through those barriers.

I need to believe in myself; Jack needs someone to believe in him.

"I'm here for you," I say firmly.

His breath shudders in his chest, and I hold him tighter, hoping my words will reach him.

Finally, his arms shift, and for a second I think he's going to push me away. But his hands move, and he wraps them around my shoulders.

Through the cold of the rain, his warmth is steady and pure, and all Jack.

I'd drawn his hands all this trip, hiding my phone so he wouldn't see. But I couldn't stop thinking about him. It's always been Jack who has been on my mind, even through all these years we were apart.

I rest my forehead against his chest, finally breathing out steadily for the first time in ages.

He whispers, "I've missed you."

It's only been a few days since we last talked, but I know he doesn't mean that span of time. He means the years that stretched out between the sadness of his mother's death, the years where we'd drifted apart, only to find each other again. Years of missed moments that we'll have to catch up on, starting with now.

I nod and whisper back, "I've missed you, too."

A set of guards walk past, talking loudly, and we break apart.

"You should get back inside," Jack says. He gently brushes away the damp hair sticking to my forehead. As I look back up at him, wonder fills his eyes, with a hint of disbelief, as if he still doesn't believe this moment could ever be real. As if he expects me to disappear. "It's too wet out."

I want to melt into his touch. "I . . . I'm not leaving you alone," I say fiercely. "Whether it's your family stuff or even if you're really busy with tutoring or tennis lessons and sometimes just need someone to hang out with as a breather, I'm not going to run away anymore."

And to myself, I promise, *I'm not going to miss what's in front of me.*

Not this time, and not ever again.

My lips curve up and, finally, I say, "Want to break this booth down?"

        ❧   ❧

A few hours later, we've packed the last box into the car.

"All done," I say as the trunk clicks shut.

His eyes drop to mine, and he doesn't break his gaze as he says, "Not everything, not yet."

"Yeah . . . I guess I do have to drive back. But . . . I have something to show you." I pull out my phone, my hand shaking slightly. "I did it."

I turn my phone screen to him. *Public Account.*

I'm sharing my drawings with the world. It doesn't matter if a bunch of people see them or even no one at all, but it matters to *me* that I'm no longer hiding.

Jack's eyes widen as he scrolls through my Instagram posts. "Ellie . . ." He pauses on a doodle I did of his hand, scar and all, and he smiles, looking between his real hand and the hand on the screen. "It was me after all, wasn't it?"

"Yeah," I admit. "I know I got mad at you, but I've been hiding too much of my own self, too. But I'm trying. I refuse to be invisible anymore."

Jack looks up, his gaze burning into mine, fierce and protective. "You're bright and charming and beautiful and anything but invisible to me."

I swallow.

"When I walk into a room, I see you," he says. "It's always been that way, from when we were kids, to when we didn't talk much, to now. I always see you first, and to me, you light up the room in color."

Words escape me. But I don't want to stay hidden anymore. So I run my hands down his arms, until our fingers meet and entwine.

Maybe I don't have to talk, sometimes.

Not when I pull him closer, so we're finally face-to-face, and one of his arms wraps around my lower back. I'm holding him around his waist, breathing in deep. Breathing in the scent of summer rain and green tea and just-washed laundry.

Breathing in the scent of Jack.

But then he looks at me, and I can't breathe.

He pulls me closer, and I lean my head on his chest, letting the steady bumps of his heartbeat erase the pain. As I hold him, my fingers curling around the cloth of his T-shirt, my heart fills with emotions that I'm only now beginning to understand the depth of.

We've been so far apart for so long and I need him close, to tell him that I don't want to ever let him go.

It's as if he hears my thoughts. Jack leans down, his lips brushing against my ear, sending shock waves down my body. "I've missed you, Ellie."

"I've missed you too, Jack. More than just this summer, I've missed being friends with you these past years."

"And I want to make up for that, today and every day after that," he whispers, his voice low and husky. "Will you let me?"

I nod into his chest, wrapping my arms tighter around him, and a tiny smile begins to tug at my lips. I'm no longer a wallflower, and I'm starting to realize that maybe my life—my world—has started to bloom after all. "I can't believe we've finished the convention and we're already heading back. I feel like I've checked off something major from my list."

"Speaking of checklists," he says, "I've been thinking . . ."

"I know," I say wryly. "I was just telling Lia—I think I wrote my bucket list on some cursed paper or something."

He tilts his head to the side. "Cursed? I don't think so."

I laugh. "Okay, fine. Tell me, how's it *not* cursed?"

He pulls me closer. "Because of this . . ." Jack slides his hands around my neck and tilts my chin up. "Because of your list, we found each other again."

The feeling of his calloused fingers—holding me ever so gently—stops my breath. "I can't argue against that."

"And we'll make new lists. Magical lists that *don't* involve revenge on me," he says.

"You have to help me finish this summer's list first."

"Is that a challenge?" he asks, and with a flip of my stomach, I *know* we're both thinking about what's remaining on my list. "We've got this whole road trip back up to make plans to knock off more items—"

He keeps talking about my list, moving his hands in small circles around my upper back, making goosebumps rise with every brush of his fingers.

I want his touch. Not in the way I want to check off an item on my list, but because of something more, because of the way I feel around him, the way he makes my heart spark with happiness, better than any spell.

I tilt my chin upward, my eyes meeting Jack's, and his words suddenly die out. There're so many emotions teeming in his eyes—all emotions that match the swirling, magical feeling in my chest.

"I don't want to be just friends with you, Ellie," he whispers. "I want more."

"Me, too." I lace my fingers behind his neck.

Then, as if he was waiting for those very words, he dips his head and his lips brush against mine, endlessly soft. My heartbeat thrums in sync with his as he deepens the kiss, his lips salty-sweet, and my heart nearly bursts as I pull him in closer.

Epilogue

The next morning, the burning-hot sun glows on the ocean waves, like any other typical summer day.

As if it had never rained last night.

But something has definitely changed.

Over a hearty pancake breakfast, my family chatters happily, talking about Remy and Cam's plans to go to Disneyland in a few hours and how Mom, Dad, and Mochi will be going into LA's Little Tokyo before they all meet up again for their flight back this afternoon. We even talk about how Lia's finished her set of magic-awareness courses, and now Jack and I are finally off the hook and can stay in magical society—as long as we don't mess up again (which we've absolutely promised). Or how Mochi's met another Shiba and she finally has her own little best furry friend.

But any time I look up, my eyes immediately go to the person sitting next to me.

Jack pauses from inhaling his stack of blueberry pancakes

to hand over the little pot of maple syrup to my mom before she even has to ask, and Mom smiles warmly at him.

Does he have to be so damn wonderful?

"Keep eating," Remy laughs, bumping me with her shoulder. "And less gawking. Between the two of you staring at each other, it's a shock you've managed to eat even one pancake."

"Who's staring?" My face heats up, but my little sister only rolls her eyes.

"What's up?" Cam asks, leaning in.

"Nothing," I say way too quickly. Remy laughs under her breath. Earlier, while we were waiting for the Yasudas to join us for breakfast, I filled her in on last night. Her instantaneous question still burns: *So, did you two kiss? How was it?*

And just the thought of that kiss—it's been replaying in my mind nonstop—makes me catch my breath.

But then I hear a voice on the other side of the table; Mr. Yasuda's talking up a storm with my father. To Mr. Yasuda's surprise, the convention has been a huge success, with Charm-Works *and* my parents' tea *and* the rest of the goods from Sorcerer Square all getting a huge number of orders and interest from customers and distributors. He probably will never admit it, but selling things together has drawn more crowds than if we were selling things on our own.

"How are things with your dad?" I whisper, leaning in toward Jack.

"He's . . . he's going to take some time to change his ways," Jack says with a sigh. "But he wants to apologize to you for the things he said. Dad blurted all of that out in a moment of anger toward me—not that that excuses what he said—but he's been upset at himself. I told him that Mom wouldn't have been very proud of him for those words, and I think that hit him hard. He'd been going to therapy to work things through, but I think he's going to add a few more sessions going forward."

I wince. Mr. Yasuda, for all his faults, worshipped Mrs. Yasuda and had spent nearly every waking hour trying to ease any part of her life that he could. "He doesn't need to apologize. Your dad's been through a lot."

From across the table, Mr. Yasuda meets my eyes. His lips tip down in a very Jack-like way. *Regret*, I realize immediately. I nod at him, and he inclines his head; it's a silent acknowledgment of the past. And to me, it's a promise to move on.

"How's Cam been?" I ask, glancing to my left where he's chatting happily with Remy.

"Now that Cam's in the loop, he's been talking about getting a part-time job to save for college. That'll help a lot."

I nod. "And I'm here, too."

"Just you being with me helps more than anything." He smiles, ducking his chin. "I'm lucky," he adds. "I'm so lucky you're here with me."

This time, his fingers entwine with mine under the table and my heart jumps like I've drunk three shots of espresso instead of demolishing mounds of nap-inducing carbohydrates.

As everyone else chats about their plans for the day, Jack and I talk to each other. We don't seem to be able to stop talking. We chat about our plans for college. Even after the time we've spent apart, our paths seem to have been made to bring us back together. After seeing the magical village, I'm kind of interested in combining my love for art and magic by majoring in Magical Architecture. He's set on going to Foothill

Community College and then transferring to the Magical Research division at Stanford University, to study cancer and maybe find ways to help prevent others from going through what his mother had to—and, according to Remy, Stanford also has a Magical Architecture department. He fills me in on his past few years, though it seems to be mostly days filled with tutoring and tennis lessons, all to make sure he has saved up enough for college tuition for himself and Cam, too. And I tell him about life with Lia. I promise myself to take him on fun dates our senior year, so that he has more to his life than trying to scrape together money for his family.

We've got so much to catch up on, but time seems to stretch out in front of us, almost like we have forever together. And I don't want to waste a single moment.

$$\sim \qquad \sim$$

After breakfast, Jack and I wander out on our own; we still have a few hours before we need to go pick up Lia from her cousin's house for the drive back.

Instead of joining Cam and Remy at Disneyland or going out to the beach, I lead Jack to the gardens of the hotel. Being that we're in Southern California, the paths are lined with luscious flowers and leafy palms instead of the redwood trees of Palo Alto. Bridges dripping with ivy and flowers arch over rivers and paths; just the gardens alone could be a tourist attraction. The owner of this hotel is magic-aware and gives the magic-aware a hefty discount during the convention, or else we'd never be able to afford a place like this.

There're a lot of people walking through the gardens, too, all milling in one direction. Jack and I are pulled into their flow, down to a lush, grassy corner filled with plush white chairs.

At an archway covered in ivy and purple tropical flowers, I pause and eye the sign: WELCOME TO THE WEDDING OF SUMMER AND ROBIN CHANG.

My gaze slides over to Jack, and he grins. "So this is why you wanted to come here?"

Number 3: Crash a wedding with a +1.

I crook my elbow. "Would you like to join me in showing up uninvited?"

One of the guests passing by looks at us suspiciously, and I feel my cheeks heat up. Okay, maybe I need to refine my wedding-crashing skills.

He dramatically bows and accepts my arm. "Where you go, I'll go, too."

We stroll under the brick archway, and I glance around, expecting someone to point and shout, "Intruder!"

But the other guests are absorbed in their own conversations or getting escorted to seats.

A sharp-dressed woman in black, with a clipboard, smiles politely. "And you are a guest of—?"

She's got a thin metal badge clipped to her shirt: *Emmie Chang, Wedding Planner.*

I freeze in panic. A guest of who? Are we caught?

Then I catch sight of the similarly suited younger boys and girls, maybe around Remy and Cam's age, standing behind her. Oh, *ushers.*

I stammer, recalling the sign outside. "We're—we're guests of Robin!"

The wedding planner frowns. "Really? I know everyone

from Robin's side—she's my cousin—but I don't recognize
you . . ." She flips a page on her clipboard. "What's your
name?"

"Look!" I say, pointing behind her. "The bride!"

The color drains from the woman's face, and she spins
around, craning to look over the guests. "But Summer and
Robin aren't supposed to walk out yet, they—"

I drag Jack behind me, out of the archway, and lead him
to a spiral staircase I spotted earlier. "Quick! Let's hide here."

The woman hurries out, her heels clicking on brick.
"Where did that couple go?" Then, there's a swell of piano
music, and she lets out a yelp. "Oh, Summer *is* coming out.
Shoot! People, in your places."

From where Jack and I are hiding, our fingers interlocked
and arms pressing against each other near the ivy staircase, we
can hear her scuttle away.

My shoulders relax as I grin up at Jack. "Success-ish?" I
crashed a wedding with my +1. Even though we almost got
kicked out.

"This is a success to me," he says softly, tucking a strand
of hair that's fallen over my eyes. My heart flips.

On the bridge over the entrance, we settle on a bench that
gives us a perfect view of the ceremony, and I lean in. "I have
an idea . . ."

⌀   ⌀

The wedding is absolutely perfect. Jack blots my eyes as we listen to the couple exchanging vows, and his sweet touch makes
me tear up even more.

But before long, it's time for the newlyweds' procession down the aisle together. My heart patters as the guests cheer and toss coral-pink rose petals at the beaming couple, who start dancing their way to the pianists' upbeat rendition of "Paper Rings."

As they approach the bridge that Jack and I are standing on, I pull out my glass vial.

"That's the bottle of luck?" he asks.

I nod. "From one of Cam and Remy's puzzles. Your brother gave it to me to survive this trip with you."

He snorts, wrapping his hand around my waist. "I can't decide if our siblings believed in us or didn't believe in us at all." Then he gestures out at the procession below. "But . . . are you sure you want to use it now?"

"As sure as a charm," I say, grinning.

"I'll join you, then." Jack pulls a cloth packet from his pocket—an omamori. "These things have caused enough chaos for us, so it'll be nice if this charm can do something as good as your list."

As the couple walk closer, step by step, I smile to myself. I'd thought my list was a way to make me stand out. To become "somebody." A girl who deserves a label. But I'm already someone worth my *own* time and my *own* labels.

I'm *me*. I'm a girl taking chances, every day. Because taking chances is what life is all about, right?

And, I've realized, I don't have to be all one thing or the other. And just because someone else has slapped a label on me, it doesn't mean that *I* have to accept their definition of who I should be.

My list was never about standing out and getting attention, but to make myself someone I admire. And I don't need a bottle of luck or a charm to change my life.

As the bright-faced couple dance their way under our arch, I uncap the vial and Jack tears open the omamori.

Together, our magical dust sprinkles down, leaving them charmed. They don't notice, but there's a glow to them.

Kind of like the way my bucket list changed things for me, making my life brighter.

I turn to Jack, and pull him closer. His lips curve up before they claim mine.

Author's Note

When will I complete my own Charmed List?

That was a question I asked myself, day in, day out. I believed my dreams were impossible. Those were the points in my life when I thought I'd never get the opportunity to live for myself, to fulfill the wishes that would make my heart complete.

In time, I realized that I'd never be able to make my own Charmed List come true if I continued to let myself be pushed and pulled by others' currents.

I fought with all my heart to carve out my wishes into reality. Now, each book I write is a Charmed List all its own, filled with my hopes and worries, my fears and doubts. And every time, when I get to "THE END," in many ways, it feels like a new beginning.

So, with each and every breath, with every word, with every new day, I'll continue chasing my Charmed List.

Now. Here. This is your moment to pursue it, to sweat, to believe in your Charmed List until it's in reach.

So, I ask you: What is on *your* Charmed List?

Credits

Editor—Jennie Conway

Associate Publisher & Executive Editor—Eileen Rothschild

Editorial Director—Sara Goodman

Agent—Sarah Landis

Agency—Sterling Lord Literistic

Art Director—Kerri Resnick

Cover Illustrator—Vi-An Nguyen

Author Photographer—Julie Vu

Production Editor—Carla Benton

Copy Editor—Laura Michelle Davis

Proofreaders—Linda Sawicki and Yasmin Mathew

Marketing and Publicity Team—Alexis Neuville, Rivka Holler, Brant Janeway, Mary Moates, Natalic Figueroa

Sales Team—Taylor Armstrong, Jessica Brigman, Jennifer Edwards, Jennifer Golding, Sofrina Hinton, Bianca Johnson, Olivia Kasdin, Jasmine Key, Jennifer Medina, Matthew Mich, Gillian Redfearn, Rebecca Schmidt, Mark Von Bargen, Kara Warschausky

Contracts Team—Sabrina Boyle

Foreign Rights Team—Kerry Nordling, Emily Miilner, Witt Phillips, Lindsay Quackenbush, Gisela Ramos, Chris Schiena

Delicious Jam Inspiration—Uncle Dan & Uncle Dave

Early Readers—Emily Colin, Eunice Kim, Lindsey Frydman, and Sarah Suk

Special thanks to—Axie Oh, Pei (@peireads), Peijin (@peijinsart), Tiffany (@readbytiffany), and Tiffany (@quilltreefox); the Wavy Discord.

Blurbers—Axie Oh, Rachel Lynn Solomon, and Sarah Suk

Real-life shops, books, and more include: Bel Canto Books, Books Inc., Books of Wonder, Kepler's Books, Linden Tree Books, Once Upon a Time Bookstore, and all of the wonderful indie bookstores that feel like a home away from home; Shuei-Do Manju Shop; Honey & Butter Macarons; *Books & Boba* podcast; *Spin the Dawn* by Elizabeth Lim; *Dear Martin* by Nic Stone; *Jade Fire Gold* by June CL Tan; *Made in Korea* by Sarah Suk; and Jagabee are truly magical (but real) potato snacks.

Road trip soundtrack—5 Seconds of Summer, Against the Current, BTS, Hayley Kiyoko, LiSA, LeonGuitar, MAMAMOO, milet, Mirei Touyama, ONE OK ROCK, ReoNa, and Taylor Swift.

This story would not have been possible without my dear friends and family, who inspire me every day—thank you.